THE FIVE FA

WHERE LOYALTIES LIE

 Created with Vellum

WHERE LOYALTIES LIE

JILL RAMSOWER

PREFACE
Emily

I had hoped dying would be less painful.

It hurt like a bitch. But even worse than the physical pain was seeing Tamir's chilling expression as he pulled the trigger. No remorse, no conflict, no question. With a single twitch of his finger, I was flying backward onto the asphalt, his callous glare ripping through me far more ruthlessly than any bullet.

In such a short amount of time, my treacherous heart had latched onto him. He'd slipped into my bloodstream like oxygen bonded with my own blood until there was no eradicating him from my system.

Despite every warning and logical argument presented by

my brain, my heart had forged ahead, leading me down an inevitable path to this exact point in time.

To my death.

I couldn't say I was all that surprised. From the minute I ran, I knew my life was over. I was just glad I was able to take out some of the evil in the world while I had the chance.

With a renewed sense of freedom in my heart, my eyelids drifted shut.

ONE
Emily

It wasn't just cold out. It was "pack up your shit and move to Florida" cold out. It was "question every life decision you've ever made to end up in this godforsaken hellhole" cold out.

Clearly, I'd made some poor freaking choices.

It wasn't the dead of winter. We'd barely cracked the door on November, but at just six in the evening, my lungs winced from the cold every time I took a breath. It was no wonder the entire population of retirees fled the East Coast every fall for the sunny shores of Florida. Temperatures this cold made even my twenty-six-year-old joints feel arthritic.

Arctic winters were the one drawback that almost kept me from making the move to the Big Apple. At least five months out of the year, you had to dress like that kid from *A Christmas Story* just to keep from dying. Not my ideal scenario, but after careful consideration, I had decided the city boasted enough pros to outweigh the one major con.

Or so I thought before I'd experienced said con. Now, I wasn't so sure.

An early storm was supposed to push through during the week, but it was just my luck the cold had already set in. I hadn't made time to buy a winter wardrobe. That meant I was stuck in my leggings and a jacket without a hat, scarf, or gloves, debating the likely onset of frostbite and how long it would take me to recover from the loss of my extremities.

I'd have to make room on my to-do list tomorrow to grab some essentials, assuming I survived until then. I hunched my shoulders and tucked my chin down into my jacket to keep my chattering jaw from cracking a tooth before I reached the Krav Maga studio.

I went to classes three times a week—as often as my shifts at the restaurant allowed. It had been three months since I started the self-defense training, but I wasn't sure I'd made a lick of progress. The instructors had told me I was getting better, but when I saw some of the other students spar, I felt horribly incompetent. There was one woman, in particular, who gave me chills to watch. She often grappled with my main instructor, Tamir, right before our class, which happened to be the case today.

A warm gush of air enveloped me as I scurried inside the brightly lit studio. I shook away the layer of bitter cold that clung to me like the residue of a bad dream and immediately zeroed in on the two individuals training at the far end of the large room. Over and over, Tamir and the woman struck at one another, taking turns attacking and defending without any discernable rhyme or reason. But their movements had a system, a flow only they seemed to understand, almost like dancers. An invisible energy connected them, linking their bodies in an effortless rhythm.

She was my hero.

Sure, Tamir could fight just as well as she could, but a woman holding her own against a man was awe-inspiring. How often did you come across a woman who could go blow for blow in a fight against a man? Maybe in the movies, but not often in everyday life. As far as I was concerned, she was a living legend.

I found a place well away from the door to set down my jacket and gym bag, hardly taking my eyes from the woman as she transitioned smoothly from a defensive block into a wicked frontal assault. Tamir had at least fifty pounds of muscle on her, but the woman didn't let that put her at a disadvantage. She was quick, vigilant, and didn't hesitate to fight dirty. Of course, they were just training, so she didn't actually follow through with the particularly unsavory strikes, but it was easy to tell the curvy beauty would be vicious if put to the test.

I wanted to be her for more than one reason. First, her skill was unparalleled by any woman I'd seen at the studio or anywhere else, and second, because she garnered instant respect from every man in the room. It was palpable. No one would dare treat her with disrespect or objectify her. She was power and grace personified. A warrior among peasants.

I had no clue how many days, weeks, years I'd have to train to reach her skill level, but one of these days, I'd get there. I wouldn't quit unless it was the only option.

A year ago, it never would have occurred to me to learn self-defense, but things changed. We either adapted or we died—that was just life. I had chosen to adapt, which meant learning to defend myself. I had no doubt I would follow through if my crap luck didn't get in the way first. And considering my track record, it was entirely possible.

Tamir and the woman called an end to their session, leaning against the wall and drinking from their water bottles. Now that they weren't preoccupied with sparring, I turned away to keep from staring. A group of my classmates gathered along the mirrored wall across from me. After greeting one another, they conversed about their days and the changing weather.

I didn't go over to say hello. It was just easier to avoid conversation than to tiptoe around subjects and gloss over questions with a thick coat of ambiguity. Sometimes, when I felt particularly lonely, I'd try to engage my fellow students, but it always left me feeling like a fraud. I wore a sugarcoated smile on the outside, but on the inside, I clung to each word like a miserly old man refusing to part with a single cent he owned.

Words were knowledge, and every conversation I had was potential ammunition in the wrong hands. I saw small talk as a series of landmines, each one a rigorous exercise in self-control.

When Jeff, the car salesman, gleefully told the others about the new job he'd acquired and how the hours of the old job made it hard to check in on his ailing mother, his words were unfiltered. Honest and forthright. There was no threat to Jeff if he said the wrong thing. He was simply happy to share his good news. Each class was mainly comprised of the same core group of people, so they grew to know one another, often inquiring about sick relatives or following up on stories told in prior classes. A camaraderie existed among them.

How could I feel a part of that when they knew so little about me? I couldn't. Every question directed my way was another reminder of the lies I'd told and how complex my life had become. A reminder that no matter how well I camouflaged myself, I wasn't like the people around me.

I used to be, to some extent, but anymore, I found I couldn't relate to them. The course of events my life had taken changed my perspective in a fundamental way that couldn't be undone. I didn't see things the way they did, and I certainly couldn't allow them to see me. The real me.

Instead, I kept my comments superficial and my smiles broad, hoping to compensate for my lack of substantive contribution to the group. If they thought I was pretty and sweet, chances were, they wouldn't examine what I said too closely. Blending in was far more important than confiding in friends. I was there to learn self-defense, not socialize.

The Krav Maga studio was roughly the size of a basketball court. Whatever existed there before had been gutted long ago to make way for the gym. Now, only the worn window frames and ancient light fixtures remained. The dense rubber material lining the entire floor must have served some purpose besides cushioning because it was one step away from asphalt in the realm of softness. A small portion of the room contained thicker mats for practicing advanced takedowns, but I had yet to advance to those lessons.

Krav Maga, known as contact combat, was both a way of fighting and an aggressive form of self-defense. When I first looked into taking classes, I quickly realized it was by far my favorite option. The skill set drew from several forms of martial arts and knife wielding—all techniques used in fighting someone up close. I'd come from an area where guns were commonplace, so I knew how to shoot, but fighting was a different matter. I wanted to know I could hold my own if I was ever in a threatening situation.

That meant coming to class as often as I could. Fortunately, Krav Maga had become the favorite part of my day.

The musky odor of sweaty bodies didn't faze me a bit. I grew up in a warmer climate, so the sultry air was refreshing in a way. A small sense of home.

My eyes drifted back to Tamir without my permission.

His presence in class certainly doesn't hurt.

I chided myself for the thought. The last thing I needed on this earth was to involve myself with a man. And *that* man, in particular? He was regret waiting to happen. Something about the predatory grace of his movements filled me with unease. He didn't have to ink tattoos on his skin or carry a gun on his hip to broadcast a threat. The lethal confidence he exuded did the job far more efficiently than any overt warning. He carried himself with a kind of self-possessed aloofness that distinguished him from every person around him.

That was probably why he was the only man who'd piqued my interest since I had arrived in New York. I seemed to enjoy picking especially challenging men. It was a talent of mine. I'd had three long-term relationships, and not one had ended in an amicable separation of mutual respect.

It shouldn't have been surprising.

My natural inclination was to gravitate toward swarthy and dangerous over demure and polite. I was drawn to intensity and an air of intrigue, even when I knew the combination was toxic.

I blamed my father. You sought what you knew, and I had only ever known a shadier side of life. But that was before. Now, I was turning over a new leaf. I would make a conscientious attempt to give demure a chance and let dangerous latch on to some other sucker.

Releasing a long exhale, I chewed on my lip as I picked at the red sweatband on my wrist. I had to stop beating myself up over the past and focus on all the progress I'd made. For three months, I'd been in the city, and I'd acclimated rather well, considering where I'd come from and the fact I'd had to start from scratch all on my own.

I'd taken self-improvement to a whole new level. Why improve on who you were when you could start over and be someone completely new? My face was the same, but that was about it. New apartment, new job, new friends, and a completely new past I'd conjured in meticulous detail.

I'd taken the term "new year, new me" to a whole new level.

My gaze reluctantly drifted back to Tamir as he greeted my classmates and initiated our session. I shouldn't have been watching him, but I couldn't help myself. Like was drawn to like, and I sensed a familiarity in him. He was just as good at playing his role as I was at playing mine.

He smiled and shook hands with the students, perfectly executing the motions of an interested instructor. No one suspected he wasn't genuine in his regard. If I hadn't been putting on a show of my own, I never would have seen his act for what it was. A front. A fake.

I knew the signs all too well because I had to guard against them every time I talked to someone. The slip of a smile a fraction too soon after the close of a conversation. Eyes that do a sweep of the room rather than focus on the person speaking. The practice of asking questions while avoiding answering any of my own.

Maybe the others couldn't tell, but it was obvious to me that his actions were guarded. Insincere. He was going through the motions for the sake of the show, and I knew exactly what that felt like. The part that made me uneasy was the motive for his veiled behavior. Someone suffering from depression might put up a front, but that scenario didn't fit with Tamir's easy confidence. He wasn't just attempting to function under a crimpling emotional illness; Tamir was actively keeping the world at bay. But why? What was he hiding?

There was a sliver of a chance I was entirely wrong and merely projecting my own complicated past onto him, but I didn't think that was the case. Something complex about him lurked beneath the surface, and that something could be summed up in one word. Danger. The precise thing I'd told myself I would stay away from.

I tried to remind myself of that each time I went to class, but it was hard for me to think when I looked at him. It was as if my brain short-circuited from an overload of hormones. I did my best to work around it when I was in class, but it was always there. My awareness of him. His ability to distract me.

He was an excellent teacher, but he also made learning ten times harder than it would have been if someone else had been issuing instruction. Someone like Creepy Carl, my building mailman, who bypassed my box and brought mail to my door out of the kindness of his perverted heart. I'd have had no problem unleashing my anger on him in the gym.

Instead, I soaked up everything I could about the enigma of a man, trying to put his pieces together and solve the puzzle. He had an unfamiliar accent that almost sounded French, but I wasn't sure that was accurate. I felt like knowing where he was from might give me some insight into why he was the way he was, but I'd never allowed myself to ask him directly about his origins. He had rich copper skin with dark hair that could have come from just about anywhere.

His coloring reminded me of the men back home. So did his intensity. But a worldliness and sophistication separated him from the men I'd known. Maybe it was the accent, or maybe our age difference—I guessed he was a good ten years older than me—but something distinguished him as being different from anyone I'd known before. He was shrouded in mystery and had the ability to pulverize anyone who crossed him. It was a seriously intoxicating combination.

Intoxicating and dangerous.

As if on cue, his eyes sliced in my direction, colliding with my own greedy stare. The ghost of a smile played over his mouth as if he knew I'd been watching him. What had I been thinking by openly gawking at him? He was far too aware of his surroundings not to notice my stalker behavior.

I cursed my normally well-honed self-control and lined up with the other students. As usual, my stomach churned with anticipation. Would Tamir work with me directly? Would I be able to execute the proper movements or just end up making an ass of myself?

It took all my concentration to ignore the melodic lilt of his words and focus on his instruction. It could have rained down monkeys outside the large plate-glass windows, and I wouldn't have noticed. Each of my senses were totally fixated on Tamir, and my brain was tasked with the impossible mission of ignoring that feedback and learning the day's Krav Maga lesson. It was a monumental challenge, but one I was slowly growing accustomed to surmounting.

Once we'd gone through our warmup and a series of drills with pads, we started the practice portion of class where we paired off and simulated specific attack defenses. First on the list was the hair-pull defense. When an attacker grabbed our hair, we were supposed to reach behind us and grab their wrist, then turn to punch them and kick them in the groin to escape. We took turns practicing the technique, both a rear hair grab and a front hair grab, then we moved on to a gun take-away drill.

That one was far more unsettling.

We had fake guns that we used, but they were heavy like a real gun. The red tip, signifying the gun was fake, did little to ease the tension in my shoulders when the barrel was pressed against my forehead.

I was paired up with a small redhead, which helped keep my fear from taking over, but my heart still began to pound in my chest, fighting its way up my throat. I ran through the motions of yanking down on her wrist with one hand and lifting the gun up with the other. Adrenaline seeped into my bloodstream, giving my hands a slight tremor and making my movements more erratic than I would have liked.

Tamir watched as we practiced, weaving his way through the small group and pointing out corrections. When he arrived at me and my partner, the gun was back against my forehead. I tried to ignore him, but it was an exercise in futility. His steely gaze was a vise around my rib cage, denying my lungs much-needed air.

I surged through the motions, wanting to get the demonstration over with so badly that I nearly hit my partner in the face with the enthusiasm of my feigned strikes. Despite successfully disarming my partner, I was embarrassed with my performance and upset at my lack of control.

"That's not bad," Tamir said. His unexpected compliment actually sounded genuine, despite my own self-doubts. The nugget of approval sent a flush rippling beneath my skin. "This time, try not to telegraph what you plan to do. You're leaning into your action prior to striking, and the motion gives away your intent. Here, try again."

He took the gun from me and did something I hadn't expected. He pressed the cool metal against my forehead, interjecting himself into the drill. Everything about the situation felt different when I looked into his eyes across from me rather than the soft green gaze of the redhead. My pulse pounded throughout my body like a determined fist against a wall, trying to break its way outside the barrier of my body.

Tamir's stare was a black void, slicing into me without a trace of humor.

I lost all sense of the drill and tumbled back into my memories. Tamir's eyes were easily replaced with the soulless glare of a man I never wanted to think about again. A feverish chill lanced through my spine, and the hairs on my arms stood straight up. Before I could drown in the panic, I banished the image with sheer force of will and flooded my muscles with cool, determined purpose.

Ignoring the growing weakness in my knees and my heart's steadfast attempt to pound its way out of my chest, I launched into my attack and disarmed Tamir. The clarity provided by a river of adrenaline racing through my veins enabled me to execute the move perfectly. I had no delusions that Tamir wouldn't beat me in a fight, but in that one single instance, I would have bested him whether it had been a drill or not.

"Very good." His fathomless gaze held mine as the world around me returned into focus. I got the feeling he was studying me, but I wasn't sure what had triggered his sudden scrutiny. Eventually, he held out his palm and turned to my partner. "Your turn."

I gave him the gun, my skin sparking where my fingers brushed his. His hard gaze flashed back to me for a heated second before he ran through the drill with my partner, giving me a chance to calm my racing heart.

I wasn't sure what had come over me. Training with Tamir made me nervous, but normally, I handled the pressure without losing myself in a panic attack. He was my instructor; he was there to help me, not hurt me. Except I saw something ruthless lurking in his eyes, giving me the sense I was truly fighting for my life and dredging up memories I preferred to keep deeply buried.

Had I been projecting my own messed-up past on him, or had the tightly reined violence I'd seen in his eyes been real? He was secretive and enigmatic, but did he actually pose a physical threat to me? Not for the first time, I wondered how and why he'd learned to fight so well. Did it matter? Dangerous was dangerous, whether he had a valiant excuse or not.

For the rest of class, I managed to plaster a smile on my face and finish training without drawing any more attention to myself. As everyone dispersed, I hurried over to collect my gym bag but startled when I found Tamir had followed me.

"Oh, hey," I offered nervously, wiping a sweaty strand of hair off my cheek.

"Your technique was nice back there. Did you train somewhere else before you started here?" He leaned against the wall casually, but somehow, the energy surrounding him felt charged. Frenetic. Anything but the indifferent air he attempted to portray. He might project a cool demeanor, but I doubted anything was easygoing about Tamir.

Intense, shiver-inducing eyes were framed above with a prominent brow. Eye contact with him was far more intimate than it was with anyone else. Holding his gaze felt like offering up my soul for his perusal. As if he could see deeper, into the darkest parts of me.

I wasn't sure casual was even in his vocabulary.

"No previous training. I just grew up with a bunch of boy cousins who kept me on my toes." We stood two feet apart, forcing me to look up to meet his gaze. Our positioning and his intensity had me fidgeting anxiously with the necklace I always wore. It was a habit I'd tried unsuccessfully to break for years. What I needed to do was grab my stuff, make my excuses, and leave, but my body refused to cooperate.

Tamir lifted his chin as if in understanding, but his eyes still searched for answers to unspoken questions. I wanted to blame his sudden interest on simple flirtation, but Tamir didn't strike me as the type. He either wanted a woman or he didn't; there was no need to dance around the subject. If my instincts were correct and he wasn't flirting, then why had he struck up this little conversation?

"Is that an evil eye on your necklace?"

His question surprised me, making me glance down as if the necklace hadn't been the same piece of jewelry I'd seen around my neck for the past ten years. "Yes, it is. My tita … my grandma gave it to me a long time ago. Are you familiar with them?"

The small gold pendant was thin and circular with the symbolic eye etched onto its surface. When I got anxious, I rolled the circle side to side between my thumb and finger. It was more of a habit than anything else, but I did find that, on occasion, it reminded me of the woman who raised me and gave me a sense of comfort.

"They're common where I'm from. Thought to ward off evil, correct?"

"That's right."

"Has it worked for you?" His voice was a sensual rumble that I could feel just as assuredly as any tangible caress.

"I wish. Then I wouldn't need these classes." I inwardly cringed at my choice of words. That was *exactly* why I shouldn't be talking to him or anyone, for that matter.

His eyes narrowed a fraction. "What do you mean?"

"That sounded dramatic," I assured him. "I just meant that if the necklace worked, nothing bad would ever happen, and that's obviously not a guarantee. I figure the classes are a good source of exercise and give me a useful foundation in self-defense. A girl can never be too careful living in the city." Words fell from my mouth like water from a burst dam.

Tamir nodded, his lips lifting in a small smile that didn't reach his eyes. "I agree. Man or woman, it's always good to be prepared. And your cousins seem to have given you an excellent background in hand-to-hand technique."

"I'll make sure to thank them." I offered him a plastic smile, equally as fake as his own. "I better head out. Great class today, thanks." I didn't give him time to respond before I slipped from the studio back into the arctic tundra.

What the hell was I thinking?

Clearly, I hadn't been thinking at all. As if his chiseled good looks had cast a voodoo spell, making me say whatever inane thing that popped into my mind. I hadn't been that careless with my words in years, and I had no valid explanation.

Sex. That had to be a part of it. I was only twenty-six years old and hadn't slept with a man in over a year. Being near any halfway attractive man probably sent my hormones into a tailspin, deregulating my breathing and causing a drastic loss of oxygen to the brain. It had nothing to do with Tamir himself and more to do with my own sex-crazed brain.

Right. I didn't buy that for a second.

Shaking my head, I hustled back to my apartment before my sweat-soaked hair crystalized in the frozen temperatures. Fortunately, I only lived a few blocks from the studio. Not a single thing about my neighborhood was noteworthy. It wasn't particularly poor or wealthy, nor crowded or abandoned, and no one race or culture dominated. Crime was low, and the rent was reasonable, as far as rent in the city went. It was the perfect place to blend in and disappear.

My standard two-bedroom apartment was more than I

thought I'd be able to afford in the city, but it still didn't feel like home yet. A few more personal touches would help. One of these days, I would settle in and make the place feel like mine. Until then, it served a far more utilitarian function than sentimental.

The place came furnished with the basics, and I hadn't added much. I could have used what little money I made to add a homey feel to the place, but I couldn't shake the feeling that it was temporary. That my attempt at escape was nothing but a childish delusion, and each day was nothing but a countdown until I was dragged back home and made to suffer for my crimes.

At some point, I'd get over that mindset, but I hadn't reached that place. Instead, I had a basic collection of kitchen supplies, clothes in my closet, and the furniture that came with the place—that was about it. That, and my little green aloe plant with red strings tied to the end of each pointy leaf to help ward off evil. It was the first thing I acquired when I arrived in the city.

My tita always had an aloe plant and swore by their power to keep away evil. Maybe evil had bad skin and hated to moisturize—I had no idea. I didn't buy into the belief, but I figured having Ned around couldn't hurt. Ned was my plant's name. I'd named him after one of *The Three Amigos*—Ned Nederlander—who was kind but also the best shot in the West. The movie had been my tita's favorite, so I grew up watching it with her on rainy days. Little Ned was the only "person" I allowed myself to talk to openly; therefore, he'd needed a name. If his powers against evil were to be trusted, then I figured it was only fitting to name him after a famous gunslinger.

Aside from Ned, the small balcony in the back was my favorite part of my apartment. By balcony, I meant fire escape, but it served the same purpose—a chance to be outside and feel the world turning around me. Today, it was too cold to sit out there, but on most days, that was where I relaxed. I brought my laptop with me and pulled up Netflix, or sometimes, I just observed people moving about in the neighborhood behind my building. It was peaceful, as was the knowledge that I could sprint down those stairs should I need to.

Not the best way to live, but it could have been worse. I knew. I'd seen worse.

Shrugging off my coat, I headed straight for the shower to wash away the nasty residue that clung to me from class— both sweat and fear—though one was far easier to be rid of than the other. The memory that had resurfaced during class left an oily smudge in my mind; a greasy imprint that wouldn't wash away no matter how hard I tried to distract myself.

Between losing myself in the memory and my accidental admission to Tamir, it hadn't been my finest evening but berating myself wouldn't help. Even if I'd stirred Tamir's curiosity, nothing would come of it. By the time I saw him again, I would have fortified my walls and made sure nothing further slipped past my defenses. If I had any luck at all, he would write me off as mildly unstable and lose interest in me entirely.

It wasn't likely, but a girl could hope.

TWO
Tamir

"I CAN'T IMAGINE ANYONE WILL SHOW UP. WE SHOULD HAVE nearly a foot of snow by the time class ends. Most of the city has already shut down for the night," Matthew noted, his voice crackling over the phone line. Bad connection. The day before had been cold, but now the city was feeling the full effects of the storm. The winds had started raging a couple of hours before, and snow fell in heavy flakes that blanketed everything in sight.

"I'm sure you're right. If anyone happens to show up, I'll let them know class is canceled." I lived in the apartment above the studio, which made me the most logical person to be there during a snowstorm. The location of my apartment and my extra duties weren't coincidental; that's how

Matthew paid me. He got to step away from the studio and focus on his family, and I got a roof over my head in a respectable part of town. Not that I couldn't afford my own place, but this made everything simpler. No paycheck. No taxes. No trail. It was an ideal arrangement for me.

"Sounds good. We'll see how the night goes and chat in the morning about tomorrow's classes. Stay inside. It's cold as hell out there."

"You don't have to tell me twice. Talk to you tomorrow."

"Night, man."

I ended the call and slipped the phone into my back pocket before taking the stairs down to the studio. The lights were still on from my earlier classes, but the warmth created by exercising bodies had already fled the building. I figured I'd wait at the desk to inform any students who hadn't seen our email that class had been canceled. I could have simply put a note on the front door and shut down, but I had nothing better to do, so I planted myself at the desk and pulled my phone back out.

I didn't even have a chance to check the updated forecast when the glass door plowed open and a snow-covered woman bounded inside. Her back was to me as she dusted off the snow, but I knew who it was the second she swept her hood off to reveal jet black hair pulled back in a high pony-tail. It reminded me of the sleek black feathers of a raven, glossy and deceptive to the eye.

Most women I encountered were fairly straightforward creatures. They valued personal relationships above most aspects in life, and therefore, put an abundance of value in honesty and appearances. Phones and social media were a staple in their lives in order to maintain those personal connections, and they rarely left the house without a coat of lipstick in case they saw someone they knew. Their mindset was often entirely focused on pleasing the people around them. Nothing was wrong with that orientation, but I found myself unable to relate.

Emily was different.

I knew so because as often as she found herself watching me, I studied her just as intently. Unlike her, I'd had years to master my skills of observation. She had no idea she'd even registered on my radar, but she'd piqued my interest from the moment she first slipped into the back of my class.

It quickly became clear that she didn't talk with others out of a desire to connect. She did it out of obligation, only engaging in minimal conversations to maintain propriety. When she did speak up, she didn't seem particularly shy or introverted, so why the reluctance to form attachments to the people she saw on a daily basis?

I rarely found myself curious about a woman, yet the sensation was a welcome reprieve from the monotony of everyday life. Emily slaked the boredom, and in response, I found myself drawn to her. Observing her. Dissecting her every action.

She stilled as she lifted her head and realized the studio was empty. Slowly, she spun around to find me staring at her from behind the desk. Her eyes rounded with surprise, making her look even younger than she already was. The brief glimpse past her carefully constructed walls only lasted a second before she regained her bearings, and her stoic mask, once again, slipped back into place.

"Were classes canceled?" she asked, an octave or so higher than her normal sultry tone. She didn't intentionally use her voice in a sexual manner, but the natural base and gravel to an otherwise female voice was inescapably seductive. It made me glad she didn't say a lot in class—a voice like that could distract a man to the point of madness.

"Yeah, Matthew sent out emails, but we knew there was a chance not everyone would receive them."

"I came straight from work, sorry. Not that I check my email anyway." She gave an impish smile.

"Not a problem. That's why I'm here."

Her brows pursed as she scrutinized the empty room. "Well, if you were going to be here, why didn't we just have class?" Her question could have been deemed argumentative, but when her eyes drifted back to mine, I could tell she was simply curious. Those dark depths contained no malice or irritation.

It was precisely that type of unusual response that had caused her to capture my attention. In a city full of the strange and unusual, she should have simply been one among millions, but something about her stood out to me. Little oddities that gave me pause.

In my experience, different was often synonymous with problematic. In my line of work, outliers were unpredictable variables that needed to be addressed. Not that my work principles were always applicable to the rest of my life, but those instincts couldn't be turned off. Nor was she necessarily a threat just because I felt like something was off. She could have been hoarding a small army of cats, but that would have had nothing to do with me.

Whatever the source, she intrigued me. In this case, she had posed a question when most would have excused themselves and left, but her point was valid. We were both at the studio at the scheduled time.

I stepped around the desk and leaned back against the elevated front counter. "I suppose, if you still want to train, we can do that."

Her eyes did an unsteady sweep of the room, and she swallowed uneasily as she seemed to realize the implications of her suggestion. "You know what? That might have been presumptive of me. I'm sure you need to get home before the weather gets worse."

"Actually, I live upstairs." I pointed at the ceiling but kept my eyes trained on her. "So unless you need to go, nothing's stopping us from getting some practice in." I should have let her retreat. I should have allowed her an out and encouraged her to leave. There were a great many things I should have done, but training alone with her wasn't one of them. Yet the lure of learning more about her was too sweet a temptation to ignore. I couldn't help myself.

"You live here? Do you own the studio?"

"No, I'm just an instructor."

A glint of amusement shone in her eyes as if she were scoffing at my statement. Perceptive. "You're probably not on the clock then, so I don't need to bother you."

"If you're uncomfortable training alone with me, I understand."

Her spine stiffened. "I didn't say that. If you have nowhere else to be, I'm up for a lesson."

"Go set your things down, and we'll get started." I moved toward the practice area, eyeing her form in the mirror. Her curves were perfectly proportioned. I'd made certain not to stare during class, but it was impossible not to notice. Women's workout clothing left little to the imagination.

Women in America often sought a lean and toned physique. I had grown up with a far different standard of women's beauty. Soft and curvy was more alluring to me than cut, lean muscle. I couldn't have imagined a more perfect female form than Emily's tempting body. The contours of her rounded breasts and hips contrasted with her slim waist were enough to make a man insane with need. I

21

had to lecture myself at least once during every class to keep my eyes from straying.

She came every Tuesday, Wednesday, and Friday without exception and added extra classes on occasion. She was consistent, dedicated, and always put in the maximum effort —all of which were qualities I appreciated in a person.

Even without the shadow of intrigue that surrounded her, I would have taken notice of her curvy physique and relentless drive. My interest would have stopped there, but at the very least, I would have taken note. It was that intangible sense of irregularity that piqued my interest to an irresistible degree. Beautiful women were everywhere, but this one had secrets. Dark secrets.

I would bet my life on it.

Most people paid their monthly fee with a credit card or auto draft from their bank account, but Emily paid cash each month. As someone who also used cash almost exclusively and faced the associated obstacles regularly, I knew how rare it was for someone to rely on cash when credit cards were so common.

Of course, I could have been wrong. Perhaps she had a credit card and used it only for emergencies or some other setup to which I wasn't privy. Perhaps. But something told me she didn't. Just like something told me the fear I'd seen in her eyes at our last class had been real. Substantive. A fear that was driving her to show up at every opportunity and learn self-defense as best she could.

I had no desire to be her champion—her problems weren't my concern—but that didn't mean I wasn't curious. I had an unhealthy desire to strip down her walls and lay witness to all her ugly truths.

Everyone kept parts of themselves hidden. A myriad of possibilities existed—unpaid bills, arrest records, abusive

spouses—and everyone had at least one of those nasty skele-
tons collecting dust in the back of their closet. Most people
pretended those black stains didn't exist. Some of us had
secrets so ugly, there was no hiding from them. That part of
her spoke to me. Captured my interest and wouldn't let go.

Emily occupied far more of my thoughts than she should
have. It wasn't healthy for either of us.

Neither was training one-on-one, but that didn't seem to
stop me.

Except for Maria, who I sparred with most afternoons, I
didn't train anyone privately. I'd been in a somewhat similar
situation when she'd first been thrust into my life. I had
already told her father that I didn't do private sessions, but he
brought her to the studio against my wishes. Once I saw the
turmoil that churned in those arctic eyes of hers, I knew I had
to do it. Something had told me the knowledge I would give
her might be the difference between life and death in her
young life. I'd been right.

But there was a big difference between Maria and Emily.
Maria had only been fifteen when we started training, so
there'd never been a sexual nature to our relationship. Our
friendship was purely platonic and one I could easily
manage.

Despite the mask Emily showed to the world, I could see
that same unrest in her gaze. Everything about training with
her would be different. She was a good ten years older than
Maria had been. Emily was a woman—young, but still a
grown woman—and an electric charge buzzed between us
already. Training privately would only make that worse.
However, just like Maria, Emily wasn't there for recreational
purposes, regardless of what she claimed. Her expressive
brown eyes told a far more complicated, harrowing story
than her words had admitted.

I was incapable of ignoring that fact.

I was no saint—I hardly expected that training her would wash my hands of all my sins. We all had a story, and mine kept me from turning my back on her. Her luscious body certainly didn't make it any easier to turn her away. In that one regard, I was a man like any other.

It wasn't like I had agreed to be her personal trainer.

One hour. That was it.

"I think we'll work on defending a chokehold attack from behind." I could have picked any number of techniques to work on—ones that would be far less ... intimate—but I wanted to see how she responded in an uncomfortable situation. Something about her reaction to me holding her at gunpoint made me want to test her limits. To see if she'd react similarly in other stressful simulations or if the incident had been a fluke. My curiosity had gotten the better of me, which didn't happen often.

I motioned her to the mirrored wall and placed a folded mat next to us. "We're going to practice what to do when an attacker places you in a rear chokehold. The best way to show you, since I don't have anyone else here to help me demonstrate, is to reverse our roles." I positioned myself with my heels against the mat, facing the mirror. "Stand on the mat behind me and bring your arm around my neck."

She bit down on her lip, but it was her only tell at any uncertainty she might have felt. The mat gave her another eight inches of height, which was just enough to line up our shoulders. Her arm snaked across my upper chest, pressing gently against my neck.

"Bend your elbow more," I instructed, using my hands to help position her correctly as I attempted to ignore the press of her breasts against my back. "You want to use the crook of your elbow to pinch at the throat from both sides. Good.

24

Now, the way to get out of this hold is to reach up and back toward the attacker's face with the hand opposite of where his face is. If his face is over your left shoulder, you reach with your right hand. Scrape down his face to surprise him, then grasp for his thumb. People's thumbs are rather weak. When you wrench down with the thumb, the wrist will follow and open space between his forearm and your neck. Tuck your chin and twist your head down through that space with all your strength." I demonstrated the motion, easily pulling free of her grasp. "The second you're able, swing that outer arm toward his gut in a series of punches, followed by a solid side kick to give you time to run. You see?"

She nodded with a growing eagerness, wiping at a bead of sweat that had formed over her brow. Oddly enough, she didn't use the sweatband on her wrist. It wasn't the first time I'd noticed the inconsistency. In fact, I wasn't sure I'd ever seen her use the red sweatband she always wore to class. Just one of the many idiosyncrasies that could mean absolutely nothing, but still activated my inner alarms, telling me something wasn't right.

I pushed the mat aside and reversed our positions, standing behind her as we both faced the mirror. Time ground to a halt as our eyes met in the reflection. It wasn't uncommon for female students to look at me with trust and sometimes, desire. Emily's eyes held quite the opposite— there was caution but also challenge.

Did she see through my façade the same way I saw through hers? Surely not, but just the thought had me instantly on edge.

My eyes hardened as I wrapped my arm around her throat. "Do you remember what to do?"

"I think so."

She swung back with her hand and feigned scraping

25

down my face before attempting to grab my thumb. Her hand lost its grip before she could free herself, and her eyes flew back to mine in the mirror.

"Again. You can't give up trying," I scolded her more harshly than I should have. "In this hold, you will only have a matter of seconds until loss of oxygen will start to inhibit your brain function. If an attacker grabs you like this, you can't stop fighting, even for a moment."

She practiced the movement again. This time, I allowed her to grasp my thumb and free herself from my hold. Going through the motions was an important part of understanding the defense before it could be practiced at full speed and force. When I returned to my place behind her, her features were etched with fixed determination.

We practiced the technique a couple of dozen times, her confidence growing with each attempt. After we finished, we ran through some standard defensive techniques for frontal assaults, each of which she excelled at performing. I encouraged her to use seventy percent of her strength in each attack. In class, when students were training with each other, it was hard to put force into practicing the movements for fear of hurting someone, but there was no way she would hurt me. It was an ideal opportunity to feel the movements at close to actual speed. To see what it would feel like to truly strike someone.

I hoped she would never have the need to experience a real-life application of her training, but something told me she might. If that was the case, I wanted her to be ready. If she were ever to face a man like myself, she'd need all the skills she could get.

"That's enough for today," I said when it came to my attention we'd worked past our allotted hour.

"I hope I haven't kept you from anything. I didn't realize

how late it was."

"I have no reason to go out in this weather." I gestured to the door. The edges of the glass window were ringed with a crown of snow.

She gave me a sheepish smile before turning to retrieve her coat and bag. "Guess I underestimated how bad it was going to get."

As if pulled by some invisible force, I followed her, ambling slowly so as not to make my compulsion noticeable. "You haven't been in town long, have you?"

"Is it that obvious?" she asked as she put her boots back on.

"No, but I'm pretty good at reading people. I'd say you arrived in the past six months."

I hadn't asked a question, and she didn't volunteer an answer. Instead, she simply gave me a vague smile and continued with her task.

"I take it you're not a native either?" she asked, changing the focus of our conversation.

"No."

"When did you move to the city?"

"About ten years ago."

"I've tried to figure out where you're from, but your accent is hard to place." She peered up at me with her gloves in one hand and her coat folded over her arm.

"I'm from Israel, but my father was from Spain, so my looks can be deceiving."

Her head drifted back. "Of course, I should have known. Krav Maga originated in Israel. For some reason, I didn't put the two together. There's a rabbi who lives right by me, but he doesn't sound anything like you."

"He probably speaks Yiddish, not Hebrew. The two are very different." I took two steps closer, bringing us to within a few feet of one another. "I take it you did some research before you started classes?"

Her coffee-colored eyes took on a serious glint that she tried to hide with a smirk. "There was no point wasting my time with crap training—blowing a rape whistle or some other inane strategy that would fail if I ever actually needed it. This is a big city. It's best to be prepared."

"You seem to think the worst of the city for someone who chose to move here."

"It has nothing to do with the city and everything to do with people—in the city, there are just more of them. I shouldn't think I'd have to explain that to you, since you're the fighting expert. I doubt your skills were acquired as a part of your membership in the Boy Scouts. Israeli military—that would be my first guess, considering that's where Krav Maga started."

I smiled at her, a bit more teeth visible than would be considered friendly. "I was Israeli Special Forces before I moved to America."

"It makes a girl wonder why you left."

"A girl would just have to keep wondering."

"Fair enough." Her lips hinted at a smirk, and her eyes glittered with an intrigue to match my own. As the seconds ticked by in silence, the air in the room grew heavy with insinuation and challenge. Neither of us was willing to be the first to shy away, but we were also unable to ignore the dangers and tempt fate by making a move.

Eventually, Emily averted her eyes and glanced toward the door. "I better get going. I appreciate you training with me." She slipped on her gloves and began to struggle with her coat.

"Allow me." I took the heavy black bundle, holding it open to help her slip her arms inside. The action brought us even closer, and when she turned around to face me, we were only a breath apart. A breath that she sucked into her lungs when her eyes lifted to mine—multifaceted eyes that hinted at acute intelligence, all hidden behind a cloying veil.

I envisioned grasping her ponytail and slamming my mouth down on hers, demanding she pull back that shroud and show me each of her precious secrets. I had a feeling they wouldn't be pretty, and it only made me want her more. She would be every kind of trouble, and I was the greatest kind of fool for wanting anything to do with her.

She must have seen the kiss play out in my eyes because her lips parted on a shuddered breath. "I need to go." Her words were no more than a whisper.

I didn't argue with her to stay or encourage her to leave, locked in my own internal battle. Fortunately, she found the discipline I seemed to lack. After a handful of agonizing seconds, she pulled away and hurried toward the door.

"Be careful out there," I called to her in a gravelly voice, heavily affected by the intense lust that had compromised all my faculties.

She glanced over her shoulder, her eyes glinting with understanding at my double meaning. "See you on Friday, and thanks again." She dropped her gaze and slipped out onto the snowy sidewalk.

I was enormously relieved when she did, unsure I could trust my own actions around her. Proving my self-doubt was justified, I went to the computer and looked up her account. Emily Ramirez. What exactly was the young Ms. Ramirez hiding? And more importantly, why the fuck did it matter to me?

It didn't. I wouldn't let it.

Instead, I shoved aside all thoughts of Emily and made my way to my apartment upstairs. I pulled out my laptop and initiated my encryption software that obscured my location before navigating to a site on the dark web. My destination wasn't a simple pornography site any idiot could find when they tiptoed into the racing current of the underworld. The unassuming site purporting to be a conspiracy theory chatroom had a back door that could only be accessed by certain individuals granted entry after a rigorous background check. Like the evil twin of law enforcement, the founders of this site were selective about who they allowed in, but with criteria rather opposite than the police or government intelligence.

As the system checked my credentials, my encrypted email server dinged with an incoming message. I opened the program and scanned the email.

To: Caracal

From: Omega

RE: Time sensitive package.

Package arriving in New York for twenty-four-hour layover. No retrieval required. Valued at $100, receipt required. Immediate response requested.

Omega was a service, rather than a person. One I contracted with when the terms were agreeable. The email was a job offer. Omega knew my particular employment stipulations and only sent me offers that they deemed compliant with my requirements, but I still had to decline on occasion. I took every job seriously, only accepting when I was absolutely certain of the risks and implications.

I downloaded the email attachment and unzipped its contents to reveal an array of photographs. The first was a shot of a lean man in his mid-fifties taken with a telephoto lens. He was dressed in an expensive suit, hair perfectly styled with a broad smile on his face as he engaged in conversation with another man, who was not fully in the frame.

The second photo gave his pertinent information—name, occupation, vital statistics, and location. The remaining ten photographs provided the background information I required before considering a job. Sometimes the documentation was less than thorough, and I performed my own research before moving forward. Today's offer came with enough nauseating detail that a secondary investigation wouldn't be necessary.

Accepted.

With one word, I had agreed to hunt down a man, kill him, and send back proof of his death in order to obtain a $100,000 payoff.

I was no longer in the military, but I'd been trained well and now made a good living for myself with my particular skill set. Most jobs came to me directly, but on occasion, I sought out work. That was what I'd been doing when the email came through. I switched back over to the site I'd opened up and began to scroll through the photographs. Now that I had a new job to work on, I wouldn't be taking on any extra work, but I had nothing better to do but scroll through the listing of individuals who had bounties on their heads. I didn't engage in bounty hunts often—too many variables involved—but I liked to keep apprised of the scene.

Every now and then, a familiar face would pop up. Rarely was it surprising. Most of the individuals who ended up on this list deserved their fate. As for me, I found it beneficial to keep tabs on who wanted who dead. Not that I got into the middle of those squabbles, but it was good in my line of work to stay informed about the power dynamic in the criminal underworld.

I scrolled until I came across a photo that sent an uncharacteristic chill through my veins. There was no questioning the face of the woman I'd been with minutes before, and above her photo, the caption: Wanted, alive.

THREE
Emily

I SPENT EVERY WAKING MOMENT OF THE FOLLOWING TWENTY-four hours breaking down each second of my time with Tamir. My inability to focus meant I was late showing up to work, forgot to refill customers' drink glasses, and even put in the wrong food orders.

I grew up working in my family's restaurant, so serving customers was as easy as breathing for me, but thoughts of Tamir had disrupted even my most basic of functions. I couldn't think straight, and I'd slept horribly. It was any wonder I wasn't drooling in a corner.

If my tita had been around, she would have insisted a hex had been placed on me and taken me to a curradero—a

Mexican healer. It would have annoyed me to no end, but now that she was no longer alive, putting up with her antics didn't sound so bad. Now, I had to figure out my own path. I had to decide for myself if Tamir was a much-deserved dip into refreshing waters or a hazardous whirlpool with the ability to pull me deep beneath the surface.

Any debate was short-lived. I knew exactly which one he was, but would it make any difference? Probably not. My body responded to Tamir unlike any other man, and I wanted to give in to that sensation. I'd been drowning in anxiety and desperation for far too long. I wanted to revel in the insistent yearning he stirred in my belly. Let go of my discipline and connect with someone, even if only physically. It could mean my downfall, but the promise of temporary pleasure was an overwhelming temptation to this starving woman.

My thoughts took me on a sickening Nascar loop of debate, round and round in circles. I told myself that just because Tamir made me feel uneasy didn't mean he was bad. Then I reminded myself what happened the last time I ignored my instincts. I was drawn to a dark place I almost didn't escape. I certainly didn't want to walk that same path, which led to convincing myself that just because Tamir affected me didn't mean it had to lead to anything. That was followed by a solid ten minutes of fantasizing about what it would feel like if we did go down that path. When I finally snapped out of my lust-drunk haze, I was back at the beginning, trying to find a way to convince myself Tamir wasn't a threat. That the smoke surrounding him was merely a trick of the eye and wasn't a sign of fire.

The fact that I had to debate at all gave me my answer. Perhaps if there'd been no foreseeable negatives to befriending him, I could have considered letting him in.

Opening up about my life was far too risky on its own, let alone opening up to a man who was potentially dangerous in his own right.

He was off-limits, no matter how badly his chiseled good looks and intriguing aura tempted me. He was my instructor and nothing more.

I didn't even have to continue training at the same studio. I could switch to another gym at any time. Of course, the possibility wasn't even worth mentioning because I knew I'd never do it. I wasn't even sure I had the strength to keep Tamir at bay, let alone walk away entirely. Being near him made me feel something more than just anxiety, which had been my constant companion for months. The electricity between us made me feel alive. Energized. Instead of trudging through each day in survival mode, seeing him gave me something to look forward to, even if it was just admiring the way his arms were corded with muscle.

I had assumed my interest was one-sided, but after our exchange the evening before, it was clear I wasn't the only one affected. For the briefest moment, I had been certain he was going to kiss me. His body went rigid with restraint, and my lips practically tasted the salt from his.

It had taken all my self-discipline and a dash of fear to shake free of the spell and walk away. From that moment on, I'd been asking myself one question: how far would it have gone if I hadn't run?

And *that* was why my boss had been scowling at me for the past two hours. My brain had punched the time clock and refused to go back on duty. However, the city had come alive the second roadway officials cleared the snow from the streets. After only one night of being forced inside, the residents of New York were out in droves. Customers had filled the restaurant since four p.m., something that shouldn't have fazed me in the slightest, but I'd struggled to keep up.

"Earth to Emily. Come in, Emily. Did you hear anything I said?"

"Huh?" I spun around to face Olivia, who stood with her hands on her hips and a single eyebrow arched high on her forehead. "Did you say something? I'm so sorry. I didn't hear you."

"No kidding." She laughed. "Where have you been today? Because it sure hasn't been here. You've been staring at the computer for ten solid minutes."

"Ay, *chinga*! Are you serious?" I started to spin toward the front of the restaurant, but Olivia stopped me.

"Don't worry, I already checked on your tables before I came back to see where you were."

I breathed out a sigh, and my eyelids drifted shut. "Thanks, Liv. I'm sorry I've been so distracted today. I think your dad's ready to strangle me." I glanced back at the kitchen, hoping my boss wasn't aware that I'd screwed up for the tenth time today.

"Don't worry about him. He was born grumpy. What's going on with you? You've never been this distracted."

Olivia was a sweet kid. Although she was only six years younger than me, I still thought of her as a kid. She was far more innocent than I'd ever been. Her parents owned and operated the restaurant. They adored their only child, and while they made her work with them by waiting tables, she was given everything her heart desired. Olivia saw the good in everyone because she'd never been exposed to the bad. She couldn't even fathom the evil that existed in the dark corners of the world.

Our proximity in age meant nothing. For all intents and purposes, Olivia was a child, and I was far older than my years would suggest. It made keeping her at arm's length a bit easier. She was the one person in the city I called a friend, but we could only get so close without my secrets being unearthed. It was safer for me and the people around me if my past stayed buried.

"It's nothing," I assured her. "I ended up training alone with my instructor yesterday and—"

"Oh my God, is he cute?"

See? Naïve in every way. My first reaction would have been worry that he'd done something inappropriate. She was chasing butterflies in a field of wildflowers while I was batting at shadows in a dusky cave. In this particular instance, she was more correct than I would have been, but that wouldn't always be the case.

"He's not bad-looking but dating him would be a terrible idea."

"Why? Does he have a crazy ex or something?"

I chuckled and shook my head. "No. Well, I guess I don't know, but I doubt it. It's just that he's ex-military and super intense, and I'm not sure I want to get into any kind of relationship so soon after moving."

"Some of those military guys can be scary," she said with wide eyes. "PTSD and all that stuff. Was he in combat?"

"I have no idea. I really don't know him at all, certainly not enough for him to be distracting me as badly as he has been. He could be a modern-day Jack the Ripper for all I know."

Liv stared at me as though I'd grown a second head. "Why on earth would you say that?"

"Because, Liv, not everyone is who they seem to be. Trust me on that."

Before I could get another word out, a loud sound

exploded from outside. I grabbed Olivia and yanked her down with me to the ground. My hand slid down my shirt to pull out a switchblade from my bra, clicking it open in one swift motion. The dining room quieted for the briefest second, then the distinct chatter of conversation and the clinking of dishes resumed as if nothing had happened, leaving me hunched on the ground holding a knife like a lunatic.

A car backfired. That was all it had been, but I'd acted as if there was a live shooter on a rampage.

When I met Olivia's gaze, she wasn't just looking at me as though I'd gone crazy. Now, her stare was infused with worry. I released my hold on her, and we both stood.

"Em, what the hell was that?"

"It just startled me, that's all. I better check on my tables. Thanks for covering for me, Liv, I owe you." I hurried back out to the dining area, unwilling to give her an explanation or time for any more questions. It didn't matter if Olivia was a work acquaintance or my new best friend; I wasn't opening up to anyone about the past.

This was my new life, and I didn't want it tainted with the stain of old memories.

After my shift, I took a detour to the shelter where I'd started volunteering several weeks ago. Olivia's dad let me take leftovers to donate rather than toss them. Sometimes, there wasn't enough to warrant a trip, but on nights like tonight, I had two large silver containers full of food that the ladies would love.

The shelter was a transitional housing and wellness center, not far from my apartment, where homeless women could go and work on a fresh start. When I arrived in New York, I quickly figured out that I needed to feel as though I was making a difference in the world. That I was doing more than living my own sheltered life and ignoring the struggles of the people around me.

As soon as I started my first shift, I knew immediately that I was on the right track. It wasn't always easy. My heart ached to know the pain each of the women had experienced. While my part in their lives was nominal, I felt better knowing I was doing something to help.

I realized that a big part of who I was revolved around who I was *not*.

I was not someone who could sit by and let horrible things happen without doing something.

The stories the shelter women told were heartbreaking and tragic, and so many of them were a result of slipping through the system. For now, I was content to participate on the tail end, helping women get back on track. However, I couldn't help but wonder what could be done to prevent them from ending up on the streets to begin with.

I talked with the shelter director about that topic and was given mind-numbing details about the extensive red tape involved in removing children from their home or stepping into domestic abuse situations. I hated to think of all the women and children hurting out in the world at any given time. There were people who wanted to help, but our society was set up to minimize government intrusion into the family.

I got it. I understood the need to keep the government in check and allow people their freedoms, but it was still hard to think about. So many innocent lives broken and lost because they were mistreated inside the sanctity of their own homes. A place that should have been a haven.

Fortunately, dropping off food was always a happy occasion. After the day I'd had, I wasn't up for much more. I brought in the goodies, managing to squeeze them into the packed refrigerator, then chatted briefly with the ladies who hadn't made it up to bed yet.

By the time I started on my walk home, I was utterly exhausted, but not quite tired enough to still my overactive imagination. As if my catastrophe of a day hadn't been bad enough, my paranoia kicked in on the way home. I could have sworn there were eyes watching me. I looked over my shoulder repeatedly, almost to the point of hysteria. I was so distracted that I walked straight into the man in front of me when he halted at an intersection. I hadn't noticed he'd stopped for cross traffic and had nearly bumped him into the busy street. I apologized profusely and scolded myself for being so ridiculous, but the feeling didn't go away.

The moment I entered my apartment, I made sure all the blinds were closed and peeked in every dark corner. Once my nerves settled, I changed into a baggy T-shirt and sweatpants, then curled up on my sofa with my two favorite men, Ned and Don Julio. Most women my age would pour a glass of wine or sip on a spritzer, but that wasn't me. I'd never been a wine drinker, and some things you couldn't erase.

When I needed a little something to calm my nerves, I went straight for the tequila. And not just any tequila—the good stuff—Patrón or Don Julio or Casa Noble. I made sure to keep one of them on hand, along with a few limes, for just such an occasion. Simply feeling the cork stopper pull free of the thick glass made my stomach warm in anticipation.

I laced the edge of my sipping glass with a swipe of lime wedge, giving the perfect hint of citrus with each taste of liquor. After starting my Spotify relaxation playlist, I sipped my tequila and munched on the tortilla chips I'd brought home from work. Salty chips were the ideal complement to the drink even though I rarely wanted any after serving them all day to customers. I had known today would be different and had gone home prepared.

Two hours later, all my worries were dried up like a summer rain. Ned had been fully updated on my day, and my whole body was toasty warm. The moment I dropped into bed, I closed my eyes and drifted to sleep, unable to fully banish a certain set of intelligent brown eyes from following me into my dreams.

FOUR
Jamir

WHEN I WAS GROWING UP, MY MOTHER USED TO SAY THAT nothing good happened after midnight. It was her way of defending the strict curfew she placed on us. I didn't understand as a kid, but after two decades of dealing with some of the worst scum on the planet, I realized she knew what she was talking about.

What was it about the cloak of darkness that set all manner of nefarious activities into play? Even when those deeds took place inside, where the degree of moonlight or sunlight was irrelevant, they still usually occurred in the hours closest to midnight. Granted, the rule didn't apply to some of the more modern criminal activity, but as for most traditional criminals—thieves, rapists, and murderers—the hours between ten p.m. and two a.m. were particularly sacred.

What did that mean for me? A fucked-up sleep schedule.

The silver lining? It gave me just enough of a window to accompany a certain mysterious brunette home from her shift at the restaurant. I'd known something was off about her but never imagined she'd have a bounty on her. There was no question in my mind that I had to learn more.

Since it was my job to be observant, I'd noticed once, in the past, she'd come to class wearing a Jalisco's name tag. It was a small restaurant not far from the studio. The perfect place to observe Emily in her daily life. I'd only meant to watch her for a few minutes to see what I could glean from her interactions at work, but when she clocked out for the night, I saw a perfect opportunity to get her home address. People's homes were always the best source of information.

She was a far cry from a normal target, which meant I wasn't going to rush into any judgments about her. Evil hid in the daylight just as easily as the darkness. If her secrets were even uglier than I'd suspected, I would turn her in for the fifty-thousand-dollar payout. It would be a disappointment, but if her crimes fit the punishment, that was her own fault. Just because I was intrigued by the woman didn't mean she wasn't flawed. I would do my research and find out why she was being hunted. If she deserved having a price on her head, I'd bring her in just like I would any other target. If the bounty was unwarranted, then this became a far more complicated situation.

In order to make a decision, I needed to learn everything I could about the woman who called herself Emily Ramirez. As far as I knew, I was the only one to locate her, but there was no guarantee it would stay that way. I would need to gather information quickly.

Unfortunately, she wasn't the only item on my agenda for the evening. Taking care of Chad McDonald, my most recent job, was far more pressing. I followed Emily home, making note of her address, then rerouted myself back uptown to The Mark Hotel.

When I read where Chad would be staying, I had chuckled at the irony. He wouldn't be able to appreciate the humor in his choice of accommodations, but then, he had no idea he was in the crosshairs of one of the most sought-after hitmen in the country. It was probably best that way. People tended to panic when they knew, making them less than dignified in their final moments.

I normally required a much longer time to prepare for a hit, but Chad was a moving target. He rarely stayed in one place for long, and the Omega had provided ample information for a quick transaction. Plus, the fifty-nine-year-old pharmaceutical executive was hardly a threat. Prosperity and privilege in the flesh meant he'd probably never broken a sweat outside of the gym in his entire life.

He was never married but had a wealth of friends who adored him—or who they thought he was. As it turned out, Chad had a secret life. More than just a closet homosexual. Darker than any pornography addiction. Chad had a proclivity for little boys.

His perverse interest had budded and blossomed over the years until he had secured an intricate network of connections who supplied him with the objects of his desire. During his stay in the city, he had an appointment with said connections that would last well into the night.

As we already established, nothing good happened after midnight.

Myself included.

Wrapped in a full-length coat with a blond wig peeking

out beneath a golfer's flat cap, I casually strolled through the hotel lobby. When I arrived at the room number I'd been given, I used a device attached to a replicated hotel key card that wiped the coding from the lock such that any key could gain entry. When I was in the service, we used a far more advanced version that reprogrammed locks to accept our key in addition to the assigned key card, making it seem as though the lock was still functional and untampered with. In this particular case, I wasn't dealing with a political assassination that would be analyzed with a high degree of scrutiny. Erasing the lock programming was sufficient.

Once I was inside, the wait began. That was the worst part of any job—the boredom. It wasn't anxiety or any last-minute misgivings about what I was about to do that grated on my nerves. It was the endless minutes bleeding into hours of forced attentiveness. I could hardly sit back and play Words with Friends on my phone when my mark could come through the door at any moment. Once I was set up, I had to keep my muscles coiled and my reflexes on guard in preparation of attack.

No, I wasn't burdened with a sour conscience or forced to question the moral justifications of my actions. I did what I believed was right—end of story.

I'd been a killer for a majority of my life, surrounded by some of the vilest humans on the planet. I'd seen evil and knew what it looked like, how it moved and where it hid. If I performed my job appropriately and determined a man was evil, I would not entertain any doubt about ending his life. The world was better off without him, and I stood by that decision. I'd experienced self-doubt in the past and learned that it only brought about misery, and that was true of anyone in any profession.

Unlike some of my jobs where I lay in wait for hours,

Chad did me the favor of calling it an early night. He let himself inside, humming softly like a chittering mouse, oblivious to the snake coiled nearby. When he passed the entry to the small kitchenette, I lunged for him.

It was almost too easy.

Chad had no self-preservation skills or survival instincts to rely upon. Instead, he froze in shock, making my job almost effortless. I came at him from behind, clasping one hand over his mouth. The other hand held an instrument to his neck that used ultrasound waves to inject medication without breaking the skin. It was important not to leave any signs of foul play.

Within seconds, the stiff form in my arms softened as the medication worked its way through his system. I carried him to the bed, making sure not to leave any bruises. At this stage, Chad was still conscious but unable to move a muscle.

"Succinylcholine," I explained to the man trapped behind wide, unmoving eyes—awake and coherent but held prisoner inside his own body. "As you're in pharmaceuticals, you're probably familiar with the anesthetic. Normally, it's used in combination with other medications for surgical procedures." I lifted his leg and began to remove his dress shoes. "On its own, the drug induces paralysis and eventual asphyxiation. It's got to be awful to be under the effects of such a powerful paralytic. To have things done to your body without your consent, all while you're perfectly aware and unable to resist." I tsked as I slid down his pants and draped them carefully over the desk chair by the window. Next, I pulled off his jacket and unbuttoned his dress shirt while foam began to collect in the corners of his mouth.

"It's an absolute nightmare but, in this case, rather fitting, wouldn't you say? I bet plenty of defenseless little boys out there would agree with me." I pulled the covers over his chest, as if tucking him in for the night, then hovered over his face so that our eyes could meet. "You've been very naughty, Chad. As you gurgle on your last breath, betrayed by your own body, I want you to understand that you did this. You brought this upon yourself."

Before pulling away, I removed his contacts from his eyes, then placed them in their case in the bathroom. By the time I returned, Chad no longer had a pulse.

I took a picture as evidence and cleaned up after myself, ensuring the room looked perfectly undisturbed upon my departure. Using a technique I'd been taught many years before, I engaged the chain lock on the door as I left, making it look as though the room had been locked from the inside. The last touch, a "do not disturb" hanger on the door handle.

I had already ensured cameras were not in use in the hallways. I might have been seen on elevator cameras arriving on his floor, but there was no proof what room I'd visited. With my hands in my pockets and a lightness to my step, I slipped from the hotel without a trace.

FIVE
Emily

Friday's class brought an onslaught of tension and awkward glances, at least as far as I was concerned. Tamir was his usual stoic self, totally unruffled and radiating cool confidence. I felt like the building furnace had malfunctioned and immersed the gym in a sauna-like heat. Judging by the fact that I was the only one drenched in sweat, the temperature spike was purely a personal problem.

I might have been a hot mess on the inside, but on the surface, aside from my fountain of sweat, I kept myself aloof and distant. Each time Tamir's cutting dark eyes turned my way, they were met with an immovable iceberg of impassivity. A sweaty iceberg, but an iceberg, nonetheless. I was stronger than my desires and wouldn't allow logic to be swept away under the guise of need. I might have *wanted* to explore the chemistry that sizzled between us, but that wasn't what I *needed*. I didn't need a man at all, but if I did open up to one, it would be to someone respectable and honest. Someone who wouldn't put me right back where I started. Someone I could trust.

I wasn't sure what that looked like, but I knew it wasn't Tamir. He had secrets, and I couldn't see how trust could be established on a foundation of lies and deceit.

With that in mind, I kept my distance the entire class. I didn't even allow myself to look in his direction when it came time to leave. I grabbed my things and ran, hurrying home to spend my Friday night alone in my apartment.

Sometimes, when I was lonely, I got angry with myself for my situation. It had been my own doing, after all. I would drink or binge watch some inane television show, and when my pity party lost its appeal, I reminded myself why I'd left. Why it had been necessary to move myself across the country and cut myself off from everything I'd known. That was when I put my big girl panties on and admitted that I'd done the right thing.

A few months of solitude was worth the outcome, and it wouldn't be forever. One day, I'd settle into my new life, and I'd be in a better place than where I started. One day. Until then, I spent the weekend alone, as I did most weekends, working and cleaning my apartment.

Monday was a long, grinding day at work. Traffic was slow, which left far too much time for internal retrospection. Tuesday wasn't far off, but at least it allowed me enough time to run home after work and change before going to class. Most days, I was forced to change in the tiny restaurant bathroom and rush from work straight to the gym, but when the restaurant was half-empty, my boss sent me home early. I lived close enough to make the quick trip home before class.

My apartment was on the fourth floor in a mostly residential neighborhood. There were six apartments on each floor, and mine was one of the two farthest from the elevator. I'd gotten to know three of my neighbors although, admittedly, not well. There was a young family across the hall who was always on the go and paid me little mind, as I was outside their tornadic nucleus. Nearest the elevator was a middle-aged man who looked to be in finance or some other low-level white-collar gig. Both tenants were pleasant enough, but I usually just smiled and walked past when I saw them in the halls.

The apartment directly across from me was a different story.

Mrs. Timmons was an elderly woman who lived alone, except for her two Siamese cats. She reminded me of my tita although Tita had never been a cat person. She'd had a vicious little chihuahua named Taco. He was affectionate to the family, but the second an outsider stepped foot near our house, Taco went ballistic. Poor thing had the heart of a pit bull in the body of a rat. When Tita passed away, my father agreed to keep the dog but refused to allow it inside. In a matter of weeks, he got out of the rickety fence and came to grips with reality when he took on an actual pit bull.

It did not go well for Taco.

I adored my tita, crazy dog and all, so it came naturally for me to form an attachment to Mrs. Timmons. I enjoyed our little visits. If my tita had been alone in the city, I would have wanted someone to check on her for me.

On my way home, I knocked at the old woman's door and waited for her to answer. As usual, her foggy eyes lit through the haze of cataracts when she greeted me.

"Sweet Emily! What a lovely surprise." She reached for my hands and clasped them both, figuring out early on that I wasn't exactly the hugging type. "You want to come in? I just got some new cherry sours." She started to turn for her candy dish, but I stopped her.

"Actually, Mrs. Timmons—"

"Honey, I've told you, call me Grace."

I smirked. "Grace, I've only got a few minutes before I have to be somewhere. I just wanted to check on you while I was home."

"Always so busy! I remember those days. No need to worry about me, honey."

"Are you sure you don't need anything? I can swing by the grocery store on my way home later."

"Thank you, dear, but I think I'm fine for now. Oh! I almost forgot. I got a glimpse of that visitor you had over earlier. He's quite the looker!" She grinned devilishly and patted her perfectly set silver hair. "I just happened to be coming back from checking the mail when he was leaving and couldn't help but notice."

My stomach dipped and rose, churning its contents. Someone had been at my apartment? A man? Could he still be in there? No, she said she saw him leaving. But what if he came back? I struggled to swallow, my throat suddenly tight and dry.

"Um, did you see him come from inside my place? Or just walking down the hall?"

Grace's eyes narrowed as she began to detect my discomfort. "Is something wrong, dear? I didn't see him come from inside, but he definitely came from our end of the hallway. I assumed he was there for you because I certainly didn't know him. Should I have called the police?"

"No, not at all. It just surprised me, that's all," I assured her. "I appreciate you letting me know, but I better change clothes and get going."

More wrinkles gathered over her pursed brow. "Okay, if you say so. I'll keep an eye out and let you know if he comes back."

I forced a semi-genuine smile. "There's really no need, but I appreciate you looking out for me. Have a good rest of your day." The last thing I wanted was to make Grace worry about my safety or her own.

"You too, honey."

I stepped out of her doorway and pulled her door shut behind me, then turned to my own door. Nothing looked any different. There were no signs of forced entry, and the door was locked when I tested it with my key. It was entirely possible a visitor had gone to the wrong floor or the man had been a solicitor even though they were not allowed inside the building. Sometimes a magazine salesman, or the like, found their way past the front entry.

I squashed the overwhelming sense of paranoia that had been ghosting me for days and made my way inside. My eyes carefully scanned the kitchen and into the living area, searching the contents for signs of tampering. Not one thing looked out of place.

It was official. I was losing my mind.

I rolled my eyes and hurried to my bedroom to change. Once I was ready, I grabbed my gym bag, which doubled as my purse on class days, and hurried out, making sure to lock my door before I left.

I arrived just minutes before the start of class and avoided eye contact with Tamir throughout the hour-long session, as was my new routine. I should have continued with that strategy and hightailed it out of there the second class was over, but of course, that's not what happened. Those good old social norms kicked in when I noticed the cluster of pads, punching mitts, and shin guards spread across the back of the room and the mass of students rushing for the exit without helping to clean up.

Dios mío. My God.

What was wrong with me? Why couldn't I just walk out with the rest of them and let Tamir clean up after us? He *was* getting paid, after all. I could almost feel my tita pinching the sensitive skin on the underside of my arm. The woman had trained me too well. Not smiling at strangers on a city street was a far cry from making someone else pick up a mess all by themselves. I couldn't do it. I had to stay and help.

I hurried over to the pile farthest from Tamir and gathered items, then lugged them over to the storage bins. When I went back for a second load, he was leaning against the wall, eyes glued to me.

"You're not running off today?" he asked with a hint of amusement.

"I don't know what you mean." I filled my arms again, keeping my eyes on my task.

He didn't move to help me. Instead, he crossed his arms and waited for me to return. "Right … and the fact that you can hardly make eye contact with me is all in my imagination."

Properly goaded, I lifted my gaze to his. "There, feel better?"

He didn't even try to tame his serpentine grin. "Not by a long shot, but I will." He bent over and picked up two of the large torso pads. "You have plans tonight?"

"I do, actually, which is why I have to get going." I needed to get out of there before my heart pounded its way out of my chest. Why was Tamir putting me on the spot? Any other man would have accepted my avoidance and left me alone, but not him. He wasn't giving me an inch of wiggle room.

"That's what I figured," he murmured as he walked toward the bins.

I didn't respond. Grabbing my gym bag, I left the warmth of the studio for the crisp night air. Our awkward conversation left me swimming in questions. Why did it feel like he was trying to provoke me? Why couldn't I have left right after class like everyone else? Were classes always going to feel that awkward in the future? Did I need to consider switching gyms?

The maelstrom of questions and internal debates occupied my complete focus, which was why I didn't notice the hooded figure leaning against the wall at the entrance of an alley. A hand shot out and clasped my arm, yanking me to the side. When I looked up in surprise, I caught a brief glimpse of the man's profile against the city streetlight. It was angular and harsh—the sharp features of pure ruthlessness.

"What the—" I didn't get another word out. His warm, calloused hand clamped over my mouth from behind as he dragged me deeper into the shadows of the alley. I squirmed and thrashed, but between my shock and being unsteady as he tugged me along, I couldn't come up with a single move to free myself.

"Peekaboo, I found you," the man cooed near my ear just as he slowed enough for me to get my bearings.

His words sent unadulterated terror surging through my veins.

I'd been found. It only took three months.

I didn't recognize the man, but he clearly knew who I was and knew I was on the run. Was he there to take me back? Or was he just going to kill me there in the alley?

My mind tried to launch into a chaotic panic, but I shoved

it all into a back room in my brain, turned off the light and slammed the door shut.

This was no time to fall apart.

I had a matter of seconds before this man either killed me or captured me. I couldn't let either of those happen.

Time stretched and yawned, dragging out each moment in clarifying detail, when in reality, our encounter only consumed a handful of seconds. In that oddity of time distortion, I flipped through my mental playbook of options and committed to my next move.

He held me in a type of bear hug, one hand over my mouth, the other gripping my chest tightly, both keeping me firmly pressed against him, with my arms forced down at my sides. I folded over with as much force as I could, bending at the waist, then slid my hips to the side to give my hand room to swing backward at his groin. I performed the series of movements in quick succession, catching my attacker by surprise and landing a perfect strike. He bellowed a curse, and his arms reflexively contracted backward, giving me room to yank myself free of his grasp.

It worked.

I had freed myself of his grasp but done so in a way that still left me trapped. The man stood doubled over between me and the street. My only chance at escape was to run past him and risk being captured again. I had no choice. I lunged forward and used all my force to push past him, but his iron grip clamped down over my wrist on my way past.

He yanked me back into the alley so hard, it felt like he had dislocated my shoulder. My natural instinct was to curl in on myself protectively as pain radiated down my arm, but he yanked me to him and pressed my front against the icy brick wall, one hand clamped over my mouth and the other grasping my hands behind my back.

The metallic taste of fear coated my tongue, and my breathing shuddered as sobs began to wrack my chest. But before the man could make his next move, a curse came from the mouth of the alley.

My attacker was yanked off me. I scurried a few steps away, but instead of running, I found myself watching in awe as my savior pummeled the other man. It was dark, and my rescuer's back was to me, but I could still see that he wore the same black track pants and red gym shirt he'd been wearing moments before in class.

It was Tamir. He'd saved me.

His strikes were perfectly clean, performed with expert precision. Like a machine. A killing machine. It was beautiful and terrible to behold. Nothing like what I witnessed in class. At full speed and with deadly intent, Tamir no longer resembled a dancer. He was a predator. Fierce and merciless.

The two men exchanged only a dozen parries before my hooded attacker collapsed to the ground, unconscious. At least, I thought he was unconscious.

"You didn't kill him, did you?" I hissed.

Tamir slowly turned, his chest rising and falling at an accelerated rate—the only evidence he'd just been in a fight. "He just attacked you. Do you really care if he's dead?"

"No … yes. Yes, I do."

He closed the distance between us and looked me up and down. "Are you hurt?"

My breath caught in my throat, and my hand flew to my necklace for reassurance. "No, I'm fine. Let's just forget this happened. I need to go." I was doused in two competing emotions—terror and relief. Seeing Tamir there in the darkness, knowing he had stopped that man from doing God knew what, I desperately wanted to launch myself into his arms. But he'd nearly killed a man without a thought. The savagery in his black gaze terrified me, keeping me rooted in place.

"This man just tried to mug you. Don't you want to call the cops?"

"*No*." My response was immediate and absolute, which I knew sounded odd. Why the hell would a woman not want to call the police when she'd just been attacked? I began to pace. "Look, I'm fine. No harm done. I know it seems strange, but can you please just let it go?"

The possible consequences of my night cascaded like dominoes before me. Was this attacker the man who'd been at my apartment? Holy *shit*. What was I supposed to do now? How had this happened? If I'd been found this quickly, would I ever be free? Was there any point in relocating and trying again? Did I have any other option? Would I have to live the rest of whatever short life I had on the run?

"Emily!" Two strong hands gripped my shoulders and shook me firmly.

I drifted back to the present and realized Tamir had been speaking to me, but I'd been so entirely lost in my thoughts that I hadn't heard a word he'd said. I peered up at his face, searching his features for answers he couldn't give me.

"He's going to wake up any minute. If we aren't calling the police, then we need to leave. Let me walk you back to your apartment."

I shook my head frantically. "No, I can't go back. It's not safe there. You don't understand."

His hands lifted from my shoulders to my cheeks, holding me in place. His forehead creased with confusion, making me panic even more.

"Calm down," he soothed gently. "We don't have to go to your place, but I'm not leaving you here. We can go to my place. You can explain to me what's going on, and we'll figure out what to do from there once you're thinking more clearly. Okay?" His hands didn't leave my face until I managed a hesitant nod.

He took one of my hands in his and pulled me toward the street, allowing me to grab my gym bag from where it had fallen when I was first attacked. His hand seared me with its heat, and I clung to it as if he were the lifeline I desperately needed.

I hadn't been far from the studio, so we made it back within minutes. He took me to the tenant entrance beside the studio, and we climbed the stairs to the second floor. An eerie fog blanketed my mind on the way over. I felt numb and distant. As if my life was no longer recognizable.

Stepping inside the warmth of his apartment helped marginally. The place was spacious but comfortable, not too different from my own home, except Tamir had clearly been living in his apartment far longer than I'd been in mine.

"Why don't you have a seat. I'll make you some tea." He motioned toward a gray upholstered sofa as he turned toward the open kitchen.

I kept my jacket on, tugging it tightly around me, and sat on the far end of the couch with my bag clutched against my chest. The adrenaline waned from my system, making my body shiver and shake uncontrollably as I peered blankly at my surroundings.

How had my life devolved so drastically in a matter of minutes? What was I going to do?

"Here, eat these. They'll help elevate your blood sugar and ease the shaking." Tamir handed me a napkin stacked with several shortbread cookies and placed a glass of water on the coffee table. He lowered himself into a chair opposite me. His stare bored into me, but I couldn't meet his gaze.

"You eat cookies?" I asked. "It seems entirely too normal

for you." It was the first thing that popped into my addled brain.

"I *am* human, Emily."

"Could have fooled me," I muttered. "I figured you'd be one of those 'my body is a temple' kind of people who lives on spinach and kale." I nibbled on the buttery goodness, the first bites of sugar instantly calming my nerves.

After long seconds of silence, I finally glanced in his direction.

"Are we really going to talk about my dietary habits right now?"

"Look, I don't know what you want me to say. I just got mugged. I'm a little freaked out."

He leaned forward, placing his elbows on his knees and steepling his hands together. "*Mugged*? Back in that alley, you told me your apartment was no longer safe and you couldn't go back. What does that have to do with a random mugging?"

I couldn't help the defeated sigh that escaped my lungs. "It's not exactly random," I admitted softly. I didn't want him involved in my problems, but I could hardly avoid it now. He'd beaten a man unconscious for me and then hadn't called the police when I asked him not to. He deserved some kind of explanation. "My ex-boyfriend is crazy, but I didn't realize how bad it was until it was too late. The first chance I got, I left him in the night and ran, riding buses across the country until I ended up here."

"That man in the alley was your ex-boyfriend?"

I shook my head. "I think he hired someone to either kill me or take me back to him. I don't know how he did it, but he found me, and now, the city isn't safe for me."

It was foolish of me to have expected anything less than cool detachment from Tamir. Surprise, concern, outrage—

those were human emotions. Tamir was Terminator-grade machine.

"Why won't you call the police?" he asked.

"They can't keep me safe from him! They'll slap a restraining order on him, and meanwhile, I'm facedown in a gutter. No thanks. I got away once, so I can do it again. I have a friend in town who can help me disappear. At some point, either my ex won't be able to find me, or he'll finally give up trying." The cookies had helped balance my system, but it was anger that brought back my determination and clarity.

Tamir examined me, breaking me down, piece by piece, and analyzing his findings. I wasn't sure I'd ever felt so scrutinized in my life. Was he judging me? Condemning me? I had no clue what was going on in that cryptic head of his. The only thing to do was wait wordlessly in the heavy silence for his conclusion.

"Very well. You can stay here tonight. Tomorrow, we'll work on a plan." He held my gaze, refusing to let me go, even when the tea kettle began to shriek on the stove. When he finally severed our connection and rose, my body sagged with a bone-weary relief.

I had passed whatever test he'd been conducting and was spared further interrogation, at least for the time being.

SIX
Tamir

DURING MY TEN YEARS IN THE SPECIAL FORCES, I RECEIVED rigorous interrogation training and had participated in my own examinations that would turn the bravest of men a sickly shade of white. There were infinite ways to get a man to talk, but none of it mattered if you couldn't tell what was fact and what was a lie. People would say anything to keep from being in pain.

My lie detection instincts had been expertly honed, and I felt confident Emily's confession was sincere. Her fear about her situation was primal, unsullied by manipulation. Did that mean everything she'd said was the truth? Not necessarily. But enough evidence existed to keep me from turning her over to collect the bounty, for now.

I had no doubt there was still more to her story.

It wasn't often an ex-lover put out a bounty to bring back his woman, but that wasn't to say it didn't happen. I knew of a Russian Vor who had hunted his lover for years because he lived for the chase. People were fucked up, which meant predicting someone's actions and understanding their motivations could be near impossible.

Emily's past was shrouded in a thick fog of mystery and deceit. I'd performed a background search on Emilia Reyes, which was the name given with her bounty. Even with her last name and knowing she'd originally resided in Texas, I couldn't scrape anything together. Her digital footprint was minuscule. The birth certificate on file for her had no father listed and what appeared to be a fake name for her mother, which meant I couldn't trace her via her family. She had purportedly earned an associate degree in finance and had a driver's license but was, otherwise, remarkably absent from the system. No debt or hospital records. No voter's registration or bills in her name. Not even a single social media account could be found. She was a ghost, and in my experience, ghosts had secrets.

Perhaps her secrets were unrelated to the bounty on her head, but either way, I would need more time to ferret out the full truth. I needed those answers to decide what I would do with her. I did have some semblance of a moral code. It was my own fucked-up version but a code, nonetheless. Stealing the last breaths from my victims was easy, but only after I was certain they were unworthy of life.

I wasn't just talking about petty criminals. The men, and sometimes women, who became my targets were depraved stains on humanity like serial murderers, rapists, child molesters, and some far more creative examples of the criminally insane. My intent was never to seek out these people in a vigilante fashion, but when a contract came before me, that was my primary requirement to take the job.

Some might ask who I was to play judge and jury about another man's worth.

I would say fuck off. No one asked you.

My employers' reasons for wanting someone dead might not have been remotely honorable, but I didn't care. I was only concerned with my role in a job. If I declined a job because the target didn't meet my requirements, and the client went elsewhere, that wasn't my problem. I simply had standards by which I worked. Would the mesmerizing Ms. Reyes tick off those checkboxes?

We would find out soon enough.

As I watched her sip her tea, I had to admit that "mesmerizing" had been an apt descriptor. Not only because of the intriguing mystery of her situation, but because of her alluring beauty as well. She was some concoction of Hispanic, but there was no telling what exact origin. The slight uptick of her eyes and prominent cheekbones hinted at a Native American ancestry. She had a regal air, even when she was covered in sweat at the gym or fighting for her life in a dark alley. If she was being hunted just for her unique beauty, I wouldn't have been surprised.

"Tell me about this man who's after you."

"What do you want to know?" She sipped from her tea, her shaking reduced to a slight tremble of her fingers.

"How long were you together?"

"Long enough to figure out he wasn't a good man."

"Is he a criminal?" The question was somewhat rhetorical as he had to have criminal connections in order to put a bounty on her head. I was more curious how extensive her knowledge was about his activities.

She shrugged. "There's no telling what all he's into, but it wasn't something we talked about. Why are you asking me about him? The degree of my past screwups doesn't help me figure out a way out of this situation." The teacup clanked against its saucer when she forcefully set it down.

I'd struck a nerve.

"Just trying to figure out the full picture, but we don't have to talk about it if it bothers you. I haven't had dinner and am starved. Would you like something to eat?"

"I haven't eaten since lunch, aside from those couple of cookies, so food sounds good. Thank you."

"If you'd like, you're welcome to take a shower while I cook a little something for us." I stood to retrieve a towel but paused when Emily's eyes met mine. They were still guarded, but the defensiveness and fear had bled away, leaving her gaze tired and tinged with a wary hopefulness.

"Why are you doing this, Tamir? Why help me when being anywhere near me could be dangerous?"

"First, I'm not afraid of whatever idiots this man may send after you. And second … I had a sister who ended up in trouble many years ago. She had no one there to help her, and I regret that every day of my life."

What I said was the truth, just not all of it. Perhaps it was more than I should have said, but something about her slipped and slithered under my skin. That, above anything else, was the one thing that was starting to worry me. Crazy ex-boyfriends and other hunters out to collect the bounty just made my normally dull days a little more colorful. The soft curves of a spirited woman who needed my help? Now *that* was dangerous.

SEVEN
Emily

Wɪᴛʜ ᴛʜᴇ ᴇxᴄᴇᴘᴛɪᴏɴ ᴏꜰ sᴇᴠᴇʀᴀʟ ᴡᴀᴛᴇʀᴄᴏʟᴏʀ ᴘᴀɪɴᴛɪɴɢs ᴏɴ the white walls, Tamir's apartment was nearly as sterile as mine. They were active, lively paintings, depicting colorful cityscapes and marketplaces. They didn't seem to fit my vision of what Tamir would have chosen for himself. I would have thought he was more of a photography type of man—the city skyline at night, or something equally as beautiful but understated.

Maybe he had a decorator select them. His furniture and décor was all good quality and coordinated in a way that made the room come together. It wouldn't have surprised me if there'd been a woman's touch in the design. What did surprise me was how expensive it all looked. I knew why I was able to afford my apartment on my measly waitress's wages, but he sure did surprisingly well for a self-defense instructor.

"I've set a towel on the counter for you," he said as he showed me to the bathroom. "The only drawback about this apartment is the single bathroom. I don't have company often, so it's rarely an issue."

I stepped past him in the narrow hallway, my body wanting to gravitate toward his warmth. "This is gorgeous. Did you remodel recently?" The glass stall shower was tiled with white marble, as was the entire floor and countertop. The fixtures were crisp and elegant without being too feminine. The overall look was stunning.

"About a year ago. I like to keep busy and learn new things, and the prior setup hadn't been touched since the eighties."

"You did it yourself?"

"Don't sound so surprised. It's not all that hard, if you have the time."

"Sure," I scoffed. "Loads of people can renovate an entire bathroom by themselves."

He leaned his shoulder against the wall and crossed his arms, making his biceps stretch the fabric of his T-shirt. "Maybe they're just too scared to try."

I leaned against the doorframe and pressed my hand against the opposite side of the frame. "Maybe they just don't have any clue what they're doing."

"Maybe they should check out YouTube. You can learn anything on YouTube." He lifted a wry brow, and it was too much. I coughed out a chuckle and shook my head.

"All right, you win." I started to close the door but paused, my eyes flashing briefly to his. "Thank you, Tamir. I'm not sure what I would have done without you tonight."

He gave me a silent nod. "Try not to worry too much. You're safe here, and we'll sort out a plan soon enough." He slipped away toward the kitchen, and I locked myself in the bathroom, having a moment alone for the first time since being attacked.

I set down my gym bag on the counter and took in my reflection in the large mirror. My hair was in disarray, half-fallen out of its ponytail from class, and my cheek had a small scrape from being pressed against the brick wall. Other than that, I didn't look all that bad. My outer appearance wasn't at all reflective of the turmoil going on inside.

I was so scared that it was all I could do not to break down. Just the thought brought the sting of tears to my eyes.

That's not going to help, Em, so cut it out.

I grabbed my phone and the spare set of workout clothes I had in my gym bag and set them on the counter. When I'd gone home from work to change, I hadn't used the clothes in my bag. Thank God for small miracles.

The sound of the water turning on was soothing. Like the falling rain, the gentle hum was cathartic and cleansing. The second it was warm enough, I stepped under the heavy spray and let it wash away the sticky memories of the attack. The heat was the perfect balm on my tense muscles, but it did nothing to ease the chaos in my mind.

All of the implications of being attacked bombarded me with varying degrees of intensity.

I was going to have to walk out on my job and the shelter without a single explanation or warning. It made me feel horribly guilty, and I hated for Olivia and the women at the shelter to worry. They were good people, but I had no choice. I didn't think I could even go back to my apartment.

Leaving Mrs. Timmons was the worst part of all. She

66

would be heartbroken for me. She didn't deserve that after being nothing but thoughtful and kind to me.

It was all my fault. That was what happened when you associated with the wrong people. Their toxic influence spread and infected everything you touched, tainting the best parts of your life, even after you'd walked away.

It reinforced that I'd done the right thing, but the fallout still sucked. At least I was alive, and I would continue to fight until that wasn't the case.

I talked a big game, but there was one main reason I wasn't totally freaking out, and her name was Stephanie. As soon as I was out of the shower, I was going to text her. She would know what to do and be able to help me.

With Stephanie's assistance, I wouldn't have to rely on Tamir any further, which was important because I didn't want to drag him into my problems. Despite my adamant insistence that Tamir was dangerous, and therefore, bad for me, he had been the one to save my life. I was willing to admit I might have misjudged him. Who was I to repay his kindness by making him a target right along with me?

I stepped out of the shower and dried off only after I'd threatened to exhaust the entire building's supply of hot water. When the steam production stopped, delicious wafts of air slipped in from beneath the door. Tamir was cooking, and I was suddenly ravenous. I threw on my clothes and did my best to finger-comb my hair into behaving. A small sliver along the edge of the mirror had begun to defog, which I used to give myself a once-over and noticed the angry red scrape on my cheek.

Glancing at the door, I debated going out to ask Tamir for antibiotic ointment. It would have been the polite thing to do, rather than snoop through his drawers. Polite and not at all helpful. I wanted to learn more about the unusual man who had taken me in, and snooping was a great place to start. I might not have been evil, like some people, but I also never claimed to be perfect.

The only storage in the bathroom was a series of three drawers and the cabinet under the sink beneath the marble vanity. The top drawer contained a beard trimmer and fingernail clippers, along with a comb and an assortment of men's toiletries. The other two drawers had Q-tips, cotton balls, and other crap that wasn't remotely helpful on either front.

Squatting down, I opened the cabinet beneath the sink and found several rolls of toilet paper, as one might expect, along with cleaning supplies and a plunger. Nothing sordid and no first-aid kit. I sighed and started to stand when a glint of silver at the top of the cabinet caught my eye. I ducked my head to get a better view and discovered a small gun in a holster attached to the top of the inside of the cabinet. The sink was one of those fake bowls that sat on the counter, rather than being sunken into the vanity. It gave just enough room to attach the holster to the flat marble above.

Why the hell did Tamir have a gun hidden inside his bathroom vanity? Despite the heat still radiating from my body, tiny goose bumps perched along the length of my arms. Was it normal for someone who was ex-military to hide guns in their home as though preparing for an invasion? He didn't seem like one of those radical doomsayers or anything so eccentric, but would I be able to tell if he was?

Mrs. Timmons would swear on her Bible that I was a good girl from California with two loving parents and a thirst for adventure because that was the story I'd told her. Was that all we really knew about the people around us—what they chose to tell us? That was exactly what it meant. So what did that mean for Tamir? Nothing—it meant I knew absolutely nothing about him. One kind deed wasn't a window into his soul. He could still be just as dangerous as any other man.

One night.

I needed to survive one night in his house, then I was gone. Whatever his backstory was, it didn't matter, because I wouldn't be there long enough for it to make a difference. I quickly stood and grabbed my phone before opening the bathroom door. A wall of savory flavors swarmed me, making my stomach growl.

Before I headed for the kitchen, I texted a message to Stephanie.

Me: I've been found—someone attacked me tonight. I need help.

Stephanie: Are you ok?

Me: Yes, just scared.

Stephanie: Where are you?

Me: At a friend's for the night, but I need to leave town.

Stephanie: Of course, let me see what I can come up with.

Me: Thank you!

Stephanie: Meet me at Tops Diner off 280 in Newark. Can you be there tomorrow morning by 7?

Me: No problem, see you then.

EIGHT
Jamir

"WHATEVER THAT IS, IT SMELLS DELICIOUS." EMILY PROPPED herself against the wall, freshly showered and dressed in what appeared to be clean workout clothes.

"Just chicken and rice, nothing extravagant. It's actually done if you want to have a seat."

"Before we eat, do you have any antibiotic ointment?" She gestured to a cut on her cheek.

"Of course, let me grab it." I wiped my hands on a dish towel and slid past where she stood to go back to my room. I kept the first-aid kit in my work duffel bag to make sure it was always with me, just in case things got complicated. I grabbed the tube of ointment and went back to the kitchen, removing the cap while I walked. "Come here." My voice betrayed me, going gravelly and coarse with the bolt of lust that had assaulted me when I smelled my soap lingering on her skin.

There was something about having your scent on a woman that was beyond gratifying. And someone like Emily, who was wild and unpredictable? It made my inner beast purr with satisfaction.

For that reason alone, I needed to hand her the tube and let her apply the medication herself. Even the smallest of touches was problematic where she was concerned. It was best if I kept my distance, so I told myself to hand over the cream and step back.

Apparently, my superiors had been right.

I was insubordinate and resistant to taking orders.

I ignored myself completely, giving in to the compulsion to breathe her in, to touch her, to feel her. I put a small amount of ointment on my finger and lifted it to her face. She stood just inches from me, so close, I could feel her shaky breaths skate across my forearm as I gently spread the cream on her cheek.

"Any others?"

"No," she breathed, her eyes catching mine for a long-drawn-out second before she retreated to the kitchen table.

After slipping the tube in my pocket, I retrieved the pans from the stove and put food on both our plates.

"Thanks for cooking. I didn't realize how hungry I was until I got out of the shower and could smell the food." She dug in the second I sat down and lifted my fork.

"With enough adrenaline coursing through your system, you could have a gunshot wound and not even know it, let alone hunger pangs. It's a powerful substance."

Her curious gaze flitted to mine. "Do you know that from personal experience? The part about the gunshot wound?"

"I do."

"Does that mean you saw active duty?"

"I participated in active missions for about seven years."

She lowered her water glass from her full lips. "That's a long time."

"I'm an old man compared to you."

She barked out a humorless laugh. "That sounds like a pity party if I've ever heard one, and I've thrown my fair share."

"There's nothing pitiful about it. I was merely pointing out that you're practically a child, and I'm sure seven years sounds like an eternity to you." The tension in the room quickly escalated to a stifling degree.

"As someone who's probably been through some horrible shit, you should understand that age is just a number. Whatever you experienced during active duty would age even the youngest soldier. The same holds true for me. Unless you know what I've been through and the things I've seen, don't assume you know me. I haven't been a child for a very long time." Her eyes blazed with ferocity. Indignation. Passion. Those were the most words I'd heard out of her mouth at one time, and I wanted to lap up every bit of that emotion and drain her dry until she was languid and lost in my bed.

It was the last place my brain needed to go.

After her outburst, we both ate quietly for long minutes. I attempted to ignore the lascivious voice gaining control in the back of my mine, concentrating on more important things, like the silver watch Emily wore where her sweatband had been. Interesting. Coincidence? Possibly.

She patted her mouth with her napkin when she was done and put her hands in her lap. "That was delicious, thank you. And I meant to tell you earlier, you have a great apartment."

"It suited all my needs, including a parking spot in the basement garage. That's not easy to find around here."

"No kidding! When I first moved, I was stunned at how expensive a freaking parking spot was in the city. Needless to say, I won't be buying a car."

"I would get rid of mine, but I travel on occasion, so it's necessary."

"Where all have you been?"

"All over the world."

"Okay," she said in a sing-song voice. "What's your favorite place you've been?"

"Probably the Swiss Alps in the summer. Everything is green and blooming, and it's quite breathtaking. What about you?"

She smiled sadly. "I'm afraid I've never been much of anywhere. That's why moving to the city was such a big deal for me. I'd love to travel one day, once I get this mess over with." Her eyes dropped to her plate, zoning out for a moment before she stood and flashed an empty smile. "I'll do the dishes. It's only fair since you cooked."

I carried my own plate to the sink and helped with the cleanup. I'd been on my own far too long to sit and watch while someone else cleaned my kitchen. We worked companionably, getting the kitchen spotless in a matter of minutes.

"I'd love to offer you a guest bed, but there isn't one. The couch will have to do. I hope that's okay."

"Of course."

"Good, then I'll grab some blankets before I get in the shower, and you can make yourself comfortable." I brought out all the spare bedding I had, then headed to the shower before I was tempted to do something stupid.

I stripped down and stepped into the battering spray, hoping it would wash away the desire that sparked in my veins every time I got close to Emily. Electric shocks pricked against my skin with the need to touch her. Holding myself back made it infinitely worse. I had needed a minute away from her to rein myself in, but my plan seemed to backfire.

The soothing caress of the water only served to arouse my pulsing lust, rather than douse it. Before long, I had a stranglehold on my cock, stroking myself with white-knuckled need. The need to free myself from my desire. The need to regain my control. The need to sink myself inside her. All of it collided into a thundercloud of lethal fury and sweltering desire.

Within minutes, my abs clenched and flexed, and my thighs trembled with impending release. Two more bruising pumps of my fist, and cum rocketed out from deep in my balls. The pressure inside me instantly ebbed as endorphins coursed through my veins.

It was my belief that lust was chemical. A simple bodily function that could be controlled without subjecting myself to the cloud of drama involved in being with a woman. In the past, my assertion had held true. I was able to retain control without lust taking over and warping my decisions.

My desire for Emily seemed to be different.

Even a release hardly served to diminish my consuming hunger for her. Within minutes, the pressure coiling my muscles was back and screaming for only one thing, but I refused to give in. Instead, I walked through the litany of reasons being with Emily would be a wretched idea and regained my control by sheer force of will.

Assuaging my growing need drew out my shower longer than I would have liked, especially knowing Emily was unsupervised in my apartment. My gut told me she wasn't a threat to me—at least, not in a physical sense—but you could never be too careful.

I turned off the water and stepped out of the shower, noticing Emily had left her bag on the floor tucked between the toilet and the vanity. I wrapped a towel around me and placed her bag on the counter, unzipping the nylon duffel. At the bottom, under her wadded-up, dirty clothes, was a red leather wallet. I immediately examined its contents. Cash and no credit cards, as I'd suspected. A subway MetroCard, a reward punch card for a nail salon, two quarters, and a small key. It looked like it belonged to a lock box. I had no doubt the contents of said box would be interesting, but the key itself did little for me.

I started to close the wallet but decided to do one last search just in case. The credit card slots appeared empty, but this time, I slid my finger in each one and happened to notice a paper tucked inside the top slot. Not just a paper—a photograph. It was a picture of Emily with two small children, all three of them grinning widely, posed in front of a series of brightly colored porch umbrellas by a waterway. The picture might have been a couple of years old, but no more than that. The younger of the two kids was about three and clung to Emily like the two were very close.

Could she have children? She didn't seem like the type to have left her kids behind, but who knew the exact circumstances. Had she hidden the kids from her ex, and that was why he was after her?

I could spend all night guessing and still never know the truth. It was just another puzzle piece to add to my collection. At some point, it would all form a coherent picture, but for now, I was no closer to an answer than I was when I first discovered she had a bounty on her head.

I could ask her outright. Tell her I had seen the bounty and demand answers, but I could see that conversation devolving quickly. Explaining how I knew about the bounty would be problematic. As I'd already established, people tended to have a visceral reaction to knowing I was an assassin. I was in no real hurry, and it would be best if I got my answers from her naturally. Plus, unfolding her little mystery was the best entertainment I'd had in years—at least, that's what I told myself. If my reasons for wanting to learn more about her were more personal, I wasn't ready to admit that fact.

Once I was dried off and dressed, I stopped in the living room to check on her. "You forgot this in the bathroom."

She jumped up from her seat on the couch, where she'd made a makeshift bed for herself, and took her bag. "Thanks. Don't want to forget that." She sounded mildly embarrassed, and her gaze was a feather-light touch as it drifted from my wet hair down my damp chest and beyond.

I'd thought my little shower production had slaked my need, but with one casual perusal, I was right back where I started. Dangerously tempted. Swelling with need.

"I'm going to bed," I barked. "You need anything?"

"No. Nope. I'm all good. Thanks." She smiled tightly, and I couldn't help but notice her nipples straining through her sports bra and thin workout tank.

Fuck me.

Needing to escape, I simply nodded and hurried back to my room, closing myself inside. Tomorrow, I'd get more answers, but for now, I needed a little distance from the sexual siren in my living room.

I had a feeling she was going to be the death of me, one way or another, and I had no one to blame but myself.

NINE
Emily

I SET MY ALARM FOR THREE A.M. AND TURNED IT TO VIBRATE SO IT wouldn't wake Tamir. I thought I would have passed out the minute the lights clicked off, considering everything that had happened that day. Not even close. For nearly two hours, I lay awake as my thoughts danced from one nausea-inducing subject to the next.

Had I been at home, I would have gone straight for the tequila. I wasn't an alcoholic. I usually only drank, maybe once a week, but in times like these, a girl needed something to take the edge off. It was those precise thoughts, imagining the tang on my tongue and citrus smell biting my nose, that gave me enough reprieve from my worries to send me to sleep.

I got a whopping three hours before the alarm went off. I almost threw the phone across the room in an attempt to stop its vibrations before I remembered why I'd set the damn thing for such an ungodly hour. Once everything came back to me, my sleepiness vanished.

It was time to run.

I hated what I was about to do, but it was by far my best option. Tamir had said he had a car, and I was desperately in need. I wasn't going to ask him to take his car and risk him saying no, which was what any normal person would say. Stealing his car was my best bet for leaving town quickly without providing my pursuers a trail to follow. It was the worst repayment for his kindness, but I was desperate.

Buses and trains left a paper trail, so I needed a car. Tamir had given me the perfect solution when he mentioned his basement parking spot. I'd get rid of his car once I found an alternative vehicle, so I knew he'd get it back eventually. That thought kept my conscience from judging me too harshly. Skulking out in the night still felt like a slap in the face, but I needed to do this alone. No entanglements. No way to track me down.

Aside from gnawing guilt, my primary problem was finding the car key.

I did a cursory scan of the front door area, but there was no catch-all bowl set out or key ring hook on the wall. If his keys were in his bedroom, I'd have to leave emptyhanded and fall back on a trusty Greyhound, but I would do a thorough search of the kitchen before I accepted that fate.

As it turned out, I didn't have to look long. Like most people, Tamir had a junk drawer. His was probably far more organized than most, but he had one all the same. Inside was a BMW key fob. Any other time, I would have been thrilled to drive something as luxurious as the car that went with the fancy remote. But in this instance, knowing I was about to steal his car rather than just borrow it, I desperately wished he'd owned a rusty Chevy instead. I would just have to hope that it made it back to him in one piece and that God actually was as forgiving as I thought he was.

I might not have bought into Catholicism anymore, but I still believed in a higher power. A forgiving, kind higher power.

Please, be forgiving.

I made the sign of the cross, just for good measure, and flipped the two deadbolts that locked Tamir's front door. There was no alarm panel, which seemed odd, but when I opened the door, I was met with silence. I decided to accept my good fortune without question and hurried toward the elevator.

The second I stepped foot outside Tamir's apartment, my heart began to pound so fast, I could feel it clear down in my toes. Never in all my years had I imagined that one day I'd steal a car. Sure, I'd smoked pot and tagged a few buildings, but I'd never done anything like steal a car. I spent too many years watching people I knew go in and out of jail to walk that same path. I didn't want that for myself. Yet there I was, about to live my very own version of *Grand Theft Auto*.

Sighing heavily, I clicked the car remote to see which vehicle came to life. A black sedan flashed its lights, calling me over like the little devil on my shoulder who encouraged me to do terrible things. I would have given the angel on my opposite shoulder a chance to chime in, but her opinion wasn't welcome at the moment. Nothing she had to say was going to keep me safe, and that was all that mattered.

Tamir had reversed into the parking spot against the far wall, making my escape that much easier. Within minutes, I was exiting the parking garage and heading to my first stop.

Even the city that never sleeps was quiet at that lonely hour. Lights flashed from neon signs, and the occasional car passed by, but it was nothing like the normal frenetic activity of downtown Manhattan.

I parked at the local post office and took out the key that was tucked in my wallet. Once inside, I bought a stamp and an envelope from a vending machine, then penned a short note to Grace. She would still worry, but far less now than if I'd disappeared without a trace.

Next, I located my post office box and retrieved the go bag I kept there for just this type of emergency. I had a bag in my apartment as well, but I'd prepared this one just in case I couldn't get back to my place.

I'd never been so glad for an overactive imagination and a stout case of paranoia.

I left the key inside the box, hoping an employee would eventually find it, and ran back to the car. It took about an hour to drive out of the city and to the diner in Newark, leaving two whole hours until my scheduled meeting with Stephanie. I could either nap in the car or drive around and keep myself occupied until seven. As much as I needed to rest, I was too wired to close my eyes, so I drove. And drove. And drove.

A two-hour drive was nothing back where I was from, but considering the stress I was under and the fact that I hadn't been behind the wheel in nearly six months, it felt like an eternity. As I drove, equal parts relief and shame formed a numbing cocktail in the pit of my stomach. I was glad to have gotten away, but disappointed about how it had to be done.

The cherry on top was the odd emptiness I felt at knowing I'd likely never see Tamir again. It would have been selfish to drag him into my mess, not to mention dangerous for the both of us, but when I was with him, I didn't feel so alone. I hadn't felt that way in a long time. As though drinking the first sip of water after months stranded at sea.

I made it back to the diner with fifteen minutes to spare, only going inside when Stephanie entered the building. Spotting her at a booth by the windows, I walked over and slipped in across from her.

"Oh shit, Em, your cheek. Are you okay?" Steph reached out and clasped my hand. She knew everything about my past, and her concern brought the threat of tears to the back of my throat.

"I'm okay, just freaked out."

"You need to tell me everything, but first, are you hungry?"

"Starved, it's been a long night."

Stephanie waved over the waitress, and we both put in orders. "Okay, tell me what happened and leave nothing out."

I walked her through the timeline of events, including my night with Tamir and his stolen car. By the time I was done, our food had arrived. I dove into my chocolate chip pancakes, missing the huevos rancheros I would have had back home. Stephanie took a few bites as she processed my story, and I watched as worry lines set in over her brows.

"I can't believe you stole his car," Stephanie said through a bite of toast. "That complicates everything."

"I didn't know what else to do," I argued, my eyes pleading with her to understand.

She sighed and slouched against the back of the vinyl bench seat. "I get it. You have good reason to be worried about being tracked. I think it's probably best if you disappear with as little paper trail as possible." She reached in her purse and pulled out a fat envelope. "I gathered as much cash as I could on short notice. There's not much else I can do right now."

"I know. This is a big help, though. Thank you."

"You have my number memorized, right?"

"Yeah."

"Good. When you figure out where you're going, get me a message."

I smiled and nodded, but I knew I wouldn't. Whether the trail was paper or digital, I didn't want anything linking me back to where I'd been.

"There's one other thing I can suggest, but it's shady as shit."

I wiped my mouth and lifted my brows, signaling she had my attention.

"I know a guy. He's totally off the radar. I could give him a call and have him make you some papers to help you start over somewhere."

"Look at you. Playing with fire, aren't you?"

"It's a long story." She rolled her eyes, bringing a much-needed smile to my face. "He's in Columbus, so you've got more driving ahead of you. Get out a pen, and I'll give you his address. As soon as we're done here, I'll give him a call and tell him you need a new ID in twenty-four hours. He's a bit nocturnal, so I'll set up a meet for one o'clock tomorrow. That should give you time to get there and him time to make what you need."

"Thank you, Steph. I really do appreciate your help."

She gave me a sad smile and reached her hand out for mine across the table. "I just want you tucked away some-where safe. I would offer my own place, but I think, right now, it's better if you're totally untraceable."

I agreed and was relieved she hadn't pressured me to stay. We finished our food and said our goodbyes.

Now, I was truly on my own.

When I'd gone into the diner, the sun had just started its ascent into the crisp November sky. An hour later, the sky was fully lit and announcing the arrival of another day. I was surprised to find that starting my life over again didn't feel so scary the second time around. Not that I was happy about it or had any desire to go through the motions, but after doing it once, I felt confident that I could do it again. Having the courage and confidence to uproot my life was as valuable as any stack of money I could receive. I would need all the mental strength I could summon.

With a tiny, microscopic bounce renewed in my step, I walked to the car and slid inside to start the next leg of my journey. I pulled up Columbus, Ohio, on my phone GPS and pulled back onto the highway. It was there, among the hundreds of morning rush hour vehicles jockeying for position, that Tamir chose to make himself known.

"Where exactly are we headed?" His growled warning came from the back seat and nearly scared me to death —literally.

I screamed, and my entire body flinched, causing me to steer us within inches of the car beside me, then overcorrect onto the shoulder, a breath away from the guardrail. Once I'd regained control and was no longer on the verge of hyperventilating, I glared back at my stowaway. "What the actual fuck, Tamir? You nearly killed us!"

"You're yelling at me? *You're* the one who stole *my* car."

"Without you in it! How the fuck did you get here?" I snuck glances at him in the rearview mirror, trying to convince myself that this was reality and not just some twisted figment of my imagination.

"I followed you."

"How? I had your car," I scoffed.

He maneuvered into the front passenger seat, legs first, limber as a child gymnast, rather than six feet of muscular man. "No need for the reminder; I hadn't forgotten." He shot me a glare from beside me as he clicked his seat belt in place. "I borrowed a neighbor's car."

"Ha! You mean you *stole* a car. This just gets better and better."

"You're telling me. I'm the one who had a woman sneak out of my apartment in the middle of the night, steal my car, then lead me on a chase across Newark to catch her."

"Wait … how did you know I'd left, and how did you follow me?"

"I have a silent alarm in my apartment."

"But there was no panel!"

He smirked. "It's in my bedroom. The flashing light woke me the minute you left. When I realized you'd taken my car, I used my phone app to locate its GPS position and came after you."

As he explained what had happened, questions started buzzing through my brain like a swarm of angry bees. Would his neighbor call the police when he noticed his car was missing? Would they trace Tamir back to me and plaster my picture all over the media? What on earth was I supposed to do with Tamir? Was I supposed to take him back to the city? I couldn't possibly bring him with me. He had a life in New York, and I had no plans to go back there.

"If you keep gnawing on that bottom lip, you're going to draw blood." Tamir glared at me, silently insisting I dole out an explanation.

"I'm just a little freaked out. I know I'd already stolen your car, but I planned to abandon it, eventually, and had hoped you'd forgo calling the cops on me. Now, with your neighbor involved, I just don't know what will happen."

"Forget about the cars," he instructed impatiently. "The neighbor is a friend. I already gave him an explanation and have someone taking his car back to our building."

"Okay, but what am I supposed to do with *you*?"

"I suppose that takes us back to my original question. Where are we headed?"

"Does it matter?" I gaped at him. "I'm not going back to the city. In fact, this is ridiculous." I put on my blinker, crossed four lanes of traffic, and took the next exit. "You need to get out and Uber back home." I pulled into an abandoned gas station and put the car in park, then crossed my arms and stared at him.

He leaned toward me, placing his elbow on the center console. "*I* need to Uber home? Is this not *my* car?"

"Well … yes, but I stole it. It's mine for the moment."

His lips lifted in a feral grin. "I don't think you understand. I told you last night I was going to help you, and you're going to get my help, whether you want it or not."

"What on earth are you saying? You can't come with me."

"Why not?"

"What … why … you can't just … ugh." The words were just as choppy and unformed in my mind as they were on my tongue. He'd completely thrown me for a loop, and I had no idea what to say. Only after several deep breaths and an uncomfortably long silence was I able to communicate. "What about your job? Your apartment? You have a life. You can't just pick up and leave for some stranger. That doesn't make any sense."

"I'll let Matthew know that something came up, and he'll be able to sort it out. It's not the first time I've had to leave town for an extended period. I don't pay rent and have no plants to water or animals to feed. There is no great catastrophe that will befall me if I leave the city. And you have to remember, just because I go with you doesn't mean I can't ever go back."

I gripped the steering wheel as if it held all the answers, and if I squeezed tightly enough, I might glean some of them by osmosis. What Tamir was offering was incredibly tempting, while also terrifying. I would love to have someone keep me company and help keep me safe, but the way he'd gone about forcing my hand raised a bevy of red flags.

I didn't know what to think.

Normal people didn't just uproot their lives for a stranger. I knew that. I knew there had to be some underlying motivation, aside from his desperate need to be charitable. It could have been as simple as wanting to have sex with me. Men did a lot of outrageous things in the pursuit of sex.

Yet something told me it was more than that.

But what was I supposed to do? He had tracked me down and was there in the car with me on the side of the highway—the car I'd stolen from him—and he was insisting on coming with me. I couldn't exactly force him from the car. He had me between a rock and a hard place, and he knew it.

The tension in my arms softened, and I dropped my head to the side to peer at him. His features were inscrutable. A blank canvas of emotion, giving me no sense of what he might be thinking.

"The answer is Columbus. We're headed to Columbus."

TEN
Emily

"Who was that you had breakfast with?" Tamir asked after we were back on the highway, and the car had started to fill with a suffocating silence.

"She's an old family friend. She knew about my situation and had told me, if I ever needed help, to call her."

"Was she able to help?"

"She gave me some money and an address. That's more than I had when I woke up this morning."

"I take it that's why we're headed to Columbus?"

"Yeah. She has some friend there who may be able to give me a hand. All I know is that his name is Reggie, and I'm supposed to meet him tomorrow at one o'clock."

"You don't have any idea how this person is supposed to be helping you?"

Yes, but it's none of your business. "No, I don't," I snapped. He was pushing for answers when I had so few of my own. I couldn't help but be short with him.

"And after that?"

I glanced at him with a scowl, but his eyes were fused to the road ahead. He had to have been aware he was pushing my buttons but was clearly not interested in backing off.

"I don't know. I'm taking this one step at a time."

"Don't you think it would be a good idea to form a couple of contingency plans?"

"How exactly am I supposed to do that?" I spat at him, my anger now firmly taking hold. "This man could give me money or a place to stay or a bundle of sympathy flowers for my fucked-up life. I have no idea what to expect. Outside of that, the only thing there is to do is pick a spot on the map and start driving. There is no plan except stay alive. Don't you get that?"

He was quiet for several minutes before redirecting our conversation. "Where are you from? That takes one destination off the list of possibilities."

"A suburb of Los Angeles."

"That leaves the two coasts off-limits, but a whole lot of options in between."

"I had tossed around the idea of Chicago."

"Is there a reason you gravitate toward big cities?"

I shrugged. "Not really, they just seem easier to blend in."

"Also a lot more opportunities to be spotted."

"What are you suggesting? I'm not going to go live by myself on a farm. I'll die of boredom."

It was his turn to shrug. "Something to consider, that's all."

By some miracle of God, he let the subject rest and stopped his incessant questions. His point about a more rural setting had been valid, but there was no way I would admit that to him. He seemed to think he had all the answers. I couldn't give him the smug satisfaction of knowing he might have been right.

I turned on the satellite radio and channel surfed and sang for the next few hours. If we talked on occasion, it wasn't about anything of importance. We took a brief pit stop in Pennsylvania at lunch, gassing up and grabbing food.

"When we get back on the road, why don't I drive for a bit?" Tamir suggested as we walked back to the car. "You've been struggling to stay awake, and it's not going to be any easier once you have a belly full of fast food." Apparently, he had noticed my gallant effort to stay awake during the last hour of driving.

"I can't let you drive. The second I'm in that passenger seat, I'll pass out, and you'll turn this car around and drive us straight back to New York."

"If you get back in the driver's seat, you're going to pass out behind the wheel and drive us off a bridge." He backed me toward the car, one imposing step at a time.

"You didn't get much more sleep than I did last night." I was being difficult, mostly because I was so tired. My back stopped when it hit the driver's side door, and Tamir towered over me. His body pressed against mine, our faces inches apart, and his hands caging me in on either side.

"You can accept my promise that I will not turn this car around, or you can watch helplessly as I throw you in the back seat, but I am not letting you kill us both by driving right now. So, what's it going to be?" His voice purred across my skin, igniting my body in a lusty heat and making my lips swell with the need to press against his.

Suddenly, I felt much more awake.

I wasn't crazy about either of my options, but I had been struggling earlier, and I didn't want to chance running off the road. Accidentally killing myself would put a real kink in my plan to stay alive. I'd have to put some small degree of trust in Tamir and hope that he was telling me the truth. Even if he did reroute our course, it was better than being in a car accident.

"Fine, you drive," I muttered.

After conceding victory, I expected Tamir to step back and release me.

He didn't. At least, not at first.

Scalding coffee-colored eyes dropped to where I could feel my pulse thudding at the base of my neck, then he lowered his face to the side of mine until his lips ghosted across the skin behind my ear. I immediately turned my face away, but whether to escape him or to allow him access, I wasn't sure.

He took a deep breath, inhaling my very essence with a lungful of air, then released it on a shaky exhale of practiced restraint. Wariness battled with longing. Frustration collided with curiosity, each of us lost in our own silent, internal war until self-discipline won out.

Mine had been an epic struggle to simply keep from arching against him while molten need pooled deep in my belly. The source of his struggle was a mystery to me, but its presence was evident in the cataclysmic heat of his stare.

Then it was over.

He lifted himself off me and stepped back. I could feel his penetrating stare devouring me, but I was too overwhelmed to meet his eyes. I stumbled around to the passenger side and slipped inside. It took a solid ten minutes for my heart to stop throwing a rave in my chest. Neither of us said a word about what had just occurred between us.

Not long after I calmed down, I laid my seat back and finally got some rest. About two hours later, I startled awake, greeted by the devastating tsunami that was my reality. I'd had a bad dream while I slept, but it was nothing compared to what waited for me in the real world. Stuck in a car with a man I didn't know, running from people who wanted to kill me.

My life was in shambles.

I dropped my head back and watched the countryside fly past. It came as a pleasant surprise when I noticed a highway sign advertising Cambridge, Ohio. He hadn't turned us around. While I had hoped he wouldn't, a part of me was genuinely shocked that he hadn't. If I had been in his position, I wasn't sure what I would have done.

"I was starting to wonder if you were out for the night."

"Sorry about that."

"Not a problem, but I'm going to need directions after I make a quick phone call." He pulled his phone from his jacket pocket and selected a name in his contacts. The car immediately transferred the call to the speaker system, but to my surprise, Tamir didn't send the call back to his phone.

"You're bailing, aren't you?" The raspy, feminine voice filled the car, causing a mass of tar-like jealousy to fill my stomach.

"I had to head out of town for a while. Not sure when I'll be back."

"Don't be gone too long; I'll be big as a house and worthless," she pouted.

Big as a house? Was she … pregnant? Oh, Jesus. Did Tamir have a pregnant girlfriend back in the city? Now I felt defeated *and* slimy, lusting after a man who was already taken.

"Somehow, I very much doubt that," Tamir said with a

smirk. "I'll buzz you when I get back. Until then, try to stay out of trouble." The line clicked dead. She'd hung up.

I glanced at Tamir out of the corner of my eye. "She sounds … lovely."

"She's something, that's for sure. Her name is Maria. You may have seen me training with her before class most nights."

I whipped around in my seat to face him. "That was *her*? The badass woman you're always sparring with? You're having a baby with her?"

He threw his head back and laughed deep from his flat, chiseled belly. "No," he said when he finally calmed down. "She's married to another man; it's his baby she's carrying. I'm just her trainer and longtime friend."

Oh. Well, at least I could take homewrecker off my updated resume. That was good to hear. "She's amazing to watch. I assume she's been training for a long time?"

"I've been training her since she was fifteen, but she started five years before that."

"You two must be really close."

"Until recently, I didn't think anyone would ever be close to Maria. Things change; we mature. Now, she's married and finally settling down."

"How old is she? Twenty-five?"

"Twenty-six, I believe."

"The same age as me," I murmured.

Tamir's jaw flexed. Was that why he thought of me as a child? Because I was the same age as the woman he'd known for so long and still viewed as a little girl? He sure hadn't been thinking of me that way in the parking lot a couple of hours earlier. Maybe that was why he hadn't acted on the desire that he'd so clearly felt.

Whatever. That was on him. If he couldn't see me as the

adult I was, that was his problem, and it was probably for the best.

I crossed my arms and stared out the passenger window, no longer interested in conversation. As signs for Columbus came into view, I pulled up the address on my phone and acted as navigator. He followed my instructions for a bit, then pulled off into a Walmart parking lot before we got too far into the city.

"I have a few things with me but could still use some supplies." He gestured to a duffel bag sitting on the floorboards of the back seat. "I assume you're in the same boat?"

"You thought to pack a bag?" I gaped at him.

"You're not the only one who likes to be prepared." He raised an eyebrow poignantly at my own duffel I'd retrieved from the post office.

"Yeah, but I'm on the run for my life. What's your excuse?"

"Special Forces, remember? That kind of training sticks with you. Now stop looking at me like I'm Jeffrey Dahmer and let's get this over with. I hate these places." He slipped from the car soundlessly, leaving me speechless, mouth agape, and mind blank.

At some point, I was going to have to set aside any expectations I had for this man and just roll with the punches, because everything he said and did surprised me. If I didn't have any preconceived notions about how he should behave, maybe he wouldn't seem quite so mysterious. Possibly. But it was equally as probable that intrigue was in his blood, and nothing I could do would diminish its mystifying effects.

Tamir insisted we stayed together once we were inside. The trust factor in our budding partnership was clearly lacking. I insisted on buying a few snacks to have on the road, then we both grabbed an assortment of toiletries and a change of clothes. Tamir picked up a package of boxer briefs, conjuring a mental image I couldn't shake.

Once we were back in the car, we selected a Motel 6 not far from the address I'd been given, grabbed another round of takeout for dinner, then made our way to the motel. I was ready to get a room, shower, and call it a day.

The motel was your standard double-decker affair with a pockmarked parking lot and bad fluorescent lighting. However, for the one low price of only sixty dollars a night, we had a roof over our heads, a bed, and a moderately clean bathroom. That was the full extent of the amenities, but it was enough.

"I don't suppose you'll agree to separate rooms," I commented to Tamir as we approached the front lobby.

"With your tendency to disappear in the night, not a chance."

It was what I'd expected, although it didn't make sense to me. Why did he care whether I disappeared? Most people would have been glad to be rid of me, wouldn't they? Maybe it was just my old friend, paranoia, paying me a visit, but I felt it was odd that he'd gone so far to help me. Instead of being relieved to have company, I couldn't shake the feeling of unease at how invested Tamir had become in my plight.

"Two doubles, please," I told the clerk.

"I'm down to a single king room." The woman was somewhere between the ages of fifty and eighty—it was entirely too hard to narrow down any further. Her voice indicated she smoked at least a pack a day, and her leathery skin piled with caked-on makeup could indicate a young woman with a tanning addiction or an older woman, trying to reclaim her youth. Either was equally possible.

"You've got to be kidding me."

"Afraid not. The Blue Jackets got a game tonight, and the

rink is under a mile from here. You're lucky there's a room left at all. No one in a five-mile radius will have any vacancies."

My eyes drifted shut, and I sucked in a deep, cleansing breath. I debated going in search of another hotel with two beds, but what would that have said about my maturity? He already indicated he thought of me as a child, which shouldn't matter, but it did. I wanted us on equal ground. Wanted to be an adult who would be unfazed by sharing a bed in a less than ideal situation with another adult. Besides, if he was going to do something awful to me, would it make a difference whether we were in one bed or two? Separate beds wouldn't exactly be an obstacle to a rapist. Surely, there would be a sofa or chair one of us could sleep in, making my entire inner debate pointless.

"All right. One king bed, please, for two nights."

She took a puff of her lipstick-stained cigarette and flashed a grin of preternaturally white teeth that likely glowed in the dark.

The good news was, there wasn't carpet in the room. There was nothing more disgusting than motel mystery-stain carpet. The bad news? No sofa. Not even a chair, aside from the mall cafeteria-style two-seater table and metal chairs. There wasn't even a dresser or a nightstand. The room was one step up from a prison cell—unwelcome roommate and all.

"I don't suppose you'd agree to sleep on the floor," I muttered as I claimed the side closest to the door.

"You couldn't pay me enough." The jerk was smirking.

"You getting some perverse sense of satisfaction out of this? You could sleep in the car, you know."

"Do *you* want to sleep in the car in this neighborhood?"

He sifted through the Walmart bag and pulled out his toiletry purchases.

"I'm not even sure I like the car being left out in this neighborhood."

"Me either," he grumbled. "I'm jumping in the shower. Do I need to tie you up to make sure you're still here when I get out?"

"No." I threw myself onto the bed and stared up at the blotchy water stains on the ceiling.

"Just to be sure, I'll take this with me, along with the keys." He shook my wallet in his hand, shot me a wolfish grin, and disappeared into the bathroom.

"How the...?" I sat up and stared at my bags, completely dumbstruck at how he'd pilfered my wallet from me. He'd either taken it when I was asleep in the car, or he was magic. It was all a great mystery, as was everything else about the man.

If I thought he'd rendered me speechless with his little snatch and grab trick, it was nothing compared to my response when he exited the shower shirtless minutes later.

His dark brown waves clumped heavily with water that dripped in fat droplets down his taut chest, over the ridges of his sculpted six-pack, and soaked into the low-slung waist-band of his joggers. I could almost feel his smooth skin against my tongue as I collected beads of water like a game of connect the dots.

I'd never been so thirsty in my entire life.

I was two seconds from sexually assaulting him when I noticed two patches of marred skin—one at the top of his left pectoral and the other slashing across his right side. Scars. Gnarly, painful-looking scars.

It was the reminder I needed that this man was an

unknown. A predator in his own right. He claimed to be on my side, for now, but would that always be the case?

He would be the worst kind of enemy. Intelligent. Unpredictable. Deadly.

I didn't have much choice but to stay on my guard and hope for the best.

ELEVEN
Tamir

EMILY TOOK HER TURN IN THE BATHROOM, BUT ONLY AFTER I agreed to hand over the keys and give back her wallet. The minute the door was closed, I slipped outside the room to make a call to an old friend. Some days, I considered him my closest friend. Others, I swore I'd never speak to him again.

Uri and I went way back. We'd gone to school together before we were ever in the service together, and our years of active duty only brought us closer. He was far more proficient with computers than I was, so I had asked him to help dig for information on Emily.

"Tam, you sort out your little runaway?" Uri answered after a single ring.

"Not even a little. To make matters more complicated, she ran again."

"No shit," he huffed. "You chasing her down?"

"Even better, I'm running with her."

He huffed. "I suppose that's one way to keep an eye on the mark."

"You able to find anything more about her?" I wasn't interested in his input about my methods.

"No, she's a ghost. I'll keep digging, but it's not looking promising. You going to tell me what the hell this is all about? You've never once put this much effort into the front end of a job. If the waters are murky, you walk away. This? This isn't like you."

"Why don't you just say whatever the fuck it is you want to say?" My fist clenched around the phone, wishing it were his neck.

Silence.

"I want to know if this is still a job or if it's becoming personal."

"Not that it's any of your fucking business, but it's a job. She's a payout, like any other; I just need to get the facts before I decide if I'm taking her in or walking away. That clear enough for you?"

He grunted, and I took that as the cue that our conversation was over. I hung up and took a second to lean against the railing, watching cars come and go on the access road.

I understood why Uri was concerned about my actions. Wives and children didn't exactly fit into our type of lifestyle. Quitting was always an option, but I didn't want to quit. I loved what I did, and I was good at it. I liked to think I helped balance the scales of good and evil, one payday at a time. No messy red tape. No long, drawn-out legal proceedings. Just me, my mark, and a mountain of sins.

That was the way it had been for years, and that was the way it would stay.

We turned the lights out as soon as Emily finished her shower. She curled up on the far edge of her side of the bed after building a pillow blockade between us. It was actually more of a pillow speedbump. Had we been at a quality hotel that provided a full array of pillows, she would have had more to work with.

I had no plans to attack her during the night, so her efforts were wasted. Even if I had, I wasn't sure what she thought the pillows were going to accomplish. It was kind of adorable, which annoyed me to no end. I didn't want to find her adorable or attractive or any of the things that stirred when I looked at her. She was a job, exactly as I'd told Uri, and nothing more.

Fortunately, I didn't have to dwell on it long. The military had taught me to be a light sleeper, but it had also taught me to sleep in any conditions. I was out in a matter of minutes.

Something stirring in the room woke me early the next morning. The sun wasn't even up, but Emily had insisted on leaving the bathroom light on with the door cracked so there was light in the room.

She had annihilated her own pillow blockade and crossed over into enemy territory. She was fast asleep, curled up against my side. I rolled gently to face her, listening to the cadence of her breathing and appreciating the soft lines of her face in sleep. Most of her body was under the covers. Only her face, top shoulder, and her arms were visible. She wore her watch on her bottom wrist, and in the dim light, I was able to see the hint of a tattoo peeking out beneath the metal clasp.

I lifted my hand and gently slid the watch aside with the delicacy of defusing a bomb by hand. In pale script was the letter Z. The scrolling ink was faded enough that I guessed she was in the process of having it removed. Could that have been her ex-boyfriend's initial? As desperately as she tried to hide it, I doubted she'd want to discuss it.

It was intriguing—as if there was anything about the woman that wasn't intriguing. People had tattoos they regretted all the time, so it wasn't like a Z was particularly telling. I'd seen any number of tattoos that were far more regrettable than hers. So why had she hidden the mark like she was ashamed of it?

Everything I learned just produced more questions, like fighting my way out of a pit of quicksand. The more I struggled, the deeper I sank.

Sometimes a target was tricky because the magnitude of his or her sins floundered on my line of judgment. Rarely did I encounter someone with so little background that I couldn't even gauge their guilt. It was rare, but it had happened. In those cases, I simply passed on the job and left someone else to dole out the judgment.

Not knowing the details of their past had never bothered me, but in Emily's case, I didn't want to walk away without an answer. I could say it was because of the money or that it was also a point of pride, but it was more than that. More than I was willing to admit. I felt an unrelenting need to lay my eyes on all of her coveted secrets, to learn the extent of her corruption and see how it compared to my own.

If I didn't get some concrete answers soon, I would have to force them from her, and neither of us was going to like that outcome.

TWELVE
Emily

I LOUNGED IN BED FOR MUCH LONGER THAN I WAS ASLEEP, BUT that was primarily to avoid acknowledging the fact that I'd gravitated toward Tamir in the night. When he got out of bed, I woke up, realized I was on the wrong side of the bed, and promptly pretended to keep sleeping for the next hour. It gave me plenty of time to overthink my nonexistent plan until my stomach was a bundle of nerves.

I had wanted to take breakfast back to the motel room and continue to hunker down until it was time. Tamir had other plans. He insisted I was safe for the moment and coerced me into going to a local café to eat. The food was delicious, and it was good to get out and do something normal. However, the minute we got back in the car, my nerves rallied for a second attack.

"Where are you going? The motel is back that way." I pointed behind us, but Tamir never altered his course. After he had proved he wasn't going to take me back to New York, I'd given in to his insistence to drive. It was his car, after all.

"If you keep rolling that necklace around in your fingers for the next three hours, there won't be any etching left. I thought we could go somewhere to take your mind off everything." He raised his hand when I started to argue. "No one followed us. This is Columbus, Ohio. No one here is after you, I promise. Now, please, try to trust me."

He wasn't wrong. The chances that anyone knew I was there were slim to none. Of course, I was rightfully paranoid since I'd already been found once, but logically speaking, the odds of being caught again so quickly were right there next to winning the lottery.

"Fine," I muttered. "But if I die out there, it's your fault."

He smirked. "Even if you're hit by a train or fall into a well?"

"Absolutely. Those scenarios would never have happened if I was tucked away at the motel, so yes."

"I'll just have to make sure to keep you safe then." He peered over at me, just as I snuck a glance at him. Our gazes locked, and through that connection, the tiniest tendrils of trust passed between us. It was brief, and the threads precariously delicate, but it was a start.

A few minutes later, we pulled up at the Franklin Park Conservatory and Botanical Gardens. The entry sign boasted eighty-eight acres of landscaped grounds and breathtaking floral displays.

"How on earth did you think of this?"

"Google." His wry response drew my eyes from the landscape to see he could barely contain a sarcastic smile.

"Well, thank you, *Google*. This is absolutely perfect. It's just too bad it's fall. I'd love to see the place in the spring."

"I wasn't sure if you'd be one of those women who enjoys nature or runs from it."

"I've never been camping or anything like that, but I've always loved being outside. Something about seeing the trees wave in the breeze and the birds floating in air reminds me the world will keep spinning and everything will be okay. It's reassuring, especially when life feels overwhelming. My dad used to have a swing hanging from a tree out in the front of his house. I would sit in it for hours, just watching the world go by."

Tamir parked the car without responding. We both exited and rounded the car, walking silently toward the building entrance. I wasn't sure why I suddenly felt so uncomfortable. As though I'd presented a tiny piece of myself, only to have it rejected with Tamir's silence.

"Maybe that's just me," I muttered.

"I know exactly what you're talking about." He pulled ahead of me in three easy strides, his words drifting back to me like a warm summer breeze.

We explored the different ecosystems and their vast array of plants in the greenhouse buildings. The sunlight poured inside, and I basked in its warm rays. My body and soul had desperately missed the heavy doses of vitamin D that I was used to receiving before I moved to the city. Concentrated stints in the sun were far less common in the concrete jungle, where towering skyscrapers cast the world below into shadow.

I was so caught up in enjoying my surroundings that I was stunned when Tamir pointed out it was time for us to leave. Three hours flew by as if it was nothing, and for the first time in what felt like months, I wasn't looking over my shoulder every ten minutes.

Stephanie had set up our meet at a McDonald's in downtown Columbus. We ordered food and selected a table by a window. Tamir began to eat, seemingly oblivious to the world around him, while I barely got down a french fry as I scrutinized every person who walked through the doors.

"Do you have any way to identify this guy, aside from his name?" he asked between bites.

"No, and I'm wishing I had. How the hell am I supposed to meet up with someone without knowing anything about them?"

Within minutes of our exchange, a lanky white guy with dreadlocks gave me a chin lift from across the dining area. He was holding a plastic grocery sack full of stuff and chewing on a fingernail.

I mouthed his name with a questioning look, but instead of coming over, he just glared at Tamir.

"Um, I'll be right back."

Tamir watched me warily but didn't stop me.

I approached the man as if he were a lost child looking for his mother. "Are you Reggie?" I asked with a smile.

"Steph gave me your description; she didn't say anything about a dude. He looks way too serious for my taste." He looked and sounded like a southern California surfer who'd taken one too many hits off the bong, hopped on the wrong bus, and ended up thousands of miles from home without a way to get back.

"She didn't know I'd be traveling with anyone. He's fine, I promise. You want to come sit with us?"

"No, brah. That's how dudes like me get locked up." He glanced around nervously. "I know what I'll do. I'm gonna hit the little boys' room. You get me?" He flashed a smile, then spun around and disappeared into the bathroom hallway.

Was he expecting me to follow him? I glanced at Tamir, who admittedly, looked ready to interrogate Reggie, and shrugged. When I turned back, my paranoid contact exited the bathroom less than a minute after entering, the bag no longer in hand.

It hit me that the Bob Marley wannabe was worried it was a setup. He didn't want to be caught handing over anything incriminating, so he'd left it for me out of sight.

I hurried back to the men's restroom and retrieved the sack that was waiting for me on the counter. Without chancing a peek at its contents in public, I went directly back to Tamir.

"Did you open it yet?" he asked.

"No."

"Good. Finish eating and we'll have a look in the car."

Once we were safe from prying eyes, I sorted through the bag's contents, one item at a time. A woman's sweater and a pair of joggers. One disposable phone. A visa debit card with one hundred dollars on it. A sudoku puzzle book and a hardback book—*The Path Made Clear: Discovering Your Life's Direction and Purpose* by Oprah Winfrey.

"That's it?" he asked, brow furrowed.

"You can see it just as well as I can. There's nothing else in there."

"What about the books?"

I flipped through the pages, keeping the new driver's license and birth certificate tucked safely out of his view. Knowing what Reggie would be giving me, I had guessed the documents were in the book. I was glad Reggie was just as paranoid as me and hadn't handed them over in a manila envelope. That would have made things complicated.

Something kept me from telling Tamir the purpose of my meetup. He'd done nothing but help me, and a small part of me was starting to trust him, but some troublesome questions about him still lurked in the back of my mind. Those shadowy doubts kept me from fully relaxing around him.

"You saw how he was. I'm pretty sure his elevator no longer goes to the top floor. It's fine. I hadn't expected much. Let's go back to the room, and we can figure out what to do from there."

He put the car in reverse and directed us toward the motel without a comment.

"You know what?" I blurted. "There was a liquor store around the corner from the motel. Stop there first."

He quirked a brow.

"Don't judge me. It's been the week from hell."

Now that I had my new identity, it was time for me to get away from Tamir. I couldn't allow him to tag along forever, no matter how much I dreaded the idea of leaving him behind. In part, I was hesitant to be alone, period. But the majority of my reluctance was founded in an unwillingness to admit I'd never see Tamir again. The thought of leaving him had been the true inspiration for my impulse stop at the liquor store. Being found and having to go on the run had sucked, but the booze would be nursing a fresh, much more sensitive wound. The anticipated loss of someone who was quickly finding a home in my subconscious. Regardless of my doubts about him, I would miss Tamir.

Fifteen minutes later, we were back at the room with my good friend, Señor Patrón, and a bag of limes. Drinking with Tamir nearby wasn't the smartest idea I'd ever had, but I trusted myself when it came to tequila. I knew where to draw the line, and I certainly wasn't novice enough to be giving up secrets just because the burn of liquor warmed my belly. In my mind, I would be toasting to our final night together. Then I would have the strength to find a way to disappear.

"I didn't think about glasses, so we're stuck with plastic coffee cups."

"We? It's two in the afternoon."

I ignored his comment and set out two clear plastic cups on the half-circle table and poured two fingers of tequila in each. "Do you have a knife?" I glanced back at where he watched me from across the room. "Dumb question, huh?"

Tamir smirked and went to his black duffel that I hadn't seen him open yet and pulled out a switchblade from the side pocket. My blade that I normally kept with me had been left at home in my haste to get to class the night of my attack. I loved having that knife on me. I would have to replace it. It wasn't foolproof, but it gave me a degree of security.

I set one of the limes I'd purchased on the table, then sliced it into wedges with Tamir's knife. I secured a wedge on the rim of each glass, sat back in the metal chair, and raised my glass to Tamir. "Let's drink."

He towered over me and stared with equal parts wariness and amusement. "You really think drinking is a good idea?"

"It's as good an idea as any other. It's not like we have anywhere to be."

"No, but it might be a good idea to have the use of our faculties should something unexpected happen."

"I thought you said I was perfectly safe here with you?" This time, I did the smirking.

In a full display of silent protest, Tamir slowly lowered himself into the small chair and lifted his cup. "Salud."

"Look at you with your Spanish toast," I teased.

"My father was a Spaniard, if you'll recall."

We clinked our glasses, tapped them on the table, and downed the tequila. Tamir handled his well, refraining from wincing or coughing from the burn. I let my head fall back-ward as I savored the warmth trailing down my throat.

"This stuff is too good to shoot, but I needed that," I said, bringing my gaze back to his.

"You handle tequila like a pro."

"When we had family gatherings, there was beer and tequila, so I grew up on the stuff."

"Where did your family originate?"

"My dad was from Mexico originally. Never knew my mom—she died in childbirth. What about you? Tell me about your family." I refilled our glasses and anxiously awaited his response. It hadn't slipped my attention that I knew almost nothing about him. I was hoping a little tequila might fix that problem. There wasn't much point if I was leaving, but I was still insanely curious.

"I had a pretty standard, happy childhood. Two parents, a sister, and a cat."

My brow furrowed, and I looked him up and down. "So, what went wrong?"

My question drew a chuckle from him. "The military changes everyone, and my parents dying in a car crash was rough, but it was my sister's death that derailed things entirely."

"Oh, *shit*. What happened?" His admission took me aback. I hadn't expected him to be so forthcoming.

He smiled, helping to keep the mood light. "It's a long story, but the result was me leaving the military and being dishonorably discharged."

"Damn, that had to hurt." I sipped from my cup, and he followed suit.

"Our lives all take unexpected turns. I would have loved to have had my sister back, but aside from that, I wouldn't change what happened."

"You going to tell me about it?" I lifted my brows.

He shook his head with a smirk. "If I told you everything about me, there'd be no mystery left."

"I've already contemplated that one and decided that mystery is in your blood. You probably even blow your nose mysteriously." I grumbled the last part.

"You've contemplated me, have you? Any other conclusions I should know about?"

How did he do that? I was supposed to be learning about him, not the other way around. And I certainly shouldn't be admitting my thoughts about him. Yet while I wasn't officially even tipsy, something about the burn of tequila made me want to talk. Probably just habit, but either way, I found myself sharing more than I had expected. Nothing of critical importance but an admission, nonetheless.

"You're dangerous. I sensed that from the moment I first saw you. Other instructors at the studio knew how to fight like you, but none of them made me nervous. You, on the other hand, you scare me sometimes." I tipped back my cup, emptying its contents.

"You're perceptive," he admitted.

"Are you saying I should be afraid of you?"

"I'm saying I can be a very dangerous man in the right situations." He finished his drink before he continued. "We all have parts of ourselves we keep tucked away from view. Things we're not proud of, or things we think others won't understand. I happen to have more of those parts than most. Would you like to know what I've concluded about you?"

I poured us a fresh round of drinks. "Of course."

"I think you know exactly what I'm talking about. There's more of you that you keep tucked away than what you show to the world."

I swished my cup around, sloshing the tequila to start it

spinning in a tiny whirlpool. "I'd say you're probably right." I held Tamir's gaze and lifted my cup. "To all our dirty little secrets."

The next hour was a blur.

I was heavy-handed with the tequila, even for me, and quickly started feeling the effects. Our conversation, thankfully, returned to the shallows, which was where we found ourselves at almost four in the afternoon, arguing over the likelihood of a South American versus European champion in the upcoming World Cup.

"Spain can do it. I'm telling you. This is going to be their year." Tamir pointed across the table at me, elbows planted as he leaned into his argument.

"Don't be absurd," I scoffed, a Spanish accent coloring my words. "France is favored to win, but even if they don't, Brazil will win over Spain."

My father was passionate about soccer. We were never particularly close, but we were able to connect over his love of the game. I adored watching games with him, decked out in our Mexico jerseys, regardless of who was playing. Mexico was always our favorite when it came to international teams. Should Mexico be out of the running, we cheered for the Central and South American teams over European. It was a matter of Latin pride.

"Eh, you don't know what you're talking about," he grumbled, waving his hand flippantly in my direction. He'd had just as much tequila as me, if not more. I gave him props for being able to handle his liquor, but a person could only do so much before the tequila took over.

"Don't tell me you're one of those men who can't stand to lose to a woman." I stood from my chair, entirely too unsteady to pull off my desired level of coyness.

Tamir swiftly rose, looking far more surefooted than he

should have been. He slowly closed the distance between us, his wolfish grin making my drunk heart flutter against my ribs. "I wouldn't know. It's never happened before."

I threw my head back in a fit of laughter and would have ended up on the floor had two strong hands not steadied me. I gasped, and my gaze snapped back to his. All humor had fled from his eyes, leaving unadulterated lust in its wake.

He walked me backward, hands still fixed around my upper arms, until my back was pressed firmly against the wall.

"What are you doing?" I didn't need to ask. A devout nun could have felt the waves of desire rolling off Tamir. But his actions caught me off guard. He was a study in discipline and self-control, but at that moment, he looked almost feral. A man who had surrendered to his basic instincts.

"I'm crossing that fucking line we've been dancing around for days—weeks even. That's what this was about, wasn't it? The tequila? You needed something to blame when you let go and gave in to this maddening pull between us."

A vicious defense bubbled up in my throat but never made it past my lips. Down in my gut, despite the small reservoir of tequila attempting to drown the truth, I knew he was right. If I was being brutally honest with myself, this was exactly what I'd wanted, needed. To let go of my fears. To set aside my doubts. To stop fighting the magnetic chemistry that popped and sizzled between us.

But I hated the way it sounded. That I'd used liquor to get him into bed as if I didn't have the courage on my own. I didn't want to admit to being so needy. So manipulative or brazen.

"You're twisting my intent. I wanted to relax and forget my troubles for an evening. My sole purpose wasn't to get you in bed."

In an instant, he flipped me around to face the wall. My hands came up, pressing flat on either side of me, and a gasp slipped from between my lips.

His hard body caged me in, and I could feel his engorged length pressing into the curves of my bottom. "So, you weren't hoping I'd do something like this?" The seductive, quivering heat of his breath danced along my bare neck before his teeth sank in and ignited all of my delicate nerve endings.

My addled brain attempted to compose an objection, but I could only vocalize a ragged moan. His touch turned me into a willing slave to the sensations he stirred inside me. And when he gently soothed my burning skin with the caress of his lips, my body arched of its own volition, pressing back into his hard length.

"Look at you." He groaned, his firm hands digging into my waist, holding me immobile against him. "You're sex incarnate, dripping seduction to distract a man beyond reason. But then what, my little Venus flytrap? What happens once you have them in your clutches?"

"I don't know what you're talking about." My reply was breathy as I struggled to wade through the thick waters of lust and intoxication.

His hand slid from my waist up to my breast, massaging and kneading, before pinching my nipple with just the right amount of delicious force. "Don't play coy. It doesn't suit you."

A rush of anger electrified my blood and briefly burned through the haze fogging my thoughts. I pressed against the wall, launching myself backward and freeing myself from his grasp. "I'm not playing coy, and I don't know what you're insinuating. Yes, I was interested in being with you, but not if you're going to degrade me and suggest I'm something that

I'm not." I retreated until my legs bumped against the bed, but my body still pulsed with awareness for him. My pebbled nipples ached for the return of his touch, and my panties were embarrassingly wet. His provocative touch and god-like body were hard to resist, but I had just enough wherewithal to remember my dignity.

A normal man would have seen my anger and backed down—offered apologies and fed me banal platitudes—but not Tamir. He wasn't just a man; he was a predator. With the prowess of a jungle cat, he stalked toward me and invaded my personal space, denying me free thought with his intoxicating presence. When he was close enough that I could breathe in the masculine scent of his skin, he clasped his large hand under my chin and lifted my face to his.

"You are too fine a work of art to degrade. Would it be degrading to praise a fox for its ability to hunt? You're just as clever and far more beautiful, and you have the survival instincts to match the most majestic of creatures." His lips seized mine, possessing me with unabashed hunger.

The offense I'd felt seconds before disintegrated beneath the crushing desire he stirred inside me. I willfully surrendered to the electric current that sparked so fiercely between us.

His velvet tongue danced around mine, licking me and drawing me further into his thrall. When I followed his lead and lost myself to the rhythm, a guttural rumble vibrated up from his chest and stole my remaining breath.

I could feel his control slipping, and that knowledge was the headiest aphrodisiac imaginable. His hands wandered my body while his kisses devoured me until I had to pull away to fill my burning lungs with air. Both our chests rose and fell in a chaotic struggle for control, drawing my eyes down to the broad expanse of his pectorals.

My hand rose unbidden, drawn to the contours of the masculine body hinted at beneath his shirt. Needing to feel the dips and valleys for myself, I slipped my hand beneath his shirt, mapping out the sheer perfection of his body as if committing it to memory.

In a flash, he swept the shirt up and over his head, treating me to an unobstructed view of his perfect torso. He was breathtaking. Even his scars added to his perfection.

"It should be impossible for something so deadly to be so beautiful," I mused, feeling his smattering of hair beneath my fingers as they explored his chest.

"And what about you?" he murmured, reaching for the elastic band in my hair and freeing my long dark locks. "Doesn't that apply to you as well?"

I shook my hair, allowing it to cascade around my shoulders. "I think you give me too much credit."

"Then what about our toast to dirty little secrets?"

"Dirty, not deadly," I whispered, peering up into his midnight eyes. They'd been lit with passion before but suddenly appeared shuttered and closed off. It was the reality check I needed to remind me that I was playing with fire.

"You don't have to be deadly to be dangerous."

"I've never hurt anyone in my life."

He lowered his lips to my ear, causing my heart to catch. "Then why the secrets? Secrets are born out of shame. If you've never hurt anyone, what is there to be ashamed of?"

His words were a knife straight into my gut, stirring up a wave of self-loathing that pressed against my chest and squeezed my throat. I could do nothing but gulp down the tears that burned at the back of my eyes.

"Sometimes, the pain we cause is circumstantial and unintentional, but that doesn't erase the guilt." I maneuvered past him and walked out the door, slamming it behind me. I needed space from Tamir and his presumptive accusations. I would have found it hard to keep my emotions in check had my liver not been swimming in alcohol. As it was, I felt swept away in a flood of remorse, fear, and anger.

What had he been trying to accomplish by prodding me like he had? Did he think I was going to confess some great crime I'd committed? I wasn't sure how our sensual exploration had devolved so quickly, but after our exchange, I desperately needed space from him.

Thank God he didn't come after me. I didn't know what I'd have said if he did. I took the time he'd given me to sober up and clear my muddled thoughts as I walked the streets of downtown Columbus. Maybe by the time I was ready to go back, I'd have the tiniest clue about how I was going to get away.

THIRTEEN
Tamir

I HAD TO ADMIT, EMILY COULD HOLD HER OWN WHEN IT CAME TO tequila, but there was no way she could go drink for drink with a man almost twice her weight. I wasn't sure she was even aware, but Spanish words began to infiltrate her sentences, giving her speech a seductive cadence.

She wasn't the only one who had been overly ambitious. I never stood a chance against the tipsy version of the Latin siren. She was alluring on a normal day, but after we had downed the better part of a bottle of tequila, she was a fucking goddess. She owned her sexuality and basked in it without even trying. Her confidence was unusual because it was so natural. She didn't flaunt herself. She didn't have to,

117

just like a diamond would easily outshine a mountain of glitter.

She was refreshing. More than that, she was intoxicating, and it had nothing to do with the tequila.

I respected her, or what I knew of her so far, which was why I'd pushed her like I had. She hadn't taken the pressure well, but that was often the case. People got angry and defensive when faced with a truth they were reticent to admit. Once the emotion had processed through her system, along with the alcohol, maybe we'd have a real chance to get some answers.

She took more time than I had expected, but I never doubted her return. Everything she owned was here in the room. It gave me the perfect opportunity to go through her things and see what I could learn.

Everything about our meetup earlier had felt off. She was lying about something, and I was done with waiting patiently for her to be forthright. Whether it was the tequila or the way her body softened against mine, something had allowed me to realize how frustrated I was at her reluctance to let me in.

It was hypocritical. I knew that well enough. What gave me the right to be upset if she was keeping secrets? I had plenty of my own. In fact, there was a good reason for her not to trust me.

It didn't matter. Logic didn't seem to matter where she was concerned.

I was pissed, and it brought on a renewed sense of purpose. I still had a job to do, and she was still my mark. It was time to get back to work.

We had the drapes pulled shut across the small front window, but a halo of light broke through around the edges, giving the room a soft glow. I had yet to go through the bag she'd brought with her, but I was more interested in the grocery sack Reggie had given Emily. I set each item on the small dining table and sat down to examine them. The book was, by far, the most illogical item to have been included, so that's where I started. One simple flip through the pages, though, and the book instantly revealed its secrets. A professionally made driver's license and matching birth certificate for one Emily Rogers.

I wasn't sure what I'd expected. Possibly a gun or a plane ticket abroad but definitely not illegal documents. How the hell was she hooked up with people who could provide her with false identification? That wasn't something ordinary people could pull out of their back pockets.

I was fucking sick of the games.

Frustration and anger clawed greedily at my skin. She was either in a world of trouble, or she was even more of a professional con artist than I could have imagined. If that was the case, I was done being played.

I stood so quickly that the metal chair legs scraped across the vinyl floor, nearly tipping it over. I paced for close to a half hour before I finally settled back into the chair facing the door and waited for my pretty little mark to return.

By the time the lock clicked over and the door slowly swung open, I was tempered steel, cool and resolute. "Come inside. I think it's time we talked."

Her eyes narrowed as they adjusted to the dim light of the room. "What's going on?" She allowed the door to close behind her but kept her hand on the knob.

I reached out and slid her documents forward an inch on the table. "This is what's going on." I tossed the photo of her and the two children on top of the documents. "You don't want to tell me the truth, but I'm sick of the lies. Did you think I would buy your attempted cover-up and believe that Reggie had given you a bag of worthless crap?"

"You dug through my stuff?"

"Only because you gave me no choice. If you'd be fucking honest with me, I wouldn't have to."

"I didn't see these, okay? How was I supposed to know?" Her voice rose as she regained her bearings.

"There was no way you could have missed those. You're fucking lying, *again*." My fingers twitched to wrap around the delicate column of her neck. It took all my control to keep my hands to myself.

She abandoned her post at the door and came to the table, charging at me angrily. "Even if I am, don't you think I have my reasons?"

"What reasons? I'm the one trying to help you." I lifted my arms in a gesture of surrender. "Do you see anyone else here doing that? How am I supposed to help you when you won't even be honest with me?"

"The truth changes nothing. I'm still in danger, and I'm still on the run."

Standing, I closed the distance between us, then traced my knuckles down her cheek and along her jawline. "The truth can be the difference between life and death." My words were only a whisper, an admission of my own, though she'd never know it.

This was why I'd never considered going into the security business. Other colleagues of mine had done so after leaving the service, but I hated the business. Protecting the client from themselves was just as difficult, if not more so, than from whatever outside threats existed. I wasn't sure how I'd gone from seeing her as a mark to seeing her as someone to protect, but that was becoming more evident by the minute.

I was starting to realize the best thing I could do for both of us was to let her go. She felt safer on her own, and I was only opening myself up to disappointment by sticking around.

I walked away and lifted my duffel onto the bed with Emily at my back. Gathering the few items I'd left in the room, I stuffed them in the bag, totally distracted by my own dark thoughts when she began to speak. What she said stiffened my spine and reminded me why feeling anything for her was a horrible idea.

"I'm in the witness protection program, WitSec." She spoke in a low, sure tone, and all traces of alcohol were gone. "Stephanie isn't my friend, not exactly. She's my handler. She's been helping me from a distance ever since I moved to New York. I haven't told you because one of the conditions of the program is absolute secrecy. I'm not allowed to contact anyone from my old life, but I'm also not allowed to tell anyone from my new life about the program."

I lifted my gaze to find her staring at the birth certificate in her hands. "WitSec wouldn't need to get you documents through some stoner in Ohio." Was she still lying? Had I somehow fallen in with a pathological liar?

"The only way I was discovered so quickly was if there was a leak in the program. Stephanie had told me from the beginning that if the program was compromised, then I'd have to run on my own. She said it's rare but possible. I don't know how she knows Reggie, but I'm sure it was the only thing she could do to help me without a record on her end."

I walked over and pulled the document from her hands, waiting until her eyes lifted to meet mine. "WitSec is comprised of ninety-five percent criminals who have rolled over on their fellow associates. You don't end up in the program because your boyfriend is after you." I wanted to see her reaction to my questions to help gauge whether she was finally telling me the truth.

"He was a biker. A part of a large motorcycle club. I provided testimony against him, and now his club is after me."

"Why would you turn in your boyfriend?"

She took a deep breath and sat down on the edge of the bed. "At first, I thought it was a simple motorcycle club. There were plenty of them around, and I'd grown up around them, so I didn't think anything of it. One day, I went looking for him and accidentally walked in on him doing some illegal business. He freaked out." She swallowed hard, not meeting my eyes. "He threatened me—made sure I understood that I was to keep my mouth shut. But after that, I couldn't see him the same way. I didn't want to be any part of his club or that crowd, but I wasn't sure how to leave. I was terrified. A few weeks later at a club party, one of the girls was joking about the feds watching them in a car outside. When it came time for me to go home, the car was still there. I scribbled my number on an old receipt and slipped it to them as I walked past. I had no idea what would come of it; I just knew I needed help. As it turned out, they were already building a case against the club, and they needed my testimony. I was able to negotiate my way into WitSec in exchange for testifying, but I've lived in a constant state of paranoia ever since."

Her story was sufficiently detailed, and I got the sense she was telling the truth, but I still wasn't sure what to think. I'd believed she was telling me the truth before, and while it wasn't entirely a lie, there was far more to her story than she'd divulged.

"What about the picture of the kids?" I asked.

She leaned forward and picked it up where it had been discarded, smiling fondly at the memory. "That's my half brother and half sister, Isaac and Averi. My dad remarried when I was seventeen, the same year my tita passed away. It was a rough year. His new wife was a worthless sack of shit, but those kids meant everything to me. She was too lazy to bother with raising them, so I took care of them. That was by far the hardest part of walking away. I wasn't supposed to take anything with me, but I had to take the picture. It's all I have left of them."

Something grated at me. The incessant chaffing of a rock inside my shoe.

Guilt.

I rarely suffered from that ugly emotion. My father used to say, "Measure twice, cut once." I liked to think I practiced that philosophy in all areas of my life, which meant I rarely regretted my actions. Emily was proving herself to be my exception in all things.

I'd injected myself into a far bigger mess than I had expected. I certainly wasn't interested in showing up on the federal government's radar, but I also couldn't leave her to deal with this on her own, not when I was partially responsible for her situation.

I walked to where she sat and cupped her cheeks, tilting her chin up to face me. "I think what we need to do is go somewhere remote and let things settle down. I know you were thinking about going to a new city, but you're safer where you won't be seen. It'll buy us some time, which we could both use to clear our heads. Maybe then, we can come up with a long-term plan."

Her eyes grew glassy, but she kept her composure as she nodded.

"Why don't you get showered, and we'll grab some dinner. First thing in the morning, we head north."

FOURTEEN
Emily

Few things are more difficult in this life than admitting aloud the ugliest parts of ourselves, especially when that admission is made to someone we respect. The words taste rancid and shameful after being swallowed back and festering down in our bellies for so long.

Sometimes, we want to spit out the words so we can be free of the bitter aftertaste, but when the opportunity arises, we get scared. We think no one will understand, and that maybe, if it stays in the dark, it'll be like it never happened.

But we should know better.

Secrets have a way of bubbling to the surface.

It is the one epic battle almost everyone fights at some point—whether to keep a secret to protect your reputation, letting the knowledge eat at you internally, or to divulge the secret, thereby relieving the burden at the risk of ostracization. The two arguments war with one another, a bloody and corrosive battle that only intensifies as we tell further lies to protect that hideous little secret.

When I told Tamir my story, I was relieved but still so incredibly embarrassed and ashamed. He had been so understanding and helpful, and I had done nothing but lie to him. During that brief window when we'd been drinking and kissing, it felt like those barriers between us had begun to drop. We were free to be two people exploring the attraction between them. After my confession, those barriers felt reformed and fortified, an almost physical presence.

When he placed his hands on my face and suggested our next course of action, I was begging and screaming on the inside for him to kiss me. To show me that what I'd told him didn't change the way he saw me. To reinforce that connection we'd shared hours before. Instead, I felt like an inmate locked behind iron bars and denied all but the most paltry scraps of affection.

That evening, we went to dinner, but our conversation was subdued and superficial. Neither of us seemed to be interested in addressing the status of our complicated relationship or the maelstrom of questions that hung over our heads. Instead, we called it a night early, neither of us straying from our sides of the bed. We both rose at five a.m. without complaint when the alarm went off, and within a half hour, we were on the road.

"When you say we're going north, does that mean you have a destination in mind?" I asked as we pulled away from the motel.

I had thought about asking during dinner, but we'd kept our conversation on anything but our situation. My mental and emotional sponges had been thoroughly saturated during the day. By the time dinner rolled around, I couldn't take any more substantive discussions. Plus, it hadn't made one bit of difference where we went. It was a small relief to offload that one decision onto his shoulders so that I could better carry the remaining burden of my current circumstances.

"I have a small cabin up in Wisconsin not too far from Lake Superior. It's about eleven hours from here, thus the early alarm. We can make the drive in one day, but it's going to be a long one."

"You have a cabin? In Wisconsin?" That was probably the last thing I had expected him to say. What New Yorker kept a cabin in northern Wisconsin? Vermont or Maine, sure. But Wisconsin? Had I inadvertently teamed up with an ax murderer who was playing the long con to lure me to my death? Was I going to end up in a wood chipper like that guy in *Fargo*?

Maybe my story would be sensational enough to find its way onto Netflix. *Emilia Reyes: Woman on the Run*. We all had to have goals—I supposed that could be mine. At least my story would live on in infamy.

"It's just a small hunting cabin I use when I need a break from the city. I only go about once a year, so keep your expectations reasonable. It'll be dusty, and it's tiny. Don't go imagining some romantic cottage on a lake. You'll be in for a disappointment."

"I don't have anything better to suggest, so it works for me. Do you hunt when you're there?"

"I do but only for food. I don't need to kill things just for sport."

Well, that's good to know.

"My family didn't hunt much, but back where I'm from, it's a huge pastime."

"Texans and their guns. Every man, woman, and child own one," he mused.

An icy chill skittered down my back. Had I told him where I was from? I had gotten used to telling everyone I was from California. Had I slipped and mentioned Texas at some point? I thought I remembered everything that had happened while we'd been drinking, but maybe I'd said something and didn't remember.

"Yeah, actually. I don't remember telling you that."

"I could have sworn you did. Probably while we were drinking." He played it off nonchalantly, but I couldn't escape the feeling that something was off.

Moments like this made me wonder about myself. I knew Tamir was dangerous. I knew he had secrets and was swathed in mystery like a real-life James Bond. How unstable did a woman have to be to truly want a man like that? I'd only ever have what little of himself he was willing to give, and he probably had a different woman in every city he visited. Why was I attracted to a man who was potentially so bad for me? Considering my background, I supposed it would have been more shocking if I was drawn to a normal man. But still, I worried about myself sometimes.

"Tell me about your life in Texas," Tamir said after I'd been quiet for a while.

"I did the bookkeeping and helped manage the restaurant my grandparents started when they were younger. I loved that place; it reminded me of my tita. When I moved to New York, I knew I wanted to work at a restaurant because that's all I'd ever known. That's about it. I worked and hung out with friends when I wasn't taking care of my brother and sister. My life was pretty simple. What about you? Tell me about your life in Israel."

"I went straight into the military after school like every Israeli."

"Everyone?"

"Yes, Israel has a mandatory conscription of its male and female citizens with a few limited exceptions. Currently, women only serve for two years and men for three before they can be released. The government anticipates it won't be able to continue that practice, but for now, it's the law."

"Wow, I had no idea. How did you feel about joining?"

"I was young and idealistic, eager to serve my country. Israel and the Palestinians had signed the Oslo Accords to move toward peace. I'd grown up in the shadows of the war between our two nations and seen the hatred that festered from one generation to the next. It might sound counterintuitive, but I wanted to serve to be a part of the solution. To help with the peace accords. I was eventually deployed into the West Bank and witnessed how violence still prevailed. It was horrible. I quickly realized the only way to stop the violence was from the top down, not by policing the everyday people on the streets. We needed leaders who would genuinely want things to change and rally the people in that direction."

"It's better over there than it used to be, isn't it?"

"Yes, but there's still much room for improvement."

"I take it you're Jewish?"

He glanced at me, probably feeling like he was under interrogation. "Yes, but I'm not exactly practicing. I assume if you're Hispanic, there's a good chance you're Catholic."

"Technically, but I'm not sure I'm anything anymore. I've been questioning everything lately."

"We all grow and change. There's nothing wrong with that."

"I know, but my tita was devout, and that's the one way I still feel like I've let her down. She raised me, gave me love and a moral compass she would attribute to her faith in God, and it would break her heart to think I'd abandoned my faith."

"That the same Tita who gave you that evil eye necklace?" he asked with a smirk.

"Yeah, why?"

"It's been a while since I learned about Catholicism in school, but I don't recall that being a part of their teachings. It seems to me your tita had quirks of her own."

I smiled as I recalled all the old wives' tales we had lived by. Times when my tita would rub an egg on my back, then crack open its contents into a glass and put it under my bed at night to help keep me from getting sick when a sniffle would set in. Our magical aloe plants and the almighty power of the red string. Her beliefs were definitely patchwork, and Tamir's assurance was a great reminder of that.

The sun was slipping beneath the horizon as we pulled onto a dirt road, winding our way through a forest of evergreen pines mixed with other types of trees that had lost their leaves for the winter. Traces of a recent snowfall remained on the ground and in the crooks of branches. It made the place look utterly magical in the twilight of the setting sun.

The dirt road wound through the trees for about two miles before a small wooden building came into view. The outside didn't give the best first impression. Boards covered the two windows, and the forest undergrowth was attempting to swallow the cabin whole. I tried to reserve judgment, but a part of me was very concerned. The cabin didn't even look big enough for one occupant, let alone two.

"Just give it a chance," Tamir interjected, reading my thoughts. "It actually cleans up pretty well."

I was dubious, and I shot him a look that said so.

Once he showed me inside, I had to admit, I could see the potential. The entire cabin was one room, save for a tiny bathroom in the corner. One double-sized bed, a sofa, a two-seater table and chairs, and a corner kitchen, all encompassed in one room.

"Let me get the lights on. I'll be right back." Tamir left me inside, and after a few minutes, a generator out back came to life, then the lights flickered on.

Unfortunately, having light didn't help the situation. It only highlighted the severity of the cleaning job required. On the bright side, the place was so tiny, there wasn't all that much to clean, but what was there, was filthy.

Tamir popped his head back inside and rapped on the door to get my attention. "Let's get our stuff inside, along with some firewood, before the sun sets. You've never seen dark until you've been in the forest at night. There will be plenty of time to clean later."

We grabbed our few bags and the supplies we'd bought from yet another Wal-Mart and dropped them just inside the front door. Then I followed Tamir toward the pile of wood he kept in a covered stand. He placed three logs in my arms, and I made my way back to the cabin, placing the wood in the metal grate next to the stove. When I crossed paths with Tamir on my way out, he had twice as much wood in his arms as I'd been able to carry.

I started pondering why exactly lumberjacks and outdoorsmen were so damn sexy when I heard a flapping noise in front of me. All I saw was a glowing set of yellow eyes before an enormous owl swept by me so close, I felt my hair stir from the movement of its wings.

"*Aye, chingao!* La Lechuza!" I wailed hysterically, running back into the cabin and slamming into Tamir on my way in. "I swear to God it was La Lechuza! She swooped down and tried to take my head off, and now, I don't even have Ned to ward her off. We are sitting ducks in this place."

"Slow down," he chuckled, clearly not taking matters seriously enough. "What happened?"

I stepped back and put my arms on my hips. "There was an owl, a huge, angry owl, that just swooped down and tried to kill me."

"So, what were you saying about la…"

"La Lechuza. They're witches that turn themselves into owls. *That* was one of them, I know it. I saw her eyes."

The corners of Tamir's mouth twitched. "And Ned? Who is Ned?"

I glowered at him, not happy about being his source of entertainment. "He was my aloe plant. They keep away evil spirits."

"Your plant's name was Ned?"

"*Pinche cabrón!* You aren't even listening to me. Yes, my plant's name was Ned, like you've never named a plant before. Whatever. You can get the rest of the wood yourself. I'm not going back out there." I whipped around but then stopped, as I had nowhere to go without being covered in a mountain of dust.

Before I could make another move, Tamir pulled me back flush against him. My heart rate had just started to settle from my scare outside. With his arms wrapped around me and his lips near my ear, the poor organ in my chest lost all pretense of a rhythm.

"I told you I'd keep you safe," he said in a rumble that had me clenching my thighs together. "Whether it's from a man or a train or a well or a witch. Nothing is going to happen to you while I'm around. Got it?"

What about you? Who's going to protect me from you?

I nodded my head in agreement, but my mind had been wiped blank by a potent wave of lust like a flashflood surging through a dam. He could have told me I was the Queen of England, and I would have agreed because I had no brain-power left to dispute him.

It took me a solid five minutes to regain cognitive function after he pulled away to continue stocking the firewood. There was no avoiding this man's effect on me. It was chemical. Primal. And now, we'd be spending who knew how long together in a cabin the size of a dollhouse. We'd either kill one another or … I wasn't sure I was brave enough to entertain the alternative.

FIFTEEN
Emily

BETWEEN THE TWO OF US, WE WERE ABLE TO MAKE THE CABIN presentable by bedtime, which was good because, after an eleven-hour drive and cleaning, we were both exhausted. Tamir gallantly offered me the bed, but he was way bigger than me, and I would feel awful forcing him to stay on a sofa not much bigger than a loveseat. I made myself comfortable on the couch, and we passed out without hardly a word.

It was the next morning when the reality of our situation sank in. I lay there listening to the birds coming to life outside our windows and wondered what I was supposed to do with myself out here in the middle of nowhere.

"You up?" Tamir's morning voice was sexy as hell. Deep and raspy. It wouldn't take much more than a few words to initiate a delicious round of morning sex, had our relationship been in that place, which it wasn't. But if it was…

Get a grip, Em.

"Yeah, I'm awake."

"I thought I'd go hunting this morning if you're interested in joining me."

"I'm pretty sure my calendar is open … so sure." If the man was going to kill me, he could do it just as easily in the cabin as he could a mile into the woods. I might as well take advantage of the opportunity because I didn't think activities would be easy to come by.

We each took a turn getting dressed and freshening up in the bathroom, then put on our new coats and cold weather gear. Before we left, Tamir retrieved a rifle he kept in a gun safe beside the bed. He sighted the scope, using an old coffee can on a log, and then it was just the two of us alone in the woods.

Down in the Hill Country of central Texas, there were no forests—not like the one we were in. Texas had cedar trees and scrub, live oaks and mesquite, but nothing like the towering army of trees around us. It was breathtaking.

"See these trees with the white bark?" Tamir asked, drawing me from my reverie. "Those are aspen trees. A lot of them will have chunks of the bark peeled off because the bark has pain-relieving qualities like aspirin. The deer somehow know that and will gnaw at the bark, especially during rutting season. If you spot fresh marks on the trees, it's a great way to help determine if deer have been in the area recently."

"How on earth do you know that?"

"I spent some time with the forest rangers up here after I bought the place. They gave me all kinds of information about the local wildlife."

After we walked for about a half hour, he found a spot

beside a bush for us to use as a makeshift deer blind. I hadn't been on a hunting trip before, but I knew the general principals. Sit. Be quiet. Wait. There was no pressure to talk, as that would have been counterproductive, so we were able to simply enjoy the silence and the beautiful setting.

We were there for about an hour when Tamir slowly lifted his gun and took aim. I hadn't seen a thing, but when I squinted in the direction the gun was pointed, I made out something brown moving slowly in the distance. It looked entirely too far away to shoot. Between the trees being in the way, its movement, and the sheer distance, I couldn't imagine it was possible.

One shot. That was all it took.

The blast rang out, slashing through the silence and echoing into the far corners of the forest. I flinched but kept my eyes trained on the deer long enough to see it slump to the ground. He'd done it. Located his prey, locked in on it, and brought it down with a single shot.

I was equally impressed as I was terrified.

We made our way over to it, and I was stunned to see just how large the deer was. "This thing looks like a mutant compared to the small white-tail deer we had back home. How are we supposed to get it back to the cabin?"

"With this." He pulled out a blue plastic tarp with rope tied to two of the corners from his backpack. "All we have to do is roll the deer onto the tarp, then we can drag it back."

What he proposed was far more difficult than it sounded. I had been pondering, when I first woke up, how I was going to occupy my time, but I started to realize roughing it might be more time consuming than I anticipated. The hunting trip alone was going to be an all-day affair.

We eventually got the deer loaded up and each took a rope, dragging the carcass behind us.

"That shot was pretty impressive. What exactly did you do in the military?" The question had been bouncing around in my head after seeing him use the rifle like it was an extension of his own body.

"Special Forces."

"What does that mean? Like our Army Rangers or Navy SEALs?"

"Very similar, yes."

"But not the same?"

Tamir slowed his steps, coming to a stop. When I peered back at him, he'd gone eerily still, his entire body chiseled in stone.

"Have you heard of the Mossad?"

The gentle breeze seemed to still at his words as if the forest itself feared what he was about to say.

"It's a super-secret organization," I offered, barely above a whisper. I sensed we were entering dangerous waters between his change in demeanor and what I could recall from my research of Krav Maga.

"Its existence isn't a secret, but its actions are. The Mossad is Israel's chief intelligence agency, the same as other countries have, except the Mossad has near limitless autonomy. It reports only to the Prime Minister—no one else. Its actions and operatives are not subject to judicial inquiry, nor are its operations disclosed to the public. The institution is given absolute authority to act in the best interest of Israel."

"And you were a part of the Mossad?"

"Yes. There are eight departments for purposes such as espionage, research, and technology. One of those departments contains a top secret unit called Kidon. I belonged to that unit."

I felt like a child about to ask her parents about the existence of Santa Clause. Somehow, deep in my heart, I knew the answer to my own question, but I had to ask it anyway.

"What does the Kidon unit do?"

"Assassinations." He said the word without any emotion. No remorse or shame.

Tamir was a killer.

Not just a man trained to fight. He specialized in ruthlessly ending lives without a second thought. That was why he could shoot as easy as breathing. That was why he had a silent alarm in his apartment and kept a gun beneath his bathroom sink. That was why my survival instincts begged and pleaded with me to stay away from him.

I didn't say a word in response.

We continued walking, a heavy silence blanketing us all around.

What did a career as an assassin do to a person? Could someone remain sane after that? When he'd told me earlier that he was in the Special Forces, I imagined something like *Blackhawk Down* or *Lone Survivor*—a unit of soldiers busting into a compound to save innocent civilians. Something grand and heroic.

An assassin sounded far more ominous. Stealthy and ruthless. When I thought about it, the description fit him, but it wasn't the only aspect to him. He was also the man who had offered a private training session when class had been canceled, saved me from an attacker, helped me on the run, and even took me to a botanical garden to help ease my nerves.

What was I supposed to think? What was I supposed to do? I could try to get away from him, but if I was being hunted, wouldn't it make more sense to stay with the man who claimed he wanted to protect me? He was certainly capable, if I could manage to trust him.

I glanced to where he walked along side me, rope slung over one shoulder and gun on the other. I'd sensed he was dangerous but had never truly felt threatened by him. Every one of his actions spoke to his effort to keep me safe. As far as I could tell, my best move would be to trust that his actions accurately depicted his intentions.

Besides, it wasn't like I had a decent alternative. I was in the middle of a forest without any mode of transportation unless I attempted to steal his car for the second time. Somehow, pissing him off like that sounded like an especially bad idea.

He was there to help me, and I would stay with him as long as he didn't give me reason to run. He was definitely the lesser of two evils. If he could keep me from falling into the hands of the men who were after me, I'd gladly accept the risk of staying with him.

Should he change his mind and want to harm me, then I was a goner.

I'd never stand a chance against a man with such lethal abilities. I would just have to hope he would continue to use those gifts to protect me, rather than punish me.

When we got back to the cabin, after we both had lunch, Tamir strung up the deer on a pulley and began to butcher it. I didn't have the stomach to watch, so I stayed inside and experimented with the water tank shower system.

I'd gone camping in a friend's RV one time as a teen. The cabin shower reminded me of using the RV shower. The water sprinkled out, barely penetrating my thick hair. On top of that, there was no conditioner, which meant my hair would be a tangled mess for the foreseeable future. The one main difference between the RV and the cabin showers was the water temperature. I'd never in my life showered under such ice-cold water. It inspired a new level of efficiency in my routine.

Despite those drawbacks, I felt enormously better after cleaning off two days of grime since I hadn't bathed after we arrived at the cabin the night before.

By the time Tamir finished and joined me inside, the clear sky had melted into dusk. He handed over two venison steaks, which we put in the tiny oven, and I began to cook dinner while he took his turn in the shower.

Dinner was better than I ever could have imagined. I had insisted on getting ranch-style beans for Tamir to try when we bought groceries on our way to the cabin. I cooked those and a can of green beans to go with our steaks. We were limited to canned goods and items that didn't need to be refrigerated, but the meal tasted amazing.

After we finished every last bite, neither of us left the table. My belly was full, and the fire had kept the cabin toasty warm, which helped me feel more able to continue our discussion.

"As you can probably guess, I've thought about what you told me for the past few hours. I'd really like to know what happened after … what happened when you left the service." He'd said that he was dishonorably discharged. I didn't want to form any judgment until I knew exactly what had happened and had the entire picture.

Tamir stood and went to the kitchen shelf where an ancient bottle of whiskey had been collecting dust. He poured us each a small amount before returning to his seat. "Eleven years ago, my world came crashing down around me, and it was all my fault."

SIXTEEN

Tamir

Past

"I heard the commander talking about commendations for the mission." Uri clapped his hand on my back as he announced his good news. Our team had spent months gathering intelligence and planning the assassination of a top enemy general, who had been a key proponent of suicide bombings of Israeli citizens.

"It would be well earned," I replied, closing my front door after my friend had entered.

"Why don't you sound pleased? That would be an incredible honor."

I wouldn't feel comfortable talking to many people about the thoughts I'd been struggling with, but Uri was one of them. We'd been through so much together; he was more of a brother than a friend. We walked farther into my house as I began to explain.

"When I chose to stay in the service, I thought what I was doing would make a difference. I know, it sounds ridiculously naïve. But at the very least, I thought we'd be working toward peace for our nation. An end to all the killings. After ten years of service, I don't think there will ever be an end. Just a bloody river of retaliation and death. And what's worse? I can feel hatred and intolerance growing inside me."

"Should we not hate evil? Think of all the civilians—*the children*—these terrorists kill every day."

"And do we not send airstrikes and bombs that result in undesired casualties? Six months ago, we targeted an enemy compound and ended up killing six innocent children inside and wounded thirty other people in the vicinity. What makes us so different from them?"

Uri's fist came out of nowhere. Pain blistered across my cheek, but I'd experience so much worse in my life that it barely registered.

"Say that shit again," he warned in a low growl. I had pissed him off even more than I'd expected.

"Look, I know we're not the same, but lately, I'm struggling to see the point."

"The point is, as long as there are terrorists on our doorstep trying to kill us, we fight. We aggressively defend our people. That doesn't make us monsters like them."

I dropped down onto my leather sofa. "I know, I know. It's just getting to me lately."

"You need to figure out a way to get past it. You have one

week to get that shit sorted out, then we get back to work."
He stormed out of the house, slamming my door behind him.

I understood why he was upset. The atrocities we'd seen were horrific. It wasn't that I felt guilt over our actions; I just didn't want to be perpetuating the problem. At some point, when you continue to slam your own head against a wall, shouldn't you stop and ask why?

I'd already been struggling with my doubts, but something that happened on our last mission truly shook me. A small team of us were raiding an enemy stronghold under a "no survivors" order. The timing was crucial, which meant a daytime attack, rather than a preferred strike under the cloak of darkness. Because of that, our gear was different. We'd had to arrive at the compound undetected. A fully decked-out team of assassins would have blown our cover. Instead, we wore flack vests under everyday clothes and left our helmets and other gear behind.

I'd gone in through the back, making sure to eliminate an escape attempt. When I entered the small kitchen near the rear entrance, I aimed my gun at an enemy soldier sitting at a small table, eating his breakfast. His eyes lifted to mine, and I instantly recognized him as the adult version of a boy I'd lived next door to growing up.

I froze in shock.

How had this member of our community become one of the enemy? We'd played soccer together and traded player cards. When I looked at him, all I could see was that same boy. It was the same way children never age in our minds when we don't see them for long periods. To me, he was still that same person.

I could see the same recognition in his eyes. I had no mask or helmet to obscure my identity. We both remained locked in our moment of surprise until chatter sounded in my earpiece, urging me to move forward and join my squadron. My orders were to leave no survivors, but I couldn't make myself to do it. To kill this man I'd grown up with. Forced to make a quick decision, I went with my gut. I ran past him, allowing him to escape out the back.

Our mission was successful. We killed the primary target and obtained more intelligence about future planned attacks on Israeli citizens. But I couldn't celebrate our victory. I was too bogged down in worry about whether I'd made a mistake by letting the man live, along with a new myriad of doubts about the entire principle of our war.

After the mission, I didn't tell anyone what I'd done. It was good to at least confess to Uri about my internal struggle, but there was only one person I could confide in completely. If there was anyone who could help me sort my thoughts, it was her.

Aliza wasn't just my sister; she was my twin.

We had a deep-seated bond that was usually only found in identical twins who shared the same DNA. I could sense when she was upset, and she was the only one who could calm my razor-sharp temper. She had cried for days after I decided to stay in the service and set my sights on training to be in the Mossad. She was proud of my choice but extremely worried for my safety. When I struggled with the realities of my job, she was the one who brought me back into the light.

I picked up the phone and dialed her number. She'd be thrilled to know I was back on break. Even though she was engaged and busy starting a new job after graduating from the university, she always made time for me when I was between missions.

She didn't answer, which wasn't unusual. I left a message and began to tackle the chores that accumulated while I was away. By the next morning, I still hadn't heard from Aliza and was starting to worry.

Throwing on my clothes, I made the hour drive to her apartment and pounded on her front door. Nothing. As I pulled out the spare key she'd given me when she moved in, a tremor shook my fingers.

I was a Mossad assassin. Trained using waterboarding and the most ruthless tactics to erase any hint of nerves from my system, but all of that programming vanished as a horrifying certainty settled into my gut. Something was horribly wrong.

As it turned out, I didn't need the key. The door was unlocked.

Inside, Aliza lay in the living room, surrounded in a giant pool of her own blood. Her pale, slim throat had been sliced open. She had been cooking when it happened, our mother's patchwork apron still tied around her waist.

My knees shook and trembled, but I refused to fall. This was no accident. No random hate crime or burglary. My old neighbor had told his superiors who I was, and my sister was made to suffer for my role in the war.

Maybe they thought it was a message. A threat to back off. Regardless of their intent, all it did was solidify my resolve. These cowards didn't scare me. Quite the opposite. They had erased every hint of doubt I'd been struggling with. Erased every remaining shred of my humanity and empathy.

They created a monster, and I was going to bleed every one of them dry for their sins.

I left the scene without calling the authorities—Aliza would be discovered soon enough. I had a war to prepare for. Not just a counterstrike or a simple revenge killing, I would rain down the holy wrath of God upon every one of the enemy soldiers I could get my hands on.

Our department knew far more about the enemy than we'd acted upon. We were only given authority to strike in certain limited situations, but we knew all about their camps and their numbers. We knew who their officers were and how they liked their coffee. The general we'd killed a week earlier? I knew exactly who he reported to and where that man lived. It would be easy to walk up to him and rip his heart straight from his chest, but that was the problem—it would be too easy.

I ran by my house and collected every weapon and supply I might need, then found a cheap apartment to set up my base of operations. What I was doing would end my career and possibly get me killed, but I didn't care. If the other side had no scruples, then neither would I.

For two weeks, I raided enemy weapon stores, killing whoever was present. I needed the firepower, but I also figured it would be poetic justice to kill them with their own weapons.

After that, I set out on a methodical manhunt, working my way up the enemy chain of command. When I came across my old neighbor for a second time, he received no mercy. By the time I stood face-to-face with the senior leader who was calling the shots, the raging fires of revenge had devoured me, leaving an entirely new creature standing in the ashes of who I used to be.

While I would have liked to have killed them all, even in my most enraged moments, I knew that wasn't possible. Once I was satisfied with my body count, I planned my escape. The Mossad was an independent agency, but my actions were unauthorized. I was subject to prosecution under the penal code just like any other Israeli citizen. There was no way I was going to prison for killing scum terrorists.

Two weeks later, I used a fake passport to immigrate to

the United States, where I could create a new life for myself. My past would always be a part of me, but I could never be the idealistic man I'd been before Aliza's death. Instead, I would welcome the man I'd become by harnessing the ruthless violence and embracing my power to do what so few could—bring evil to its knees, one merciless kill at a time.

SEVENTEEN
Emily

A CYCLONE OF EMOTIONS PICKED ME UP AND SPUN ME IN EVERY direction as I listened to his story. I had known he was a killer, but to hear that he'd gone rogue and annihilated an entire battalion of enemy soldiers was entirely different. Unpredictable. Homicidal. At the same time, my heart broke for the excruciating guilt and anguish he must have felt at discovering his sister dead.

My siblings meant the world to me, so if I'd been in his shoes, I wasn't sure I wouldn't have done the same thing. I worried every night when I went to sleep whether they were being taken care of properly. When I first decided to leave, I had to carefully consider whether my actions would be taken out on them. Whether they would be used to get back at me.

My father was far from Father of the Year, but I had to hope and pray that, at the very least, he would keep my brother and sister safe.

"I'm so sorry," I whispered. As my emotions settled, I realized that the overwhelming sentiment that remained was sorrow. My heart ached for what Tamir had lived through.

"It was my own fault. My punishment for not following orders when I allowed my old neighbor to live. I won't grieve my career; it was over anyway. My loyalty was to my family, as it should have been. I don't regret one thing I did to avenge my sister."

"Yes, but you also can't blame yourself for her death." I placed my hand on the table and sat forward, horrified that he would carry around that kind of guilt. "You were showing a man compassion, and he ratted you out to his superiors. He's the one responsible—he and whoever killed her—not you."

The firelight from the stove glinted off the obsidian shards in his eyes, and the corners of his mouth twitched. "I appreciate your perspective, but I see it differently. Regardless, I've walked through the fire and come out stronger on the other end."

I smiled softly. "'A certain darkness is needed to see the stars.' That's what my tita used to say."

"She was a wise yet highly superstitious woman," he teased as he sipped from his glass. "I would have liked to have met her."

"You know what? I think she would have liked you, Tamir …" I paused. "Wait a minute. If you used a fake passport to get over here, does that mean your real name isn't Tamir?"

"Technically? No, it isn't."

"Well, what *was* your name?"

He stared at me for a solid minute. Until I could almost

feel him sifting through the thoughts in my head. "Does it really matter? I'm not that man anymore."

I thought about what he said and realized that, regardless of whether my license read Reyes, Ramirez, or Rogers, I was still the same person. "No, I guess it doesn't." I sat for several minutes, absorbing everything I'd learned. He'd lived an extraordinary life before coming to the States, and now, his life was far simpler.

"Was it hard letting go of that life? Becoming an instructor and giving up years of a military lifestyle?" I'd heard that integrating back into society could be difficult for ex-military.

Maybe it was just the flickering light of the stove, but an ominous shadow seemed to cross his features.

"Actually, the transition was rather seamless." His eyes broke our connection and dropped to the glass in his hand.

"Is the Israeli government still searching for you?"

"There are still warrants out for my arrest, but no one is actively looking for me. So long as I stay under their radar, I shouldn't be at risk. I think that's enough story time for one night. It's time to get some rest." He stood and walked to the kitchen sink, effectively ending our conversation.

I felt like something had bothered him, but I wasn't sure which part. He was generally very even-tempered. It wasn't like him to be mercurial, but we all had our moments, so I didn't press him.

An hour later, as I lay snuggled on the sofa under a pile of blankets, I felt my outlook shift. Tamir's story had confirmed he was a dangerous man, but it had also explained the odd feeling of safety I got when I was around him. He might have disagreed with my assessment of him, but I was starting to believe the beautiful soul of a worthy man was tucked deep beneath his stoic, harsh exterior.

Would a man, who loved so deeply as he had loved his

sister, hurt me for no reason? Surely, not. Knowing what I now knew about his past, I felt even more confident he truly was there to help me. A dizzying realization settled over me that there was a chance, no matter how small, I just might survive my ordeal unscathed.

For the first time in ages, I fell asleep with a smile on my lips and a lightness in my heart.

The next morning, I woke to the thunk of Tamir chopping wood outside the cabin. The sun was well into the sky, making it probably close to nine in the morning. I had to guess at the time because I refused to turn my phone on. I'd seen enough movies to know that phones could be used to gather information about me.

After rolling out of bed and tidying up the blankets, I headed to the bathroom to get dressed for the day. Back home, I always showered in the morning, but after only a day and a half at the cabin, it was quickly clear to me that showers in the wilderness were an evening activity. There was no way I could go to sleep covered in sweat and dirt from a day in the forest, and I certainly wasn't about to take a second freezing shower in the morning. One a day was plenty.

Once I was dressed, I set about washing our dishes from the night before. We'd been too tired to mess with them after dinner. It was amazing how chores piled up even in a 500 square-foot shoebox of a house.

The rhythmic thuds of Tamir's ax continued while I cleaned. I wiped away the remnants of dust that had settled after our initial cleaning and made Tamir's bed, mostly just to keep myself busy. When I reached to pull the sheets to the headboard, my foot bumped something under the bed. I squatted down and discovered that it was Tamir's black duffel stuffed beneath the mattress.

It was hard and bulky, piquing my interest about what could be in it. He'd hardly touched the thing while I'd been around. But I wasn't an idiot. I didn't expect it to be clothes or something equally normal, especially knowing what I did about Tamir. That precise knowledge was exactly why I was so curious about what *was* in the bag.

I set aside all expectations and pulled back the main zipper. On top was a large first-aid kit, which was probably why I couldn't find one in his bathroom back at his apartment. Below that was a laptop and what appeared to be two handgun cases, both with fingerprint locks. The bottom was lined with a heavy wool blanket and a plastic tarp along with a length of rope.

A part of me wanted to be upset because a normal, healthy individual wouldn't carry around this type of gear. But after what he'd told me the night before, I didn't think any of it was all that surprising. Not only that, but my own convoluted past blurred the lines of acceptable versus unacceptable. It wasn't like he had torture devices or a severed head tucked away. If he needed to keep a stash of guns and a tarp in a go bag to feel prepared for any situation, I wouldn't hold it against him. Then again, I was from Texas, and our views on firearms and personal property were a bit different than most.

I shoved the bag back under the bed and finished cleaning. As I did, I wondered what I was missing in civilization. It was odd to think that the world was continuing on, outside our little wooded bubble. Without my phone, a world war could have broken out, and I would have had no idea. Tamir had his phone with him, but now that we were beyond cell service, it did him little good.

I had to admit that there was something peaceful about knowing the real world couldn't get to us. The reprieve wouldn't be forever, but it was a relief while it lasted. The same was true for my struggles, though. They wouldn't last forever. I had to remind myself, on occasion, that this was just a chapter in my life and not my entire story.

One day, I'd have my life back, and it would be up to me to do something worthwhile with it. I didn't go through hell to wait tables and drink myself to sleep at night. It had taken a good amount of soul searching, but I had started to construct a plan. Now, I just had to live long enough to see it through.

"That should keep us in good shape for the next several days." Tamir joined me inside, slumping into a kitchen chair while I continued to cook lunch at the stove.

"I noticed the clouds were heavy this morning. Is it going to snow?"

"Looks like it might. I figured I'd rather be prepared just in case."

"I appreciate that. If you want to clean up before lunch, there's time. This won't be ready for another ten minutes." I glanced over my shoulder when he didn't respond.

Tamir's painfully intense and equally fathomless gaze bore into me. I couldn't tell if he wanted to bend me over the kitchen table or filet me like the deer out back. The latter, I was adamant against; the former, sounded more appealing each day I was with him.

He eventually stood and eased the sultry tension in the room. "After lunch, we can do some training if you're interested."

"I'd like that, thank you." My words were rushed, making me feel like a rabbit in the presence of a wolf. I chided myself not to be so affected by him, but it was innate. My instincts told me to fear him, but I was starting to wonder if it wasn't for the same reason I'd initially thought.

He was still dangerous to me but not in a lethal way. He had the power to derail my life. To turn on end everything I'd worked so hard for. Tamir wasn't the type of man you had a crush on, dated, and married. A relationship with him would be life itself. He would become the air I breathed and my reason for waking each morning. That type of power was terrifying.

I didn't know if I ever wanted to give that kind of control over me to another human being, but the longer I was around Tamir, the more I worried that I had no say in the matter. He was a force of nature. His effect on me wasn't something I could moderate or filter. The only options were to prepare for the devastating effects or to run, and the latter no longer felt like an option. That was how I knew I'd already fallen into his orbit. The pull toward him was too great to resist. I didn't want to run and risk never seeing him again. The only thing left to do was to prepare for the fall and pray it would be worth the long descent.

An hour later, we squared off outside the cabin, both layered in comfortable clothes that allowed movement but kept away the increasing chill in the air. We both did a round of warmup exercises, our breath puffing out in small clouds, and our footfalls echoing loudly beneath the canopy of trees.

"Our options are somewhat limited without the proper training pads, but we can still practice plenty of techniques. Let's start with some simple punch defenses—just the motions with little force—more for muscle memory than simulation."

Tamir rotated randomly through jabs, hooks, and upper-cuts at a reasonable speed, allowing me to adjust to his attacks and produce the proper defense, whether it be a redirect of his strike or a block. Going through the motions was incredibly empowering even though it wouldn't be the same as defending myself against a real attacker. I remembered all too well how hard it was to think clearly back in that alley when I'd been grabbed. The hope was that, if I practiced enough, the movements would become second nature, and I wouldn't have to think about them. If a hand came toward my face, I would deflect it instinctually.

We segued into kick defenses, which often involved a built-in counterstrike. Feign to the side, block the kick, then flow directly into a punch to the face. Even practicing at a fraction of the speed, my muscles quickly grew tired from the exertion. A part of me wanted to call an end to the session, but I also hated to wimp out when Tamir was still going strong.

"Had enough for one day?" He smirked. Apparently, I hadn't hidden my fatigue as well as I thought.

"It's been a week since I've trained. I can tell I'm going to be sore tomorrow."

"It doesn't take long for the muscle to atrophy. If we practice a little each day, it'll keep you from regressing in your training."

"What about you? I hate for you to get soft while you're out here with me," I teased.

Tamir arched a brow. "Soft?"

"You know what I mean. Slow your reflexes or whatever."

"At this point for me, it's like riding a bike. Even a short absence doesn't tend to affect me. But if you're worried, you can always put me to the test. See if you can actually lay a finger on me in my softened state." A challenge. He was suggesting we reversed our roles, and I attacked him for a change.

The corners of his eyes creased at the excited anticipation of demonstrating his skills. How could I deny such an atypical display of enthusiasm on his part? Plus, if I could actually land a strike, I'd feel on top of the world.

I closed in until he was within striking distance and lifted my fists on guard. We both stayed light on our feet, eyes locked on one another with grins on our faces.

"Don't be scared," he goaded me.

"You're going to be awfully embarrassed when I bring you to your knees." I launched two quick strikes as I spoke, hoping to catch him off guard. It was little surprise that it didn't work. He easily evaded my attacks.

"Come on. Surely, you can do better than that. I thought those cousins of yours would have taught you something you could use."

"They fought dirty, literally. I doubt you want me to throw dirt in your eyes so I can sneak in a punch." This time, I feigned a punch but swept out with my leg, almost catching his ankle.

"Not bad. If I'd been an ordinary man, that would have done its job."

"If you'd been an ordinary man, I wouldn't be here."

I'd be dead in an alley … or worse.

As soon as I finished the words, I rushed forward to shove my shoulder into his sternum. I fully expected him to block me and send me flying by him, but something about what I'd said made him lose focus. He didn't evade in time, which meant my strike hit home and sent us both crashing to the ground.

"Oh, shit!" I yelped. "Are you okay?"

He lay on his back with me half on top of him, eyes cast at

the clouded sky. "I'm never going to hear the end of this, am I?"

"Not ever, so long as I'm around to remind you."

His gaze dropped to my face, where I wore a smile worthy of the red carpet. Those calculating eyes briefly strayed to my lips. "It's definitely good for a man to stay humble ... I wouldn't want to lose that." His words hung in the air between us, a sultry curtain of innuendo.

Feeling awkward and uncertain, I lifted off him and dusted the dirt from my knees and hands. Tamir followed suit, stretching out his back as he stood.

"I really am sorry about that," I offered with a grimace.

"Don't worry about it. I deserved it." His words were grumbled, and he didn't meet my eyes again before he disappeared back inside the cabin.

Tamir was quiet for the rest of the day. I got the feeling what I'd said had upset him, but I had no idea why. I gave him a wide berth, or at least as much space as two people in a tiny cabin can give one another.

A heavy coating of snow transformed the landscape overnight. It was a spectacular sight. The early morning sun glinted off millions of tiny snowflakes on the open patch of ground in front of the cabin. It was magical. Surreal.

The best part was how undisturbed it remained. In the city, the snow was hardly on the ground a minute before it was sullied into a gray sludge. Tamir had enough firewood inside that we didn't even have to mar the perfection with a single boot print.

After we ate breakfast, I pulled out the deck of cards I'd found while cleaning. "Let's play a game. I don't think either of us can sit in the cabin all day without going a little crazy if we don't do something."

"You'll have to teach me. I doubt we know any of the

same games." He sipped on his coffee across from me at the table.

"If I managed to teach Isaac and Averi a few games, I'm sure I can teach you." I dealt out seven cards to each of us. "We're going to start with a classic. This one's called crazy eights. The objective is to get rid of your cards first. You have to play either the same suit or the same number as the top card in the discard pile, and eights are wild. See? Easy peasy."

He fanned out the cards in his deft fingers. "I probably shouldn't agree to this. My sister always beat me at games, and I wasn't exactly gracious about losing."

"I thought you said you'd never lost to a woman," I teased about his drunken comment back at the motel room.

His eyes flitted up from his cards to meet my challenging gaze. "I may have massaged the truth a bit."

"I see." My eyebrows rose to my hairline. "Fortunately, I never believed you for a second." I started the game, playing a seven of hearts onto the two of hearts in the discard pile.

Tamir played next, discarding a spade and making me draw a small stack of cards.

"It's not looking good for you," he prodded. "Maybe you should just surrender this hand."

"Surrender? Don't be absurd. I'll draw the entire pile before I concede defeat to you."

Two minutes later, Tamir played his last card and won the round with a smug grin.

I collected the cards and began to shuffle. "Beginner's luck. Get ready to go down, tough guy." I dealt a new round and won it along with the following two games.

"As much fun as it is to lose, I think I'm done."

"I'd goad you about being a sore loser, but my head is killing me. I think I'm done too."

His brows drew together with concern. "You have a headache?"

"Yeah, but it's just because of my damn hair. Sleeping with damp hair makes my curls wild when they dry. I've been keeping my hair in a bun to tame it, but after a while, that gives me a headache." I massaged my temples, but it was only a temporary fix.

"Why don't you braid it instead?"

"I can put it in a ponytail and do a braid from there, but that still bothers my head. I've never learned to French braid. Tita couldn't because of the arthritis in her hands, and I didn't have many girlfriends growing up."

Tamir rose from his chair and went toward the bathroom. "Take down the bun."

Confused, I did what he said. When he came back over, he held my brush in his hand.

"I don't know, Tam. It's pretty knotted right now." I was petrified he was going to tear my scalp to pieces and make my headache ten times worse.

He pulled his chair behind mine and sat. "My sister had hair a lot like yours," he said as he ran his fingers through my unruly waves. "She used to cry when our mother would brush her hair, so I started brushing it when we were little. As we got older, I taught myself to braid her hair. It was a part of our evening routine for a long time. I'd brush out her hair and braid it as we talked about our day at school." He took only the ends of my hair and gently worked the tangles out, then moved upward, one section at a time.

"I can't say I'm not a little envious. It sounds wonderful to have a sibling you were so close to."

"She also loved to tease me and push my buttons, but for the most part, we got along well growing up." He worked at my hair for long minutes until he'd brushed out every tangle.

The feel of the strokes all the way down my long hair soothed the tension in my neck and eased the pain in my head, but when Tamir set down the brush and ran his strong fingers through my hair, I positively melted.

In fact, a moan might have slipped past my parted lips.

"This feels too good; you're going to make me drool."

Tamir chuckled. "It's been a while since I've done this, so don't expect miracles the first time." He gathered the hair near my forehead and began to weave strands together, slowly working his way downward. "Braiding your hair at night will keep it from being unruly in the morning, and hopefully, it will also keep you from having headaches."

The juxtaposition of having this fierce, dangerous man caring for me in such a gentle manner warmed me from the inside out. I wasn't used to being treated so tenderly. It was addicting. I wanted to latch on to the feeling and never let go.

Each night, I got a dose of Tamir's affection, and like a junkie, I looked forward to the time each evening when I was the sole focus of his attention. I craved it. I dreamed about the feel of his hands sifting through my hair. It was the one window in time when we had no secrets between us and no baggage to sort through. It was pure and innocent, although the feelings it stirred inside me were anything but.

My need for Tamir grew rapidly each day, but I wasn't willing to risk crossing that line. Not while we were stuck together with no way to flee potential rejection. Instead, we established a new normal over the next two weeks as we lived at the cabin.

Tamir took a trip into town to load up on supplies, but otherwise, we stayed alone in the woods. Thanksgiving was commemorated with hot dogs over a campfire and the last swigs of our remaining whiskey. We spent our days on home improvement projects or hunting, working companionably side by side.

I would have thought enjoying some normalcy would have brought me peace, but each day, I felt further from it. In fact, the closer I felt to Tamir, and the more I enjoyed his presence, the more distraught I became. Sexual tension mounted to a boiling point, but I couldn't go there with him. Not when I hadn't told him the whole truth. And every day that passed, the guilt gnawed at me like an angry piranha, trying to devour me whole.

EIGHTEEN
Emily

WHILE TAMIR HAD GONE INTO TOWN TO DO A WEEKLY RESTOCK of our supplies, I decided to take a walk on one of the trails. It was amazing how a person could learn to recognize specific trees or clusters of rocks. At first, I wouldn't wander out of view of the cabin without Tamir present to make sure I could find my way back, but as each day passed, I grew more comfortable with the winding pathways.

I had to bundle up to ward off the crisp morning air. We were now a week into December, which meant I'd been dealing with the fallout of what I'd witnessed for almost a year.

It was closer to eight months, but it felt like a year. It felt like an eternity.

I was in a dramatic frame of mind, but that was because it was the day before my birthday. I had told myself when I took the leap and entered WitSec that by the time my birthday rolled around, I would be well on my way to a new life. Instead, I was turning twenty-seven in a shack in the woods, hiding out to stay alive.

Not where I wanted to see myself at this point.

Every day, the crushing weight of uncertainty bore down on me just a little bit heavier. On top of that, I missed my brother and sister. It had torn a hole in my heart when I left, and the wound only seemed to worsen rather than heal. Even out in the wilderness, where I should feel invigorated and refreshed, I felt small and lost.

But the thing that ate at me the most was my suffocating guilt over lying to Tamir. I was falling for him more and more every day, allowing him to help me under false pretenses. It made me feel like I couldn't breathe.

I was swimming in a sea of negative emotions, unable to see my way to the surface. They compounded one another, magnifying their effect until I had to get out. Get out of the cabin. Get out of my head.

A branch cracking, not far away, startled me from my thoughts. As I honed in on my surroundings, I realized I'd been standing in one place for some time. I hadn't even realized I'd stopped. Turning only my head to stay as quiet as possible, I scanned the area all around me but saw nothing unusual.

"Found you," Tamir's deep voice rumbled behind me.

"*Dios Mío*, you scared me," I shrieked and jumped to the side, unsure how he'd transported himself so close to me without making a sound. "You shouldn't sneak up on a girl like that." I swatted at his arm, but he easily evaded me.

"I thought you'd hear me coming, but when I realized you

162

were zoned out, I decided to have a little fun. I had to snap a small tree in half to get your attention. What had you so preoccupied?"

My eyes wandered to a nearby tree. "Lots of stuff, I guess. My birthday, my *real* birthday, is tomorrow. I knew back when I got into this mess that it wouldn't be easy, but I didn't expect it to be so difficult either. I'm turning twenty-seven with no family, no home, no job, and if I'm not careful, I won't even make it to twenty-eight. It all just got to me, and I don't think the self-imposed isolation is helping. Don't get me wrong, I'm incredibly grateful for your help. I'm just not used to so much time away from civilization." I turned and started us walking back toward the cabin.

Tamir fell into step beside me. He didn't say anything right away, which I appreciated. Nothing he could say would change my situation. If there was an easy solution, we would have assessed it already.

"You know what? I think you're right. I think it's time for you to get away from the cabin for a bit."

"Really?" My heart began a gentle dance to the tune of excitement and trepidation.

"Right by the market is a little restaurant. I think it's more like a bar, but either way, it should do the trick. Let's go out for dinner tonight to celebrate your birthday."

I jerked to a stop, and the second Tamir turned toward me, I flung my arms around him in a crushing hug. "Oh my God, you don't know how happy that would make me to pretend everything is normal just for a night." When I pulled away and realized what I'd done, I felt awkward. I dropped my gaze to the ground and my mud-caked shoes. "Oh, hell," I moaned. "I don't think I own a single thing that doesn't stink or isn't covered in dirt."

"I picked up a couple of new things for each of us at the

store this morning. I'm starting to look like a lumberjack, but at least they shouldn't kick us out from the stench." We washed our clothes by hand every few days, but it felt like a thankless task because they were stinky and soiled again in no time.

"I don't suppose you have any scissors here? I could help you with your hair, but only if you want. I used to trim my dad's hair and sometimes, my cousins."

He peered at me briefly with a smirk, then started us walking again. "I think I have something that should work."

"You want me to trim your hair with utility scissors? I don't know, Tamir. What if it looks terrible?" I held the heavy steel scissors in my hand like I would a dead fish. They were a far cry from the delicate shears I'd used previously to cut hair.

"Then it'll grow back. The waves just get tangled out here when it's long. As far as I'm concerned, we could just shave it all off."

"No! Your hair is entirely too pretty for that. Fine, sit down, and let's get this over with."

We pulled one of the dining chairs outside. It was low, but Tamir was tall enough to make up the difference. I stood behind him and hesitantly wove my fingers through his thick hair. It was interesting to have the tables turned. The act felt intimate, and I wondered how Tamir felt when he did my hair in the evenings. If he felt a fraction of the desire I felt for him, it was a wonder he hadn't tried to take our relationship further.

I began at the bottom, trimming away the hair that covered his neck. He'd needed a haircut before we started our little adventure, and now, it was downright shaggy. When I worked my way toward the top, I had to stand in front of him to check the length of my cuts, something that had been unremarkable when I'd cut my father's hair. But with Tamir, it was an entirely different experience.

Standing before him, my legs touching his so I could get close enough for the proper angle, I tried to focus on my work. I tried to ignore his hungry stare pressing against me, but I was weak, and my eyes were repeatedly drawn to his. When our gazes would collide, it was a hit of heroin straight to my bloodstream. Exhilarating. Powerful and disorienting. Like the bindings that held me to the earth were stripped away, and I might float off into the sky forever.

I wanted this man so badly that my muscles ached with need.

But I couldn't. I wouldn't. Not unless he knew everything. I hadn't planned to tell potential boyfriends or even a husband about my past, but Tamir was different. He already knew so much, and it felt like a betrayal to keep the rest from him. To build something with him under a false pretense. It felt wrong, dirty.

Yet I couldn't make the words form on my lips to admit the final truth. I could imagine his dark eyes turning harsh, judgment twisting his features. Just the thought doused my desire with an icy bucket of water.

"All done," I breathed, a knot of emotion balling in my throat. I gripped the scissors in my fist as I walked around to face him, making sure to keep several feet between us. "You're welcome to grab a shower first if you want to get the hair off." Each of my words and movements reeked of awkward tension.

I could see the confusion in Tamir's face, but he didn't press the matter.

"Your hair takes longer to dry, so you go ahead. A little bit of hair trimmings won't bother me."

"All right, thanks." I gave him a tight smile and fled for the cabin, feeling every bit the coward I was.

NINETEEN
Jamir

Birches was a local restaurant and bar hangout filled with rugged individuals in flannels and canvas work pants. There was a bar close to the entry, a pool table on the opposite end of the room, and a crowd of tables in the middle. They served standard small-town American fare in poor lighting while an ancient jukebox played songs from decades past.

By the look on Emily's face, you'd think I'd taken her to the Russian Tea Room back home.

Seeing her so happy was worth whatever minimal risk was associated with our outing. Her happiness made me happy, and that was a dangerous response for me to have. All of my emotions and reactions were slipping from my control. I wasn't sure if she noticed, but I had to grip my hands in my lap while she cut my hair to resist touching her. I'd been involved with plenty of sexy women in my life, but no one compared to Emily. The way she ran her hands through my hair. The rub of her legs against mine. Even something as simple as a haircut had felt borderline pornographic.

When she was lost in the process, her lips would purse and plump. It killed me. For once, I was glad the water in the cabin shower was ice cold. It forced my mutinous body back into submission.

Being with her would complicate things, but I wasn't sure I cared anymore. Unfortunately, it was obvious that she *did* care. She wasn't ready to go there. I didn't understand it, but I would respect her wishes without argument. For now.

"What are you getting?" she asked, drawing me back to our dinner.

"I think I'll have the salmon plate."

"That's very health conscious of you."

"Why? What are you getting?"

She grinned mischievously. "The chicken fried steak. I haven't had one in ages."

"I didn't grow up eating fried food, so it doesn't appeal to me much."

"Oh, man. You missed out. We used to fry everything. TexMex isn't the healthiest dietary culture to be born into, but man, is it delicious."

The waitress arrived to take our orders. Emily ordered a beer, so I did the same. I could tell she was tickled to see me do something so normal as drink a beer. It wasn't my drink of choice, but if it helped her lose herself for a bit and pretend she was living an ordinary life, beer was an easy sacrifice.

Much like Cinderella, Emily's fairy tale would end when we left this place and went back to the cabin in the woods.

Equally as unfortunate, I was no Prince Charming. I didn't know what I was to her, but regardless, I felt protective of her.

It was excruciatingly fucked up.

I had lied to her, led her away from her home on false pretenses, and now, I wanted to get in her pants? I could honestly say I was walking a very fine moral line—one I had been all too eager to judge others for crossing in the past.

At the very least, I needed to admit that I had feelings for the woman and that I wasn't going to be collecting her bounty. Nothing was deplorable enough about her to justify the price on her head.

That being the case, our time at the cabin had come to an end. But what did that mean? If I took her back home, there was a very real chance another hunter could find her and take her life. Could I live with that? I'd grown to know her, care for her. The more my feelings for her morphed, the longer I'd kept her at the cabin because I couldn't, in good conscience, throw her to the wolves.

If I was being honest, that wasn't the only reason.

I liked Emily. I enjoyed learning about the complicated woman and found myself fascinated with every new facet I unearthed. But most importantly, I respected her. And if I had any hope of her respecting me in return, I needed to tell her the truth. Tell her about the bounty. If I was walking away from her, she ought to know there was a price on her head so she could protect herself. I would also need to tell her about my role in her situation. She would be furious, but if we were parting ways, her anger would be inconsequential.

But what if I wasn't willing to let her go?

A primal, selfish part of me demanded to consider that alternative. I could keep her for myself, and then, I would know she was safe. In that case, telling her about my interest in her bounty would jeopardize any chance we had to be together. Could I keep my profession and the lies I'd told from her if we tried to have a relationship? Did I want to keep such a monumental secret?

During our entire evening out, I was consumed with questions. I tried to keep the mood light, but inside, my gut twisted with indecision—something I rarely struggled with. I kept those conflicted emotions to myself and was pleased to see Emily having a wonderful time. That was, until a pair of bikers swaggered into the restaurant and sat at the bar. She visibly stiffened in her chair, and I watched as the blood drained from her face.

Both men wore black leather vests over their clothes and had tattoos peeking up from their collars. I could see how they might be intimidating at first glance, but their posture was easygoing, and they were more interested in the food than a fight.

"Emily, look at me," I commanded softly, waiting to continue until her eyes were on me. "There's nothing to worry about. Everything's going to be fine, okay?"

She nodded and put a smile back on her face, but she wasn't the same after that. We finished our food, indulging in a rich dessert, then paid our tab and left. Only after we were in the car on our way back to the cabin did the tension in Emily's posture ease.

"Thank you for an amazing night," she said as I helped her from the car once we were home.

"It was dinner at a dive bar, but you're welcome," I replied in a playful tone, still trying to pull her back from whatever dark cave she'd descended into.

"As far as I'm concerned, it might as well have been a day at a tropical beach because it was an escape just the same. A chance to get away from it all." She leaned in and placed a chaste but heartfelt kiss on my cheek. Her eyes were lit with moonlight and regret as she smiled, then walked away without another word.

The next morning, I woke to an empty cabin.

Rain pelted the rooftop and pinged off the windows, the sound keeping me in bed as I enjoyed its relaxing cadence. When I sat up and realized Emily wasn't inside, I flew from bed and threw on my clothes. I rushed outside, half expecting to see the car missing, but found it right where I'd left it. The realization stalled me, confusing me as to where Emily could possibly be in the middle of a rainstorm.

Then I spotted her. Standing among a cluster of trees, she was drenched to the bone and shaking like a leaf. I grabbed a blanket from inside, then hurried over to her, wrapping her snugly in the thick wool.

"Emily, what the fuck? You're going to end up with hypothermia." I tugged her toward the cabin, but she resisted.

"I can't lie to you anymore," she announced, water dripping from her lashes. Her words were resolute, stirring up a deep sense of trepidation inside me. "I have these feelings, and I'm not sure what to do with them. I don't want you to look at me like a monster, but I have to be honest. Seeing those men last night was too much. It was a sign." She began to rub her wrist, and I realized there was no watch there anymore. She'd been consistent, not once taking it off since we'd been at the cabin.

Her pleading eyes met mine. "I don't know if you noticed their cuts," she continued, "but those men were part of the Los Zares MC." She lifted her wrist, exposing the faded Z tattoo. "Just like I was."

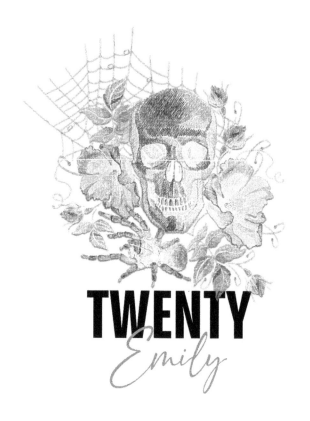

TWENTY
Emily

Past

"Hey, Tita?" I called from the kitchen. "Dad said he was going to stop by later today and finally look at that leaky sink in the bathroom."

"Eh," she spat as she joined me from the living room. "I told you from the beginning to call a plumber. I don't want your father here."

"Tita, he's your son and my dad. We can't kick him out of the family."

"We can, and I have. You're the one who won't let go. You know just as well as I do that man is no good. Neither he nor his brother—they're *not* the boys I raised." She pointed one of her gnarled fingers at me.

She was agitated. It wasn't the first time talk of my dad got her worked up. She adamantly refused to accept any of my dad's help, including his money. It was the reason we lived in a tiny house in a crap neighborhood. Not that his place was much better, but he made a lot more money than her measly government aid brought in. He tried to help, and if he gave me the money, and I didn't mention where it came from, I was free to use it to keep us afloat. At seventeen, I was a waitress when I wasn't in school, so she and I had an unspoken agreement to pretend that's where the money came from.

I had an uncle, but he never even tried to help. Dad might have had his downsides, but his older brother, Adrián, was downright mean. Even as a little kid, I had enough sense not to go near him.

"Well, it's cheaper than calling the plumber. You don't have to talk to him, just watch TV and pretend he isn't here." I finished setting the dishes on a drying rack and went to the hall closet to get a new roll of paper towels.

"Ha!" she called after me. "I'll be surprised if he even shows up. That man has never once followed through with his promises."

"But aren't we supposed to forgive, Tita?" I hollered back, using the step stool to reach the unopened paper towels on the top shelf. She hated when I played devil's advocate about my dad, but I couldn't help myself. Teasing her until she was flustered was just too easy.

This time, she wasn't taking the bait.

I snickered to myself and walked back into the kitchen to find my tita on her hands and knees, clutching her chest.

"Tita? Oh, my God. Are you okay?" I rushed over and

dropped to my knees. I couldn't think through the terror that suddenly wrapped its serpentine body around me and squeezed.

My tita rolled to her side before collapsing on her back. Her normally rich, caramel coloring drained to a pasty white, and her eyes stared blankly at the ceiling.

"Tita? No, please no. Oh, God. What do I do?" I ran for my phone, dialing 911 and hurrying back to her side. I started to do chest compressions even though I had no idea how to do them properly or if that's even what she needed. I just knew I had to do something.

The operator picked up after three rings. "911, what's your emergency?"

"My tita, she collapsed. I think she had a heart attack, but I don't know. Oh, God. I'm not sure she's breathing. Help me, *please*." Tears blurred my vision and dripped onto her yellow blouse, making dark yellow polka dots.

I felt like I was having a heart attack right alongside her because my chest ached with the need to breathe life back into her. To fix whatever was wrong and see that feisty spark back in her eyes.

The operator assured me help was on the way and walked me through how to do CPR. It took ten minutes for the ambulance to arrive. My arms burned with the strain of trying to save her life, but I never let up. Not for a second.

The two EMS workers pushed me aside and took over compressions, allowing me to step back and truly see what was happening. See my tita lifeless on her gold linoleum floor.

She was gone.

I could feel it in the shattered pieces of my broken heart. Like a part of my soul had been ripped out and stomped on.

They didn't even get her on a gurney before they turned

to me with twin looks of remorse and declared they had done everything they could.

I couldn't breathe. My lungs wouldn't allow air in or out. They simply seized up and quit, forcing me to squeak and wheeze as I tried to catch my breath. One of the men had me lower my head down between my knees and encouraged me to relax my breathing, but I couldn't understand. I didn't see how I could go on breathing, go on living without her.

She was my everything. My mother and best friend. She was my comfort and entertainment. She was my anchor when the waters were turbulent, and my compass when I got off course. She was the first person I shared good news with and the one who held me when things didn't go my way.

Without my tita, life would never be the same.

I would never be the same.

The remainder of that day passed in a blurry haze of condolences and tears. Not my tears. Tears of the family who came to help and offer their respects. I had a large extended family, and it seemed all of them felt the need to jump into action, not bothering to consider whether I might need time to process.

As for me, I slipped into a cocoon of numbness, greeting guests and answering questions with the methodical indifference of a machine. Yes, it happened at the house. No, I had no idea she had a bad heart. Yes, an enchilada casserole would be lovely.

Eventually, my father kicked everyone out and wrapped me in his arms. He'd never been involved much in my life—he wasn't the active father-figure type—but he was all I had left. His embrace was what allowed my dam to burst. The tears that had seemed to dry up flowed in heavy drops down my hot cheeks. He held me for a solid half hour, then got me in bed and gave me time to grieve alone.

Tita's funeral was just what I had wanted for her, but it was little consolation. My life had been uprooted in every sense of the word. Emotionally, I was detached and heartbroken. Physically, I was forced to move in with my dad and leave my childhood home behind. Dad put the house on the market, and it sold in a matter of days. My life was quickly unrecognizable, and I floundered to figure out my new place in the world.

I was finishing my junior year of high school, so I wasn't ready to live on my own yet. Dad wasn't opposed to me living with him, now that I was old enough to take care of myself, but his place didn't feel like home. Even more so when Dad began to bring his new girlfriend, Courtney, to the house. She was trashy and lazy, and I hated everything about her, but I had no say in how my father lived his life.

All I could do was keep myself out of the house as much as possible. I began to hang around my cousins more because they lived across the street from my dad. My tita had always warned me away from them, but now that she was gone, I felt like I had no choice. Hanging around them was also my misguided way of lashing out at her for leaving me. I knew it made no sense, but grief wasn't based on logic.

A mere five months after Tita passed, Dad got married to Courtney.

I was livid. Granted, some of my anger was likely misplaced. I was still upset at Tita for leaving me, and Dad was an easy target for those pent-up emotions. Some of the anger was justified. Courtney was a leech, living off my father and refusing to contribute anything, whether it was money, cooking, cleaning, or just pleasant conversation. As far as I could tell, she was utterly worthless, and I hated her.

I drank every chance I got to escape the cesspool my life had become. Partying with my cousins made me realize they weren't so bad. We had a great time despite getting into trouble. I was more of an onlooker than a participant and argued with myself that witnessing their actions wasn't the same as committing them. But deep down, I knew Tita would disapprove.

I told myself all I had to do was get through my senior year, and then I would be free. I could get a job and move out on my own, never having to see my worthless stepmother again. But life rarely followed the blueprints we set out. Weeks after their wedding, Dad and Courtney announced they were pregnant.

My dad was in his forties, but his young wife was still in the prime of her childbearing years. I should have known it would happen, but I'd told myself that my dad was so uninterested in raising me that he wouldn't allow more children in his home, especially now that he was older. But that wasn't how their relationship worked. What Courtney wanted, Courtney got.

I was furious when I found out. For months, I ranted and raved to my cousins about what an idiot my father was. I stopped going home. For weeks at a time, I'd stay with friends, couch surfing and actively avoiding my family.

Because of my childish protests, I missed the birth of my little brother, Isaac.

In fact, I stayed away for days after his birth. I finally returned to my father's house only when I had no other option, sneaking in at night to avoid seeing my new insta-family. When I entered the dark house, there was no avoiding that a baby had joined our ranks. His cries ravaged the night air, falling on deaf ears.

I peeked into the nursery to find it empty, except for the tiny screaming bundle. How long had they let him cry? There was no telling, knowing Courtney and my father. Neither of them was exactly the nurturing type.

Isaac's little hands scratched and pulled at his puffy cheeks as he cried. Seeing him made my heart ache. I didn't have much experience with babies, but that didn't seem to bother me. Wanting to hold him felt natural, so I scooped him up, cuddled him against my chest, and sang him a lullaby I remembered my tita singing to me.

He fit perfectly in my arms. Within a few minutes, his cries tapered off, and he fell back asleep, comforted by my touch. As I gazed down at the beautiful features of my baby brother, the pieces of my broken heart rearranged themselves until they formed a new, patchwork version of what they'd been. Not exactly like new, but far better than it had been just minutes before.

This was my new purpose in life.

This little innocent bundle was going to need me, and I needed him more than I ever could have guessed. I'd been upset with Dad and Courtney about the baby, but little Isaac was just as much a victim to circumstance as I was.

The next day, I learned how to make his bottle and change a diaper. Courtney was thrilled to see me show an interest in taking care of him, shocker. We worked out an unspoken truce—I loved my brother like he was my own, and she gave me a wide berth. My father was grateful to me for helping keep Courtney happy, which improved our relationship.

When it came time to graduate, I wasn't ready to leave. Isaac had quickly become the center of my world. My dad was more than happy for me to stay and help out. In fact, he started teaching me about the management of the family restaurant. Tita and my grandpa, who passed away when I was little, started the little Mexican restaurant when they were young. Dad took over when my grandpa got sick but had since hired managers and only checked in on occasion. I'd worked there as a waitress, but now, he taught me about the books, insurance, staff schedules, and the myriad of other intricacies running a restaurant entailed. When I took over as the general manager, I had a solid grasp of its inner workings.

I loved it, especially because the place was a part of our history. A part of my tita.

However, it didn't take me long to realize the financial records had some oddities that didn't measure up. Large sums of money would be received on days we hadn't been particularly busy, and there was an employee on the books that I'd never heard of.

My father had been in Los Zares all my life. All of his friends and most of my family were involved in the club in one way or another. Sometimes, it was hard to tell who was a real cousin and who was family through the club. When my father did spend time with me growing up, it was often to bring me to club barbecues. My tita was never happy about it, but she could only do so much to stop my dad.

When I was little, I never understood the problem. The club gatherings were great fun. I ran around with the other kids and got to spend some much-needed time with my dad. As I got older, I began to understand that Los Zares weren't exactly law-abiding. The family and friends who were associated with the club were in and out of jail. The circumstances were always downplayed to me, and the police made out to be the villains. Rarely did I hear about any major crimes, but the club members definitely weren't the Brady Bunch.

After Tita died, I had the chance to spend more time with

those people. I learned about their struggles and saw them for the dynamic individuals they were, rather than the label my tita had branded them with. They were no more good or evil than anyone else. They were just trying to make a life for themselves in a world that beat you down if you weren't careful.

In fact, some of them were the most loyal and selfless people I'd ever met. Their good intentions were sometimes misguided, but they were always there for one another. It was the club that had been providing money to help support Tita and me all those years. She might not have liked it, but my dad's other job was what kept our lights on.

I began to see the club and its activities as a way to better our lives. As just part of the world around me. I intentionally avoided any knowledge of the uglier side of my father's business, like whether it was drugs or guns or both that he bought and sold. I knew enough not to ask questions and told myself that my limited role in the club wasn't hurting anyone.

In a short amount of time, my skill with numbers allowed me to show my dad more ways he could filter money through the restaurant even more securely than before. His eyes lit up when I explained my ideas, and I yearned for that approval.

On my nineteenth birthday, after I'd been working with him for almost a year, my dad took me out to celebrate. We had dinner on the Riverwalk, just the two of us, and after, he took me to a tattoo parlor.

"What's this about? Tell me we're not getting father-daughter tattoos," I teased.

"Nah, this is way more important than that. You can't be a sworn-in member as a woman, but you're a part of Los Zares as much as any of us. It's time we let people know. By giving you our mark, no one will ever fuck with you. You'll officially be under our protection." My father wanted me to be a part of his club. A part of his life. It was so much more than any of the token outings or birthday gifts I'd received before. It felt like the first time he was truly proud of me. Proud to call me his daughter.

My heart swelled and blossomed as tears pricked at the back of my eyes. "Thanks, Dad. This means a lot to me."

He grinned, pulling me into a hug and patting me on the back. "Hey, Cinco," he called out to the tattoo artist working on a customer behind a curtain. "I have my baby girl in here, and she's ready for her mark."

"Fuck yeah," the man hollered back. "I'll be done in ten, and we'll get her inked."

It was one of the best and worst nights of my life, although I wouldn't know just how bad it was until I experienced the absolute worst night. That didn't come until five years later.

If I'd told Miguel once, I'd told him a dozen times to make sure the napkin stock was full and a backup package was ordered before the supply got too low. But no, he continued to forget, and this was the second damn time in the past six months we were stuck without napkins. It was Friday night with a restaurant full of customers. I was going to wring his fucking neck.

"Miguel, where the hell are the napkins?" I hissed, not wanting customers to hear me chewing out my day manager in the back.

"Whoa, easy, Em. I don't know where they are. I ordered napkins two weeks ago—I swear."

"If you ordered them, where are they?"

"I don't know, but I swear I'm telling the truth. You need me to run to Costco and grab some?"

I let out an exasperated breath. "Let me pull up our order history first and see what's going on." I spun around and power walked to the tiny office.

Originally, my father purchased supplies through a restaurant supply company, but I'd figured out a couple of years ago that it was cheaper and easier to simply go through Amazon Prime. I pulled up our account on my laptop and searched the past orders. When I clicked on the napkin order made two weeks prior, I realized what had happened. The napkins had been sent to our warehouse address downtown instead of the restaurant. We had a handful of addresses registered on our account since we used it for business and personal purchases. Miguel hadn't noticed the wrong address had been selected.

Rather than buy more napkins we didn't need, I decided to make the ten-minute drive to the warehouse. I asked Miguel to hang around the restaurant while I ran my errand, then hurried out to my car. My dad had bought the ware-house years ago to house the Mustang he was fixing up and for other club business that I had no desire to know about. The few times I'd been there, I noticed crates and boxes stashed on one end of the building, but they were none of my business.

He'd given me a key for emergencies, and in my eyes, this qualified. I wasn't going over to butt into his business. I just wanted to get our freaking napkins and get back to the restaurant.

The building was in the worst part of town, but the locals knew it was Los Zares property, so no one touched it. Normally, I would feel safe walking from my car to the front door, but this time, unease pricked at my skin. I had no clue what my problem was. There were no other cars out front, and no one in sight. The door was only fifty feet away, with a set of floodlights illuminating the entry. I scolded myself for being ridiculous and forced myself from the car.

I quickly flipped the deadbolt to the metal door, flinging it open and taking a confident step inside before I froze. The warehouse was one large open space with Dad's car back by the bay garage doors. Normally, the center of the room was empty, but today, a white van was parked next to the Mustang. The back doors were open wide, and a dozen women huddled inside as far as they could get from the doors. One woman was bent over the van bumper, hands tied behind her back, with a man raping her from behind. Three other men stood around watching, one of which was my father.

I took in the scene in a terrified heartbeat. The only sound was a heart-wrenching whimper from the woman being violated and the thrum of my pounding heart, pulsing in my ears.

I'd made a horrible mistake, and there was no undoing it.

Before I could say a word, one of the men had a gun pointed at my head. These weren't club members—none of them were familiar. I would have remembered. They were the seediest, most terrifying men I'd ever seen in my life. I couldn't even fathom what those women had felt being captured by such soulless creatures.

"That's my daughter," my father growled at the man. "Put the fucking gun down."

His words broke the tense standoff, sending the room catapulting into action.

The poor woman began to openly weep as her assailant resumed his rutting, laughing at her humiliation. The other women huddled even tighter into the front of the van and began to cry at various volumes. One of the men lit a cigarette and watched the scene like it was primetime TV. My father hurried over to where I still stood in shock and slammed the door shut behind me, grabbing my arm and exposing my wrist to the man.

"See, she's one of us."

The man lowered his gun and strolled over to us, his black eyes narrowed with the need for violence. His face was a graveyard of old acne scars. That didn't necessarily say anything about him as a person, but it still made him look that much more terrifying.

"You say that, but I don't like the look on her face." His voice was guttural—the sound of cigarettes and alcohol and pure evil.

"She was just caught off guard is all. Let me get her out of here, and we can finish our business."

The whole time they spoke, the man stared at me, his black eyes slicing into me and poisoning my insides. "I think maybe she needs a reminder about minding her own business." In two seconds flat, he clamped his hand around my neck, slamming my back against the wall and pointing his gun at my father.

His eyes never once left mine.

"You see that pretty girl on the van going for a ride?"

His stale breath infiltrated my nostrils, making my already rancid stomach revolt further. I had to swallow it down, past his hand and my crippling fear.

He waited until I nodded before he continued.

"You don't keep your mouth shut about everything you see here, I'll do that to you myself, then fuck you with my knife and turn you inside out. You understand?" His hand squeezed my throat so hard that black dots floated in my vision.

I nodded again, gripping his hand as I fought for air.

He flung me to the ground by my neck, kicking me in the stomach for good measure. "Get the fuck out of here, puta, before I change my mind."

I scrambled back to my feet, my eyes immediately seeking out my father. He glared at me with disdain. If he was worried about me, he hid it well. I went straight for the door, slamming it behind me and running to my car. My hands shook so badly that it took three attempts to hit the unlock button. I peeled out, driving blindly for ten minutes before I parked in the Costco parking lot and burst into tears.

The man's soulless eyes and his rank breath dominated my senses, but it was the sight of those women that haunted my soul. All I could think was, that could have been me.

It *would* be me if I couldn't find a way to forget what I'd seen.

I cried until my eyes began to burn, then pulled myself together and bought a week's worth of napkins. By the time I made it back to the restaurant, I had packaged up everything that had happened and locked it away in a box in the back of my mind. I finished the dinner shift, keeping a wide smile on my face all evening.

The one thing I wanted, more than anything, was to crawl into bed that night with Isaac and Averi, but I couldn't chance running into my dad. I couldn't face him. I wasn't sure I ever wanted to see his face again. I'd known he was a criminal, but I never dreamed he participated in trafficking women. He was so much more of a monster than I ever could have imagined.

Shame wrapped its greasy fingers around me and saturated every inch of me with its oily residue.

I'd participated in my father's enterprise. I'd helped launder money that was tainted by the sale of women's bodies. Who knew how many women I'd facilitated in being trafficked, their bodies sold and abused. Their souls desecrated and lives snuffed out.

There was no word for how wretched I felt.

For weeks, I grappled with how to live with the knowledge of what was happening behind the scenes. Drowned in shame and disappointment in myself for ignoring how my tita had raised me and contributing to my father's criminal activities. I'd known perfectly well that the club earned its money illegally—what exactly had I thought that entailed? I hadn't thought. That was the problem. I'd actively stuck my head in the sand and pretended everything was fine. But now that I knew how ugly things were, how was I supposed to continue covering up what Los Zares was doing? How could I pretend it wasn't happening?

I couldn't.

But I also needed to stay alive. The self-loathing waged a war inside me, battling daily with self-preservation. I did everything I could to act normal. To continue with my life as if nothing had changed, but it had. Everything had changed.

My father never said a word about what had happened. He never defended himself nor soothed my fears, and I was glad. As long as he didn't bring it up, I didn't have to spit in his face and tell him how much I hated him.

One day, about six weeks after the incident, I was at a party with my cousins. I didn't want to go, but it would be noticeable to others if I suddenly stopped showing up at gatherings. One of my dad's friends walked in and made a joke to everyone about the narcs out front watching the house.

It was the opportunity I'd needed, and I'd had just enough alcohol to give me the courage it would require.

I had debated about going to the cops ever since the incident, but I couldn't see how I could walk into a station without word getting around. I would end up dead without a doubt. I wasn't going to just call 911, so where did that leave me? Los Zares probably had cops on their payroll. How did I know who was good and who was corrupt? There was no way to know, but someone staking out a Zares' party was a good place to start. I would have to leave the rest up to God and what little luck I might have still had.

Before leaving the house, I wrote my phone number on a piece of paper and slipped it into my pocket. I said my good-byes and scanned the cars lining the street for the black sedan concealing the officers. As if it was meant to be, they were parked right in front of my car.

As nonchalantly as I could, I walked toward the car and deposited the note into their open window, not pausing to talk. I kept my head forward, so if anyone was watching from the house, I never appeared to register their presence. However, I held the driver's eyes the whole time I walked toward him, infusing my pleading gaze with sincerity, hoping they wouldn't take the gesture as meaningless taunting.

Three days later, I met federal agents in a run-down motel room and began to discuss the end of my life as I knew it.

TWENTY-ONE

Jamir

"I TOLD YOU IT WAS MY BOYFRIEND THAT WAS IN THE CLUB because I couldn't stand to admit that it was me. That I was a part of something so awful." Emily's teeth chattered as she talked. I'd managed to coerce her inside as she told me her story, but a chill still saturated her body.

I felt my own bone-deep chill, but it had nothing to do with the weather.

Emily had been lying to me the entire time we'd been together. Considering how well she had fooled me, she was quite the gifted storyteller.

There was no ex-boyfriend.

She was no innocent victim.

Emily had been a part of Los Zares for over five years,

laundering their money and doing who knew what else. Then she turned over, not just on the club, but on her family. She'd sent family members to prison. Had it been purely from good intentions, or was she lying again? Perhaps the only reason she'd testified was to escape her own prosecution. How was I supposed to trust anything she said when she changed her story as often as she changed clothes?

A part of me argued that it was understandable to want to hide her association with the Zares. They were a ruthless group of people, and one of the largest, most savage drug trafficking organizations in America. It was hard to picture Emily with her pet cactus, or whatever it was, living among the vicious bikers. That didn't mean it didn't happen. She'd been one of them, and not just briefly, but for five fucking years.

It wasn't the first time in my career that I'd come across a wayward criminal. There was almost always a hit put out on those who turned on a criminal organization and chose to testify rather than face the consequences of their actions in a court of law. As if testifying absolved their guilt for years of criminal activity. Just because a man threw his associates under the bus didn't mean his hands were clean. Sure, there was something to be said for repenting, but was it enough?

Had Emily's crimes been remote enough to keep her from being sullied by the darkest sins of Los Zares? Were my feelings for her enough for me to overlook her past and all the lies?

Normally, I had no problem deciding where people stood on the spectrum of good and evil. Whether their lives were more valuable than the bounty on their heads. When it came to Emily, the lines were blurred and foreign. Between the haze of my own emotions and the veil of her lies, I wasn't sure what to think.

"Did your father go to prison?"

She nodded. "He and many others. My testimony was just the final piece of a much larger case the feds had been working on for months."

"You know they'll never let something like that go. They'll hunt you forever."

"I know. It's my uncle, in particular, who will never quit searching for me. He somehow evaded all the charges."

"Do you think he's the one who sent people after you?"

"There's no doubt in my mind. To him, this was personal."

I could debate the options all night, but I knew in my gut what needed to happen. I had to take her back there. She'd fight me and try to run if I told her what I planned to do, so I'd have to be careful what angle I used. I could drug her and force her back, but it was a long trip cross country. Having her cooperation would be enormously helpful.

I folded my arms across my chest. "Your uncle is the answer. We can't stay here forever, and you'll never be free with them hunting you. The only way to be certain we end this is to kill your uncle. You have to go back to Texas."

Emily jerked to her feet, eyes wide. "You can't be serious. They'll kill me for sure. There's no way I'm going back there."

"This is one of those things you can't run from. If you'd been a simple girlfriend running your mouth, that would have been one thing. But as a protected part of their inner circle? They can't let you turn on them and not suffer consequences. It sends a message to other members that they could do the same. Your uncle will hunt you until the day he dies. You said so yourself."

"He can hunt, but he won't find me. I'll leave the country —go somewhere remote."

I stood from the kitchen chair and cupped her face with

my hands. "They found you once; they'll do it again. I know these types of people, Emily. You have to listen to me. The only way to end it is to put your uncle in his grave. The others will eventually forget you, but your uncle never will." It was time for all of it to end, one way or another.

Tears slid down her cheeks. She appeared so innocent and lost—wrapped in her blanket, hair wet and matted—but she was far from it. Lost maybe … but not innocent.

She didn't like her options, but she had no one to blame but herself. She made her bed, and she would have to lie in it now, even if it was her very own death bed.

Placing a bittersweet kiss on each of her cheeks, I tasted the salt from her tears. I didn't like seeing her upset, but my feelings were irrelevant. Facts were all that mattered. Her ties to Los Zares. Her willing participation in their organization. There was no escaping what that meant for her, regardless of how much I cared for her.

I hardened my resolve, forcing myself to stay firm. To keep with my convictions.

"I need you to trust me," I whispered against her lips, well aware that I was lying to her just like she had lied to me.

She nodded, her gaze hardening. "Promise me, if I do this, you'll help me kill him."

I'd spent more than a decade perfecting my ability to deceive, so when I smiled and lied to her face, there wasn't the faintest hint of uncertainty. "You have my word."

TWENTY-TWO
Emily

WE CLOSED UP THE CABIN FOR WINTER, AND TWO DAYS LATER, WE were on our way to the Minneapolis airport. Being in a public space brought out the worst of my paranoia. I looked over my shoulder constantly, and everyone seemed suspicious. My palms were clammy, and my stomach a tangled mess of nerves. On top of it all, I couldn't shake the feeling that this was a horrible mistake.

I wasn't certain I agreed with going back to Texas, but at least I wasn't keeping any more secrets. I'd offered Tamir the last of my ugly truths, and he hadn't turned his back on me. It was an enormous relief, but I could still feel the intangible presence of a barrier between us, and I had no idea why. I had hoped that if my confession didn't send him away, that it might give us a chance at something real. A connection. I wasn't sure I was bold enough to call it love, but whatever it was, I wanted it. I wanted him.

He was protective and passionate. Capable of anything he set his mind to and possessed an understated confidence. He was observant, understanding, and exceptionally patient. He had drawbacks, just like anyone, but nothing overshadowed the collective brilliance of his overall person. My sincere regard for him was the only reason I agreed to go back to Texas. I trusted him.

If only he felt the same way about me. I had hoped that after I'd laid myself bare to him, there would be nothing left between us. But when his hands were on my face, our breath comingling and lips only inches apart, I could feel that barrier in the air between us, keeping us from one another. For a second, I thought he might topple that wall with a single kiss. Instead, he fortified its moorings with the touch of his lips upon each of my cheeks. So close to what I wanted yet so very far away.

I didn't know what else I could do to redeem myself in his eyes but to lay my life in his hands. It was the ultimate sacrifice, and the one I made by allowing him to take me back to San Antonio.

No more running.

No more lies.

Either Tamir would kill my uncle to keep me safe, and we'd have a chance at a life together, or my uncle would kill me and put an end to the ordeal. One way or another, it would be over.

Tamir told me we'd discuss the plan once we were at the rental house. Considering his past, I had no doubt he could do the job. I just hoped I lived to see it through.

When we stepped off the plane in San Antonio, I couldn't

get my hat and sunglasses on fast enough. I probably looked like a battered woman hiding her black eye, but I didn't care. Anything was better than being spotted by Los Zares.

"I've called in a couple of my friends to help us," Tamir told me as we walked. "They arrived a couple of hours ago and have a rental car waiting for us out front."

Help was good. In fact, help made me feel significantly better, but I was curious about who he would feel comfortable pulling into such a dangerous situation.

"Who are we meeting that would be crazy enough to help us? I assumed you severed all your military connections when you fled Israel."

"Not exactly. It was risky, but I couldn't leave without reaching out to Uri. I discovered that he and some of the others who knew me well supported what I'd done. I told him where I was going, and when he got out of the service not long after, he followed me to America."

Tamir led us to a black Escalade parked by the curb at passenger pickup. The front passenger door opened, and a broad-shouldered man slid out, giving Tamir a nod and opening the back door for us.

He was rugged looking with hair buzzed close to his head. He had a beautifully savage aura to him—like he could have walked straight out of a zombie apocalypse edition of an REI catalog. He wore cargo pants with a fitted T-shirt and leather boots and a knife strapped to his belt. His eyes were so squinty, I couldn't tell what color they were, and his jaw was lined in scruff. The odd thing about him was the sense of familiarity I got when I looked at him. He reminded me of Tamir, in a way, and I could only assume that was the source.

I tore my gaze from the man and cautiously eyed the interior of the vehicle from behind Tamir, noting the driver and one man in the middle row.

"I'll sit in the back," I quickly offered.

"Uri, Asaf, Alon, this is Emily." Tamir introduced me, and all three men tilted their heads in greeting.

I gave a small, half-hearted smile and climbed in, shuffling between the two captain's chairs to the third row. It felt odd to jump into a car full of men I didn't know, but none of us were interested in a public meet and greet. As soon as Tamir was seated, we left the airport, and the mood in the car eased.

"Tam, it's good to see you," said the man in the back seat, holding out his hand for Tamir to shake. "What's it been, a year now?"

"I think you're right. Not since I was in LA."

"It wouldn't be so long between visits if that asshole would leave the city more," the driver interjected.

Tamir chuckled. "Just because I don't come see you three doesn't mean I don't get out."

It was easy to tell they'd all been in the military together. The looked the part with their muscles and serious demeanors, that was, until they dropped their guards and were teasing one another. Their comfortable familiarity eased my tension, especially seeing Tamir smile and joke.

"Emily, this asshole next to me is Alon. He was in our unit but only got out a couple of years ago."

"Only because you dicks didn't tell me how great the money was outside," the man grumbled playfully.

Tamir only shook his head. "Up front is Asaf," he said, pointing at the passenger, "and Uri is our driver. He's the one I mentioned earlier."

"I appreciate y'all coming to help us. To help me. Not many people would be willing to stick their necks out for someone like this."

"I'm just hurt Tamir mentioned Uri and not me. That's just

wrong, man." Alon was clearly the comedic relief in the group. He glanced back at me and winked, bringing a genuine smile to my face—the first one I'd worn since our dinner date back in Wisconsin.

The four men launched into an easy conversation about soccer, leaving me free to observe them. My eyes continually wandered back to Asaf, the man in the front passenger seat. He contributed the least to their discussion. Every time my eyes were drawn to him, the little hairs on the back of my neck stood on end.

I racked my brain, trying to figure out what it was about him that made me uneasy. Not until he turned back toward Alon did the pieces click into place. The car was angled in just the right direction, facing into the setting sun. When he turned, I got a perfect profile view of him with the sun behind him.

It was the man who had attacked me back in New York.

He wasn't wearing a hood like he had then, but I would never forget the glimpse of his profile I'd seen that night. I was certain it was the same man.

Adrenaline surged through my veins, spiking my heart rate. I fought to keep my breathing steady and calm as I grappled with the implications of my discovery.

Did Tamir know it was Asaf in that alley? I thought back to that day and recalled how the two men had fought while I'd stood a good ten feet away. They'd been face-to-face, and even in the dim light, Tamir would've seen Asaf's face. These men were like brothers. Tamir had to have known who my attacker was, and if that was the case, the most logical conclusion was they were working together.

Had Tamir set up my attack? Why would he do that? How had he known I was on the run? Did he somehow know my uncle? No, there was no way. It would have been too great a coincidence. But it wouldn't have surprised me if my uncle had offered money to whoever could find me. Maybe even kill me. Had Tamir somehow learned about the money and decided to collect?

My emotions stirred together in a dangerous cocktail of anger, heartbreak, and fear. I'd spent weeks with Tamir, learning about him and coming to care for him, but with the realization of one lie, I now questioned everything. Had it all been a ruse? Why keep me in the cabin if he intended to turn me over to my uncle? Was it all a ploy to get me to trust him so that I'd march myself straight to my own death without a fight? If so, he'd done a masterful job.

I thought I'd been fooling him, but it was nothing compared to the con job he'd pulled.

Betrayal was a hard pill to swallow. It left the bitter after-taste of pain and regret swirling around on my tongue. I wanted to hate him. It would have been easier to hand myself over to the emotion than to wallow in the alternative.

Grief.

For what could have been. For what I'd imagined was blossoming between us. With the utterance of a couple of words, it was all gone. My heart constricted so painfully, and I felt a sickening crunch as it collapsed in on itself.

The hour-long drive to the rental house gave me time to collect myself and gather my courage. I was going to need to remain calm if I had any hope of making it out of this alive.

The 1980s ranch-style home was well-kept on the outside and situated deep in a suburban neighborhood, where the houses lazed under enormous oak trees like well-fed cows. The interior had been updated recently, doing away with what had likely been popcorn ceilings and Formica counter-tops. Instead, white tile floors and granite gave the place a modern feel that I hadn't expected when pulling up to the curb.

There were three bedrooms and two baths. The guys paired off in two of the bedrooms, leaving me the third. I took a few minutes to freshen up, then joined them in the living room.

"What's the plan for food tonight?" Uri asked.

"I say we just order takeout," said Tamir. "We won't be here long enough to warrant a grocery trip."

"Sounds like a plan. Tell me what to get, and I'll go pick it up."

Tamir glanced at me with a glint of humor in his eye. "I'm told TexMex is delicious, so why don't we do that? Emily, you have any recommendations?"

It was a sweet gesture, which only twisted the knife in my gut that much deeper. I didn't let it show. I kept my features schooled and feigned excitement. "One day you'll have to try a quality sit-down place, but for now, Rosa's will do. I noticed one not too far from here on our way in."

Uri took our orders, and within a half hour, he was back. I could hardly eat, but considering our reason for being there, I didn't think it was all that suspicious. Tamir didn't mention my lack of appetite as the guys wolfed down their food. I got the feeling it could have been doggy kibble, and they still would have eaten every bite.

"I'm pretty wiped out," I said as I threw out the remnants of my dinner. "Think I'll call it a night, unless y'all need me for anything."

"Go ahead and rest," Tamir replied. "We're going to discuss the details for tomorrow. I can give you the rundown in the morning."

"Sounds good. Thanks again, guys." I smiled and waved

to their chorus of good nights, then made my way back to my bedroom.

The second I was out of sight, I put in my AirPods and flopped onto the bed. Relief and anxiety coursed through me as I listened to the conversation in the living room with perfect clarity. It was a trick I'd learned about from Olivia back in New York. The iPhone had a listen feature that allowed you to use your phone as a listening device, broadcasting whatever was said near the phone to your AirPods. As long as the guys continued their conversation near my phone in the living room, I would hear every word they said.

Thankfully, I'd charged the phone before we left Wisconsin, just in case I needed it. Before I came out of my bedroom, I had turned it on and activated the listen feature, making sure to pull out the sim card first so I couldn't be tracked. I then nonchalantly stashed the phone on an end table while we were eating.

If they were surprised I didn't stick around to hear their plan, they didn't show it. They probably just assumed it was a testament to my absolute trust in Tamir and were glad they didn't have to answer my questions.

I didn't want to just hear the plan as they spoon-fed it to me. I wanted to hear the unadulterated version. I wanted to hear what those four men would say when I wasn't around, and now, I had a front row ticket to the show.

TWENTY-THREE

Jamir

"SHE CERTAINLY DOESN'T SEEM LIKE THE STANDARD MARK, especially considering the pretty penny they're willing to pay for her return," Alon observed after Emily left the room.

"There's a lot more to her story than you might think," I explained.

"You've got my attention."

"Does any of that even matter?"

Alon sat back and grinned. "I don't know. You tell me." He was goading me about my feelings for her. If he thought he was going to get a rise out of me, he should have known better.

I breathed deeply through my nose. "No, her past is irrelevant at this point. We're going forward with the plan like we've already discussed."

Uri interjected, not allowing me to redirect our conversation. "She seems awfully cooperative with all this." His eyes bore into me, searching deep beneath the surface to questions that had nothing to do with Emily's level of cooperation. He knew me better than anyone, and he wanted to know just how deep my feelings for her ran.

"She doesn't know what we intend to do; that's why she isn't putting up a fight. I told her we were here to kill her uncle. It was just easier that way. She doesn't even know about the bounty on her head."

"It's a lot of cash," he pointed out. "Don't beat yourself up about all of this. Someone would have found her eventually." He must have detected the guilt I'd been carrying. Only Uri knew me well enough to see past my façade.

I appreciated his sentiment, but it didn't change anything. "The cash is irrelevant to me. I just want it over."

"I'm loving this little heart-to-heart," Asaf grumbled. "But if it's all the same to you three, I'd like to shower before we get into the nitty-gritty details for tomorrow."

"Fine, just don't pass out before we have a chance to go over everything," I grumbled.

Asaf just grunted in reply.

After food and showers, we reconvened in the master bedroom so as not to disturb Emily. We spent hours going over every piece of intel and all manner of scenarios in excruciating detail. We never went into a mission without doing our homework. It was especially important in this instance since there was such a high probability our actions could result in a gunfight.

By the time we were done, my limbs were heavy with exhaustion. I knew, come morning, the thrill of a mission would provide ample adrenaline to energize me. Until then, I was beat. But I still had one more thing to do.

I waited for Alon and Asaf to settle in their room before going to Emily's room. It was closing in on midnight, and splatters of pale moonlight filtered in through the tree outside her window. She lay peacefully asleep on her side. It wasn't the first time I'd watched her sleep. Often, at the cabin, I'd wake and find myself seeking her out, admiring how innocent she looked in sleep. Tonight was no different.

Her rich skin was flawless in the soft light. I yearned to strip her bare and lay my eyes on every inch of that supple body, make it writhe and glisten under the strain of prolonged pleasure. The one taste I'd had of her had been an intoxicating mix of sweet vanilla and pure temptation. It was a heady flavor I'd never forget.

I tore myself from her bedside, not willing to torture myself any longer. We had a big day ahead, so I needed to get some rest.

When we first arrived, I'd checked to verify the old window in Emily's room was sealed shut. Many of the finishes in the older house had been updated, but the doors and windows had not. I didn't have to worry about her slipping away in the night through her window, but walking out the front door was still a possibility. She'd been far more compliant than a woman in her situation should be. A woman who was used to going on the offensive and fighting for her survival.

She wasn't thrilled to be here, and I wasn't going to dismiss the possibility that she'd reconsider her decision to go along with my plan. Just to be safe, I grabbed a blanket and made myself comfortable on the couch with the front door in view.

As it turned out, my cautionary instincts had been justified.

Those years in the military had taught me to be a feather-light sleeper, able to rouse myself with the slightest change in the room around me. I woke up the moment the shadows shifted.

Emily had her duffel slung over her shoulder and was tiptoeing toward the front door.

I silently rose from the sofa and approached, not making myself known until I was a few short feet behind her. "I thought you said you trusted me." I spoke softly, not wanting to draw an audience.

Her posture stiffened, but she didn't turn to face me. "I thought you wanted to keep me safe." She spoke calmly, but each syllable was laced in venomous warning.

"What makes you think I don't?"

She slowly spun, her righteous glare meeting my eyes in the shadows. "It's him. Asaf is the man who attacked me back in New York. You set me up from the beginning." The air around her practically vibrated with fury.

Her accusation caught me totally by surprise. I never imagined she could have identified Asaf. He had sworn she never got a good look. It had been so dark in that alley, and she'd been terrified. People rarely recalled details clearly after a traumatic event.

I should have known she'd be different.

"Let me explain," I urged, hands up to try to calm her.

"Explain what? That there was a bounty on my head, and you wanted the money? I've been such an idiot to trust you. I knew from the beginning something was off, but I pushed those feelings aside because I wanted to believe there was more to you. But there's not, is there? You're just a fucking mercenary for hire to the highest bidder." She spat the words at me, shoving my chest with both hands.

I grabbed her wrists and forced them around to her back, bringing our chests together. "Do I get to tell my side of the story? Or are you just going to condemn me on sight?"

"As if I even have a choice."

My eyes narrowed reflexively. "I learned about the bounty and recognized you immediately. I wanted to learn more about how you'd ended up with a price on your head, but you wouldn't let me anywhere near you. I had Asaf stage an attack, hoping you would drop your guard around me so that I could get to know you and your past. That's the only way I've deceived you. In case you hadn't noticed, I've never once hurt you. And trust me, I could have."

"You told me you were an assassin, but you never quit, did you?" This time, her words were the whisper of a blade slicing through the air.

"Assassin, and a bounty hunter when the job suits."

She bucked and yanked to free her wrists. "Let go of me. You're a fucking monster. You're just the same as the rest of them."

Her flailing wouldn't stop, forcing me to press her back against the wall. The others had probably heard our tussle at this point, and I hated to air out what should have been private.

"Listen to me," I hissed next to her ear. "I know you're upset, but you need to listen. Yes, I kill people, but I'm not just some hired gun. I have a code—I only take jobs when the target has done something bad enough to earn the price on their head. I refuse jobs all the time. I'm not going to kill a woman just so her ex-husband doesn't have to pay alimony or kill some executive to enable a hostile business takeover."

"And you? Who judges your actions?" She stopped struggling, the front entry filling with a silence saturated with pleading and accusation.

"You. You are the only one, so take a long, hard look at what I've done. Not what you suspect or what you fear, but at the truth of my actions. Words and feelings can be manipulated, but actions paint a perfect picture. See the things that I've done—the ways I've protected you and provided for you—and with those truths, you decide my fate."

Our eyes stayed locked in battle as I spoke, but little by little, conflict filtered into her gaze, diluting the anger and hurt until she was completely adrift in her emotions. Her eyelids slowly shuttered, cutting off my view to her thoughts. When they lifted again, the indecision was gone, leaving only a resigned sadness.

She edged forward, touching her lips to mine in a kiss that was bittersweet anguish. There was no mistaking the kiss for what it was.

A goodbye.

There had been so many lies between us, and she had every right to hate me. I could understand her need to pull away. But if this was where things ended, I wanted more than a simple kiss. I wanted the memory of her writhing body to carry with me after she was gone.

I released her wrists and wrapped my arms around her, seizing her mouth in another kiss. Her body molded against mine. I lifted her, relishing in the feel of her legs wrapping easily around my waist. Managing to avoid hitting any walls, I walked us back to her room as we stole the breath from each other, one kiss at a time.

Once there could be no prying eyes, I set her down and made a show of slowly stripping her clothes from her body. I stepped back to admire her form, unable to help the guttural groan that ripped from my chest at the sight of her naked in the moonlight. It was just as mesmerizing as I'd imagined. My eyes devoured her as if she was the most exotic delicacy known to man, and I'd been living on bread and water for years.

She peered up at me, so brave and uninhibited. There was fear there, but she was too strong to let it bend her to its will. A stubborn reed standing tall in a raging river.

I stripped off my own clothes until we were two people, equally bare. Equally broken and exposed.

"Don't run from me, Emily. I can feel you pulling away, but you'll never make it. I'll always find you." I walked her backward until her legs hit the bed, and she tumbled onto it.

"How could I ever escape you? You're everywhere. You're in my head and under my skin." She raked her fingers down my arms as I lowered myself on top of her.

I kissed the words from her lips, devouring her admission and trying to pretend I didn't taste the blame layered within. This was no perfect union. No joining of souls, given freely with love. This was defeat. A farewell. This was two people surrendering to their need for one another, despite all the reasons to walk away.

I didn't care. I would take whatever I could get from her and deal with the consequences later.

I had no patience for tenderness or compassion. There was only blistering need. If her clutching hands and writhing body were any proof, she was just as greedy for me. She understood the urgency. The unbridled obsession that drove me to the brink of madness—the madness of wanting something so desperately and knowing it was wrong.

Lining up our bodies, I eased myself inside her, swallowing her moan with a kiss. Her knees bent reflexively, opening herself to me fully. I only gave us a moment to adjust, the count of several ragged breaths, before I began to rock inside her. My movements quickly became more frenzied, as if I could use my cock to erase all the lies and ugly that lay between us. Wipe the slate clean and find a place where we could exist beyond the heavy anchor of our pasts.

"Tamir." She breathed my name, a benediction and a curse.

I knew exactly how she felt. This thing between us was too consuming not to fear it and too dangerous to ignore.

"What is it, motek? Tell me what you need. *Tell me*." I ran my hand down her body, finding my way to the curve of her ass and squeezing, kneading her flesh.

"You. Nothing else … just you." Her words were raw as though they'd been wrenched straight from her soul.

I lifted my face so that our eyes could meet, and it was that connection, that electrical current pulsing between us, that ignited both our fuses and sent us over the edge. Liquid lightning shot down my spine and into my balls, sending cum spurting in hot jets inside her. Emily's body shuddered violently, her eyes wide and unseeing as she was swept away on a stampede of pleasure. Her inner muscles squeezed to a breaking point, keeping me snugly inside her as if her body was doing what her heart wouldn't allow.

I dropped my face deep into the crook of her neck, breathing in her essence and stamping its chemical makeup into my memory. "I'm here, and I'm not going anywhere."

I only wished the same could be said for her.

Emily was, understandably, quiet the next day. I walked her through what she needed to know about the plan first thing that morning. She didn't argue or try to run. She was braver and more disciplined than some of the soldiers I'd had the misfortune to work with.

The irony was, while she swallowed her fears and walked into battle with her head held high, I was more worried than ever that our plan was horribly flawed, and that I wasn't making the right choice.

I'd never felt so conflicted in my entire life.

We used the number on the bounty listing to set up a meet for that evening. By the time we filed into the car, even Alon had lost his trademark levity.

The neighborhood was comprised of mid-century houses in various degrees of decomposition. It always amused me that criminals, like her uncle, stayed in areas like that when they were bringing in enough money to afford a swanky estate in the suburbs. Instead, they parked decked-out Escalades and custom Harleys under carports, next to pillbox houses with the vinyl siding falling off and shingles missing on the roof.

It was the type of neighborhood where people knew when to make themselves invisible, which was good, because things were about to get ugly.

TWENTY-FOUR
Emily

I NEVER THOUGHT I'D BE BACK HERE. IT HADN'T EVEN BEEN A full year, but the feeling was surreal to see the houses I thought could only be seen in my memories. It felt like a dream or, more precisely, a horrible nightmare. I had that same sense of dread. That feeling you get while watching a horror movie when the actor was slowly walking through a dark, empty house, only to discover it was not so empty just as a psychotic murderer lunged from the shadows.

My toes curled and uncurled in my sneakers, the need to run clawing at my muscles. I was terrified of what was about to happen, but at the same time, a part of me was sidetracked with the desperate need to see Isaac and Averi, one last time. I never got to tell them goodbye, and they were far too young to understand. My heart ached to think how much my leaving would hurt them and that they'd likely be told horrible stories about me. They'd grow up to hate me, and I couldn't do a single thing about it.

Instead of righting things with them, I was going to confront someone I had hoped never to see again. The one silver lining was knowing that after this, it would all be over. No more living in fear.

I couldn't dwell on the way things could have been different. Life was rarely perfect. Losing my mother at birth, having a father who didn't want me, being raised in the shadow of crime—the only shining stars in the darkness were Tita and my sweet siblings. I focused all my nervous energy on those brilliant points of light in my memories and reminded myself that, after this was over, I'd at least get to see Tita again.

Tamir had lured me to San Antonio with the promise that we were going to kill my uncle, but that's not how things were going to play out. I'd made peace with that. I'd done what I could to fight against human trafficking. I'd given up everything for what I believed, and this was just the next step in that fight. I was proud of my choices. Even if fear wracked my body, I knew I was doing the right thing.

We parked across the street from my uncle's house. Tamir had acquired a second rental car, this one a silver sedan. I was sandwiched between Uri and Asaf on the way over, and we stayed in that formation after we exited the car. Tamir and Alon took the lead, sauntering across the street with the lethal calm of a lion prowling his savannah. I'd been instructed to keep my mouth shut and let Tamir do all the talking, which was just fine with me. I had nothing to say to my bastard uncle.

Adrián must have had men watching for us. We had

hardly stepped from the car when he ambled from the house, along with two of his men. I had no doubt there were more stationed where they couldn't be seen. Uncle Adrián was close to sixty years old, but his age only made him seem more intimidating. There was no mistaking him for young and misguided. Uncle Adrián was stone-cold evil.

He was still fit for his age, slim and far from frail. He wore his black hair pulled back in a short ponytail, and his black leather cut was always on—a show of his undying loyalty to Los Zares. Not to his family or his morals. His loyalty was fixed to a criminal organization that fed off the weaknesses of others. My father had his faults, but he loved his family in his own way.

My uncle was pure corruption.

As much as I wanted to confront him with confidence and unwavering bravery—to show that asshole he couldn't scare me—I found myself lurking in Uri's shadow, sticking close to the wall of a man. Not even my stubborn streak could override my survival instincts.

"Look what we have here," my uncle said, eyes boring down on me. "You never were very bright. It looks like now, you're even too stupid to run." He shook his head. "It's in the blood. I told your father from the beginning he should have put you in the ground with your worthless whore of a mother while you were still inside her. But no, he was soft. Too young and stupid. He waited until you were born before he put a bullet between her eyes. And now, look at him, locked away in prison because he let you live."

His words filtered through my brain, one at a time, and I struggled to weave them together. When the full picture finally formed, my world tilted on its axis.

"Ahh, now she gets it. Seeing your face right now was worth all this bullshit. I'm glad I got to be the one to tell you.

Your mother was a dirty *puta*, just like you. We put that bitch in the ground, just like we're going to do to you." His eyes were maniacal as if his lust for blood fueled his existence.

I didn't want to give him the satisfaction of seeing my heart break, but a person could take only so much pain without it bleeding onto the surface. There was absolute truth to what he'd confessed. I knew it in my gut. My father had killed my mother. Her death hadn't been the byproduct of my birth. That was why I'd been born at home. That was why he would never tell me anything about her.

I'd always wondered how Tita could hate her sons so much, but now, it made perfect sense. I'd desperately wanted to see my father as something better than his brother, but he wasn't. They were both equally monstrous, and I hated them with the vastness of all the oceans.

He'd betrayed me in the most elemental, malicious way a person can be betrayed—he stole a mother from an innocent child. Ripped apart a sacred bond and stole that relationship from me, then lied to me all those years. Knowing it had come from him, from my own flesh and blood, made it that much worse.

That was the saddest thing about betrayal.

It never came from your enemies. It was the people you cared about the most who could cut you the deepest, and I felt that knife, jagged and sharp, pierce straight into my heart.

Off to the side, Tamir stepped forward and put an end to the show. "Let's wrap this shit up. We brought her in. Where's the money?"

TWENTY-FIVE
Jamir

EMILY'S FACE CRUMPLED WITH AGONY, AND I WAS GLAD. IT WAS raw and pure and spurred on her anger. Like a living, breathing phoenix, she rose from the ashes. Her transformation from scared to broken to rebuilt lasted only a handful of seconds, but they were glorious to behold.

Her ferocity was breathtaking.

When she turned toward me and focused that majestic rage in my direction, pride thrummed in my chest. It took all my self-discipline to squash it down and remind myself that she wasn't mine. Remind myself of what had to be done.

"You were supposed to help me!" she screamed, her righteous ire palpable in the air around us. "You were supposed to kill him for me—to set me free. You're nothing but a greedy

213

bastard. That's all I was to you—a fucking paycheck?" Tears filled her eyes, but she wasn't about to go down without a fight.

With lightning speed I hadn't known she was capable, she snatched the gun Uri had tucked in the back of his pants.

Acting on instinct, I already had my fingers feathered over my own weapon. It was ingrained after too many years in the trenches. I had my gun leveled at her, and the trigger pulled before she even had a chance.

The shot rang out across the empty street, but I didn't hear it as I watched her body fall back to the ground, rich crimson blossoming across her chest. Time slowed to a crawl as her body stilled.

Seeing her motionless on the cracked asphalt made me insane with rage, but I couldn't let it show. This was not the time or place. With decades of practiced control, I bottled up every unhelpful emotion and tossed them back into the vast ocean, deep inside me.

"What the fuck, man?" her uncle shouted. "I wanted that bitch alive."

My gun still raised, I flung my arm around and redirected my aim at him. One of his guards lifted his pistol and trained it on me. In just a few seconds' time, our meet had devolved to a standoff in the middle of a residential neighborhood.

"I had no choice. She was going to shoot me," I replied calmly, then lowered my gun to help control the situation. "How about you bring us the money, and we'll be on our way."

"Nah, man. I said I wanted her alive."

"You backing out of the contract? Because my associates and I don't take well to that, and we're not the kind of men you want to piss off." I spoke with a deadly calm and could feel the wall of menace emanating off my men around me.

He glared at us, then shouted over his shoulder. "Trae me el dinero."

A fourth man stepped from the house with a gray duffel bag. He handed it to Adrián, who tossed it to us in the street.

"Take your money and get the fuck out. And take *that* with you. She's no use to me now." He spat on the ground in Emily's direction, then led his men back inside.

"Clean it up and let's go," I murmured, eyeing the neighboring houses for hostiles as I walked back to the car.

I didn't watch as Uri and Asaf retrieved the tarp from my duffel bag, then wrapped Emily inside and put her in the trunk. I had known exactly how the day would end, but I still hated to see it. I just wanted to get out of there and put the whole thing behind us.

TWENTY-SIX
Emily

I HAD HOPED DYING WOULD BE LESS PAINFUL.

It hurt like a bitch. But even worse than the physical pain was seeing Tamir's chilling expression as he pulled the trigger. No remorse, no conflict, no question. A single twitch of his finger, and I was flying backward onto the asphalt, his callous glare ripping through me far more ruthlessly than any bullet.

In such a short amount of time, my treacherous heart had latched onto him. He'd slipped into my bloodstream, like oxygen bonded with my own blood, until there was no eradicating him from my system.

Despite every warning and logical argument presented by

my brain, my heart had forged ahead, leading me down an inevitable path to this exact point in time.

To my death.

I couldn't say I was all that surprised. From the minute I ran, I knew my life was over. Between that bitch, Fate, and her bestie, the Grim Reaper, I never stood a chance. Better to face the music. To turn and fight, rather than cower like a fucking dog. I was just glad I was able to take out some of the evil in the world while I had the chance.

Fear had been my constant companion for the better part of a year. It was time to kick her to the curb. To hell with the consequences. I knew the second I exited that car what was about to happen.

I would have liked to have seen my uncle killed in the process, but he needed to stay alive. It was an important part of the plan. And our plan had gone off without a hitch, right down to my tragic death.

TWENTY-SEVEN

Emily

15 Hours Earlier

I WASN'T SURE HOW IT WAS POSSIBLE TO HAVE SUCH VISCERAL, contradictory emotions about another person, but I did. Nothing I felt for Tamir was simple or demure. My need for him was desperate and untamed, but I also harbored enough anger, frustration, and pain to fill a mighty yawning cavern.

I didn't know how to reconcile the two.

I was furious that he had played me. Furious and heartbroken and confused. I couldn't understand how he could have done such a thing after he'd helped me for weeks. How my heart could fall for someone who was willing to end my life for money. None of it made any sense.

When I confronted Tamir in the dimly lit entry of the rental house, and he reminded me of all the ways he'd protected and supported me over the prior weeks, my surging anger receded, leaving my drowning heart clamoring for reassurance that it hadn't been wrong. That I hadn't given a piece of myself to someone so callous and heartless.

I recalled snippets of the weeks we'd spent together. The times we'd laughed, and the moments we'd shared. I refused to believe I'd imagined it.

Even if I had, I wanted one last taste of the illusion.

If Tamir was set on handing me over, and I had no chance of escape, I wanted to spend my final hours feeling loved, even if it was a lie. I offered myself to him, infusing my kiss with all the bittersweet longing I felt churning inside me. I pleaded with him not to betray me and urged him to surrender himself to the bond that had formed between us, all without a single word. Our communication was purely physical. Instinctive. Primal.

Back in the bedroom, neither of us lasted more than a handful of minutes. Our hunger for one another had been building too long to burn slow like a candle. We both went off like fireworks, a cataclysmic explosion of pent-up desire.

After, we lay in my bed on our sides, his muscled form wrapped snugly around mine. My mind drifted from one question to the next, unsure how I'd found myself at this juncture in my life. Of all the things I could be thinking about, the thing that stuck out the most was something totally irrelevant considering my circumstances.

Tamir hadn't worn a condom.

I could feel the sticky residue of our passion slowly seeping from inside me. The reason it garnered my attention was because it highlighted my one big regret in life. I hadn't gotten around to having children. I'd been lucky enough to help raise Isaac and Averi but hadn't experienced the joy of bringing my own child into the world. And now, I'd lost that opportunity. Tamir was going to turn me over in less than twenty-four hours, and then, I was a dead woman.

Tears filled my eyes, and my breathing shuddered.

"Why are you crying, motek?" Tamir asked softly.

"There's just so much I didn't get to experience in life. I'm not ready to die." My voice broke, and I squeezed my eyes shut in an attempt to hide from reality.

Tamir rolled me onto my back so that he could see me, his brow furrowed. "What are you talking about? Nobody is going to die. You are far too precious to me, and I am far too selfish to let you die."

"But … I heard you all talking. You're going to turn me over for the reward."

As understanding dawned, he ran his knuckles along my jaw. "No, no. There's been a horrible misunderstanding. I'm not letting anything happen to you. I wouldn't even have you here if it weren't necessary."

I was so confused. "What are you talking about?"

"I have a plan, but I knew it would worry you, so I hadn't told you. I figured we'd go over it in the morning, so you'd have less time to stress over it. I'm also not sure you're going to like it because it doesn't involve killing your uncle."

"If we don't kill him, then who?"

"You." He let the word hang in the air before explaining. "The only way to truly end this is if you are dead, at least, as far as Los Zares is concerned. If they see you die in front of their own eyes, they'll have no choice but to terminate the contract for your life and move on. It's tricky, but it's our best option. In order to make it believable, we'll have to look like we're legitimately there to collect on the bounty."

"So you truly don't plan to turn me over?" More tears slipped from my eyes.

Tamir wiped at them, then scattered reverent kisses across my face. "Never. I'd die before I let them have you. Is that what this was about?"

When our eyes met, I could see how ardently he cared for me. He pulled back the mask he normally wore, and what I saw made it hard to breathe. Respect. Passion. Devotion. He hid nothing, and I was overwhelmed with such honesty.

I reached up and pulled his face to mine in a grateful, ardent kiss. I was still too shaken to be able to return his exact sentiment, but I hoped the kiss would express that my feelings for him were just as potent and real. When I ended the kiss, Tamir lay back down and pulled me close until my head rested on his chest over his heart.

Once I had a minute to start processing everything, one question stood out. "How on earth are you going to make it look like I die?"

He smirked. "Alon has taken up a new career as a stuntman in Hollywood. I went to LA a year ago and watched him in action; he's actually brilliant at what he does. He brought all the necessary props to make even the most critical eye believe you were shot. You'll have to pull a gun on me in an escape attempt. I'll have mine loaded with blanks and will fire at you the second you raise your gun. Alon will trigger the gunshot props. The only other crucial element is your ability to pull off the necessary acting, and I happen to know you are rather adept in that department." He was teasing me, but I still felt embarrassed. Between pretending to be an entirely different person for WitSec and all the half-truths I'd fed Tamir while we were together, it was any wonder he trusted me at all. It was a good reminder that nobody was perfect.

I'd overheard parts of their conversation but been unable to hear the entire plan when they finished their discussion back in the master bedroom. From what I did hear, I had assumed the worst. I was confident most people would have responded the same as I had—the evidence had appeared awfully damning.

"I suppose that sounds like a good plan, but I hate that my uncle gets away again. I'd wanted the feds to get him, but I had no direct proof of his involvement in the trafficking like I had my father's. But I knew. There was no way in hell he wasn't involved. He's an evil man, and the world would be a far better place without him."

"We need him alive to end the search for you. He's your biggest threat but also your only way out. I knew how important his death is to you, which is also why I hesitated to tell you my true plan. The most important part is getting you out of danger. We can handle your uncle later."

I nodded, and we both kept to our thoughts for long minutes as I processed what I'd learned. So much had changed, and I appeared to be breaking free of Los Zares, but was any of it even necessary? It ate at me until I had to say something.

"I can't help but think if you'd never staged my attack and come after me, I'd probably never have been found. It was a crazy coincidence that we already knew each other, but what were the chances anyone else would happen to find me? I could have been fine in New York forever." I didn't want to point fingers, but it was an important fact that needed to be discussed.

He breathed out a long sigh. "I've carried so much guilt over that fact, and I have no defense. All I can do is tell you how sorry I am. But I also want you to know that I still think this is necessary. I debated the entire time we were at the cabin about whether I should tell you the truth and simply send you back to the city. Once you told me the full extent of your involvement in Los Zares, I knew you would never be truly safe unless we faced them."

I nodded. "That's true. I felt it every day back in the city. I couldn't get comfortable knowing they were probably searching for me. Stephanie assured me I would settle eventually, but I couldn't imagine it. As it was, I felt like I was already half dead, constantly terrified of my own shadow and hiding out in my apartment."

We both lost ourselves in thought for one pregnant moment until his rumbling voice broke the silence.

"I thought you were shutting me out because of Asaf, that you couldn't forgive me for such a manipulation. But you thought I was going to let them kill you. That's why you were saying goodbye," he mused somberly.

I nodded against his chest. "I can't totally fault you for the ploy with Asaf. I would never have told you what was going on in my life without a compelling reason, and it wasn't like I didn't lie to you as well. Now, if I were Asaf … I'd be awfully pissed at you for knocking me out."

His chest rumbled with gentle laughter. "He wasn't knocked out, but he did bitch me out for hitting him harder than necessary. I got a little carried away when I saw how rough he'd been with you."

I had to smile when I imagined the surly Asaf grumbling to himself after we left that alley. I didn't feel too bad about it. He did put a decent scratch on my cheek and scare the shit out of me. Once I thought about it, I was a little disappointed he hadn't been knocked out.

"After that"—I continued my thought process aloud

—"you stole me away to your cabin. Why on earth did we have to spend two whole weeks in the wilderness if there was no real threat?"

My head rose and fell as Tamir took a deep breath.

"A mix of reasons. Curiosity. Intrigue. Parts of your story didn't add up, but I wasn't sure if that was relevant to the bounty on you or not. If I'm honest with myself, all of it was, in good part, founded in my desire to keep you and had very little to do with you being on the run. I wanted to get to know you and learn all your secrets. I still do. I want to know every little thing about you."

Tamir slipped from beneath me again and rolled on his side, peering down at me from where he leaned on his elbow. "None of this is ideal, but I want you to know that I wouldn't have changed a thing because in these weeks, I've fallen in love with you, Emily. Your perseverance and strength are the fucking sexiest thing I've ever seen. You're optimistic in the darkest of circumstances, and your passion for life is inspiring. There's no need to make any long-term decisions now. Just know that I'm not going anywhere."

My breathing shuddered at the full impact of his words. A storm of emotions raced through my veins, but I wasn't sure what to think. Tamir had admitted he loved me, and I had deeply complex feelings for him, but he was an assassin. He was firmly planted in a world I'd given up everything to escape.

How would I be honoring that sacrifice if I walked straight back into a life of crime?

Tamir kissed at my tears. "Let's get some sleep. We have a big day tomorrow."

I started to turn onto my side but paused. "If everything works out tomorrow and I do manage to live through this—"

"Don't even go there. I wasn't joking when I said I would die before I let them touch you."

His sincerity brought my heart into my throat. "Well, when it's over, do you think we can go by my tita's grave before we leave town? I'd like to give her a final goodbye."

He smiled softly. "I think that can be arranged."

TWENTY-EIGHT
Emily

THE HEAVY PLASTIC FELT AS IF IT WAS TRYING TO SUFFOCATE THE life from me. I couldn't move, pinned with my arms at my sides in the pitch-black confinement of the trunk. I had to keep my cool, but it took every ounce of mental strength not to panic. It was important for Tamir to make sure we weren't being followed before he could stop and let me out. Fortunately, the cool December air removed the threat of heatstroke, which would have been a real danger had we done this when it was any warmer.

When the car eventually came to a stop, frantic hands unwrapped the tarp and extracted me from the trunk. Tamir checked me over with clinical precision before taking a deep breath and meeting my eyes. "Are you okay?"

226

"Yeah." I nodded. "Just glad to be out of there. We did it, right? It's over?"

He ran his fingers through my hair, pulling our foreheads together. "It's over."

The words seemed so much more finite than they truly were. My troubles with Los Zares might have been over, but things with Tamir were far more uncertain.

He placed a kiss on my forehead, then directed me to the back seat of the Escalade. We were in an alley downtown, secluded from view while we switched vehicles. Uri took the silver car to the rental place while the rest of us made our way back to the house. Once we were safely there, Tamir helped me remove the bullet wound rigging Alon had secured to my chest and back so that I could shower off the crusted fake blood. By the time I got out, Uri was back with food.

We toasted to the completion of a successful mission with two Texas originals, Dr. Pepper and Whataburger. As I gazed at their smiling faces, I realized that, after only a short time together, they felt almost like family. Something about sharing a near-death experience brought people closer together, so I could only imagine the bond these men shared after serving in the military together. Tamir might have seemed like a loner, but he had a support system anyone would envy.

He followed me back to my bedroom after I excused myself for the night. I curled up under the covers, giving him room to sit on the edge of the bed. We'd had sex the night before, and he'd told me he loved me, but we were far from ready to jump into being a couple. I felt awkward about not being able to return his sentiment, but at least he was gracious enough to give me the room I needed.

"What's the plan from here?" I asked.

"We need to book some flights home, and in the meantime, I thought we'd go to the cemetery first thing in the morning when we're less likely to run into anyone."

"Home?"

"There's no reason you can't still live in New York. As you mentioned, no one there knows your past. You can claim a family emergency and slip right back into the life you had started for yourself."

I chewed on my lip, hesitant to accept that it could be that simple. The room filled with the debilitating weight of the words that were going unspoken until I caved to the pressure. "What about us? What happens when we go back?"

"I told you how I feel. Being back in the city won't change that. I know you're struggling with it all, so I have no problem giving you time to sort it out."

What he was offering was incredibly generous and kind. I felt awful for keeping him dangling.

"I'm so sorry, Tam." Tears burned the back of my throat. "The emotion's there, and I want to give in to it, but you kill people for a living. You saw the life I left behind. I don't want to walk back into gunfights and hiding from the law."

He clasped my hand and squeezed gently. "I understand. That's a decision you'll have to make, but there's no rush. I'd rather you took the time to think it through than walk away without giving us a chance."

I could see his pain, even through his expertly schooled features. It made me feel like utter shit. I felt like I was the rope in a vicious tug-of-war of my own making, torn between giving in to my feelings for him and continuing on my charted course to an honest life.

"I don't suppose you're open to retirement?" I decided to ask even though he hadn't offered. Normally, I wouldn't have considered asking a man to end his career for me, but this was different. I wasn't asking him to quit being an accountant. I didn't want to have to wonder every day if the man I loved was coming home, or if he'd end up shot or in prison.

His lips thinned. "Would it make a difference? What's been done is done. Quitting now won't erase the blood on my hands. What I do is a part of who I am, and I'm not ready to give that up. You'll have to either find a way to reconcile that in your heart, or we'll have to go our separate ways." He lifted my hand to his lips and pressed a bittersweet kiss to my knuckles. "The past twenty-four hours have been too emotional for you to make any decisions now. Get some rest, and we can talk again once we're home." He lowered my hand and stood, turning off the bedside lamp and casting the room into darkness. "Good night, motek."

"What does it mean? Motek. You've said it before, but I don't know what it means."

He trailed his fingers through my hair with a sad smile illuminated by the moonlight. "It means darling or dear one." His hand slipped away, and I felt the loss of his touch deep in my bones.

"Wait," I called out before he reached the door. "Please, don't go. Can you stay with me, just for tonight?" It was selfish and wrong, but the words were out before I could give them a second thought.

Tamir made his way to the other side of the bed, and I could hear him strip off his shoes, pants, and shirt, dropping each article onto the ground. Without a word, he slid beneath the covers and pulled me against his chest, wrapping me in warmth and security and crippling heartbreak.

I felt wretched knowing I cared for him so deeply, and that it might not be enough. I might have gotten my life back, and we might have been going back to New York, but nothing was going to be the same.

Tita's headstone was a heart wrapped in beautifully carved angel's wings. I'd insisted on the design, and my father had come up with the money to pay for the monument and the perfect plot under an enormous live oak tree. Maybe he'd felt guilty about hurting her for so many years, or maybe it was just easier to let me have what I wanted. There was no telling what went on in that man's head. I had thought I'd known him before, but I would never make that assumption again.

Tamir drove me to the cemetery just after sunrise. He escorted me in but stood at a distance to give me privacy. It had been years since Tita had passed away, but seeing her again when I thought I never would, and knowing this would be the last time, brought a lump to my throat as I crossed the uneven ground to her plot.

I placed the bouquet I'd grabbed from a grocery store at the base of her headstone. I would have preferred yellow since that was her favorite color, but I'd had to make do with what they had available.

"Hey, Tita." I struggled to get the words out past the emotion clogging my throat. "I'm sorry it's been a while, but life got a little crazy. You'd be so proud of me. I walked away from Dad and the club. I know you had to have hated those years I spent with them. I'm so sorry I hurt you. I miss you every day, and even though I won't be able to see you anymore, I want you to know that you will always be in my heart. Te amo, Tita." I blew her a kiss and turned back to look at Tamir through tear-filled eyes. "Let's go home."

That night, I went back to my New York apartment alone, and I'd never felt lonelier in my life. Not when Tita died. Not when I first left Texas. There was something about knowing the person you loved was near, but just out of your reach, that felt far more disturbing than had they been totally unreachable.

When I did finally get to sleep, I dreamed I was watching through a telescopic lens as a young woman with dark flowing hair walked along a cliff's edge. The red dirt wall had no grass or vegetation to help keep it together, and when she got too close to the edge to examine something, the ground beneath her broke free, and she slid straight down the cliff face. As if I had no power to look away or close my eyes, I watched in horror as she struck outcroppings, and her body bent and twisted in unnatural angles. Only once she'd completed her horrific descent to the bottom did I startle awake.

It was early but not too early to get up, so I wrapped myself in a blanket and moved to the couch. Little Ned, the aloe plant, still sat on the windowsill. I'd given him some water when I got home the night before and was pleased to see that he wasn't in too bad of shape. It was past the two-week watering schedule, but he was still green, albeit a little droopy.

Grabbing a pen and paper, I started working on a plan for myself—short-term goals first. I would need to touch base with Stephanie as soon as I could. Rent and other bills would need to be paid. Tamir had insisted I took the money from my uncle, but there was no way I'd touch that blood money. It sat in the duffel bag in my closet, and it would stay there until I figured out what to do with it.

I was going to need a job, but I was too embarrassed to go back to Jalisco's. Olivia was sweet, but her father would never overlook the fact that I walked away without any notice. I would also need to call the shelter and apologize for disappearing. I wasn't sure if I would go back to volunteering, but I had to at least let them know I was all right.

The only other part of my life in New York worth addressing was my Krav Maga lessons.

I still wanted to learn, but I wasn't sure it was a good idea to go to Tamir's studio. I needed space from him, but it made me heartsick to think of not seeing him at all. Unable to commit to an answer on that one, I left it for reconsideration later.

It was still early, but I went ahead and texted Steph.

Me: I'm back in the city. It was all a misunderstanding. I'll explain in person.

Her reply was immediate.

Stephanie: Starbucks on 54th, how quickly can you be there?

Me: An hour.

Stephanie: I want to hear every tiny detail.

That would be a problem. I wasn't crazy about lying to her, but I couldn't tell her about Tamir. Not the full story, anyway. I needed her to know I was back, and everything was all right, but that put me in a sticky situation. I had to spend the next hour carefully outlining what I could and couldn't tell her.

The second I stepped into the coffee shop, Stephanie threw her arms around me. "I was so freaking worried about you."

We'd had a professional relationship before my disappearing act, but I got the feeling the trauma of it had changed our dynamic. We put in our orders and claimed a small table in the back corner where we could talk privately.

"Now, tell me, how the hell was there a misunderstanding that made you think you'd been made, and where have you been for the past three weeks?"

I went with a good chunk of truth and simply omitted the parts that she didn't need to know. She knew about the attack in the alley, but I explained how Tamir had tracked me down and helped me. I told her he was ex-Special Forces and how he ended up coming with me on the road at the last minute. How he'd tracked me down and his reasons for doing so were irrelevant. I explained that we went to a cabin of his, and while we were there, a detective friend of his tracked down the attacker and discovered he was just some gang-banger looking to rob me for cash—a little white lie in the middle wasn't going to kill anyone. I continued to explain that I was still so anxious about being found that I had jumped to conclusions and thought I'd been tracked down.

"So this man you were with, he knows you're in the program?" She eyed me warily.

"He does." I nodded.

"Do you trust him?"

"With my life." No hesitation. No doubts.

She smiled softly. "I hate that you had to go through this, but it's an enormous relief to know we didn't have a leak. We've been tearing the department apart, trying to figure out how your location could have been identified. WitSec hasn't experienced that kind of breach in over a decade. Everyone will be relieved to hear it was a false alarm."

"I know I wasn't supposed to tell anyone. Will that affect my enrollment in the program?" My stomach churned as I waited on her answer. In theory, I didn't need their assistance, now that Los Zares thought I was dead, but I wanted all the protection I could get.

"Secrecy is important, but if you trust this man, his knowledge shouldn't affect your security or our ability to protect you."

"Thank God. I'd been worried sick that you'd kick me out."

She placed her hand on mine and gave me a warm smile.

"Emily, we're here to keep you safe. We aren't walking away from you unless you do something that makes our job impossible."

"Thanks, Stephanie." This time around, I was going to have to do a better job of getting to know her. She was a few years older than me, but I truly liked the woman. My time on the road made me realize how important friends could be, even when opening up to others was scary.

"Now, are you going to tell me about this man you spent three weeks with?" Her words were loaded with innuendo.

"Not even a little, but *you* are going to tell me where in the hell you dug up Reggie. That guy was a piece of work, and I'm dying to know how you two crossed paths."

She burst out laughing, segueing our conversation into much more lighthearted topics.

When we wrapped up, I walked home rather than taking the subway. It was shaping up to be a mild winter's day, and I needed the outdoor air. It wasn't the same as the refreshing feel of walking through the woods, but it was better than nothing. I'd gotten used to walking among the trees to help clear my head, and a part of me longed to go back to those simple days.

Once I was home, I googled local restaurants and started to make a list of places to submit job applications. This time, I wouldn't settle for a waitressing job. I was capable of more, and I would use the degree paperwork WitSec had provided to get a managerial position. With the stipend the government was paying me to get by, I had enough time to secure a job I was proud of, and I wouldn't settle for less.

I sat with my thumb over the shelter's number in my contacts for the longest time. They'd ask if I was going to resume volunteering, and I didn't have an answer to that question. Something was holding me back, but I wasn't sure what. I wanted to help. I wanted to see the women again and be a part of the solution. So why was I reluctant to go back?

Without a forthcoming answer, I shook off the unease and dialed the number. The director answered and was far more welcoming than I felt I deserved after disappearing unexpectedly. She assured me there were no hard feelings, and I always had a place as a volunteer at the shelter.

Two days later, I was back in the kitchens, helping prepare an industrial-size batch of spaghetti and catching up with the ladies. There was a new addition to the group. A young girl, around the age of nineteen, who kept to herself, still not settled in among her new family. It grated at me to see a girl so young who had already been out on the streets. I knew it wasn't uncommon, but it nettled that part of me that felt powerless. She was just another glaring example of how little was being done to fix the problem.

Everything we did was reactionary. Each day I worked at the shelter, I felt increasingly frustrated rather than fulfilled. I wanted to know my efforts were proactive. That I was helping to prevent the abuse and trauma before it even started and not just sweep up the mess that was left behind.

TWENTY-NINE
Emily

Two weeks after I returned, I secured a new job as a daytime manager at a small Brazilian steakhouse. It was family owned, which suited me perfectly. It also provided the perfect distraction from my situation with Tamir.

I never made it to any Krav Maga classes. I couldn't go to his gym, nor could I stomach going somewhere else. It would have felt like I was walking away, and I couldn't commit to that decision, which left me at an impasse.

I hadn't seen him in the two weeks since we'd come back, but sometimes, I could swear I felt his eyes on me. It wouldn't have surprised me if he was there, watching. At times, I wanted to demand he show himself just so I could see him.

See those intelligent dark eyes and remember what it was like to have his full lips on mine.

On Christmas Eve, I came home to find a package waiting for me. Tamir didn't even celebrate Christmas, but he'd been thoughtful enough to bring me a gift. Inside the beautifully wrapped box was a silver cuff bracelet with an evil eye engraved on its surface. It had a hinge on one side so that it could close all the way around my wrist, completely covering my tattoo. It was perfect—the most thoughtful gift I'd ever received.

Tamir might not have been in my life, but he was always with me. In my thoughts. In my heart.

It felt wrong to be without him, but shouldn't being with a killer feel wrong too? My chest ached to be near him, but what surprised me was how crushed I felt when I started my period that night.

In the back of my mind, I'd wondered what might come of our night of unprotected sex. I'd been on the pill in New York but hadn't brought them with me when I left. After two weeks in the cabin without birth control, I'd had no idea what would result from our slip. It had been risky and reckless. Having a child with him would have been a terrible way to start a relationship, yet my heart shattered when I discovered it wasn't to be.

A part of me had been hanging on to hope that a pregnancy would tilt the scales and make it that much easier for me to run back to him. That shouldn't have been the reason I decided to be with him, but somewhere down deep, I'd been hoping. Hoping that, the whole time, I'd still had a part of him with me and assurance that we could still be in each other's lives.

Now, there was no reason to go back to him, except for the

excruciating pain in my chest when I thought of never seeing him again.

I spent the rest of my evening draining my eyes of every tear. I didn't allow myself the numbing reprieve alcohol would have provided. Feelings were there to be felt, and I was doing a disservice to Tamir if I hid from the pain of being away from him.

Three days later, I was back at the shelter. I wasn't scheduled to volunteer, but we'd had a particularly large amount of food left over at the restaurant, and I decided to take it by so that it wouldn't go to waste. It was late when I arrived and found the director and her assistant sitting at the dining table together. Both wore matching expressions of worry.

They explained that the new girl had disappeared. She'd started her GED program and had seemed to be settling in well with no hint that she was interested in going back to her abusive family. The ladies were concerned the girl had been picked up by traffickers who targeted young women at shelters.

Not only was there nothing they could do but they couldn't even contact the authorities until the girl was gone for over twenty-four hours. And even then, she would likely be seen as just another runaway. Forgotten as easily as yesterday's news.

I was enraged. A righteous ball of fury looking to rain down my wrath in a storm of vengeance.

But I had no target. No outlet for my anger and frustration.

I had no idea how the other shelter workers kept from slipping into a murderous rage. By the time I made it back to my apartment, my blood was boiling with the need to act. I was so distracted with thoughts of destruction and spite that I didn't realize I wasn't alone.

At the sight of Tamir sitting in my living room, my heart took a giant swallow of fresh air and infused liquid coolant into my veins. I didn't question his sudden appearance or scold him for scaring me to death. The second he stood, I raced into his arms. His lips slammed down on mine, and I seized the opportunity to have him close. His unexpected appearance was the lifeline I needed, and I didn't have the wherewithal to push him away.

"Fuck, I missed you," he growled between kisses.

"Missed you so much." I wrenched his shirt up, initiating a frantic removal of both our clothes as if they were infested with ants, and we couldn't get them off fast enough.

In a matter of seconds, Tamir had me in his arms with my back against the wall. His hard length was warm against my belly, making my hips ache to roll and grind against him.

"I know I need to give you time, but my patience is wearing thin. I had to see you if only for a few minutes." He scraped his teeth against the skin of my neck, sending a storm of goose bumps down my arms and legs.

I didn't know what to say. Answers to my questions had evaded me, and with him naked against me, my brain was completely dysfunctional.

He angled his hips, preparing to press inside me.

"Wait!" By some small miracle, one clear thought penetrated my lust-filled haze. "Condom."

He slowly pulled back and met my eyes. "Have you slept with someone else while we've been apart?" The air around him could have crystallized from the arctic chill in his words.

"No, Tam," I whispered. "I just don't want us screwing this up. What we did last time was reckless." Fortunately, I'd just finished my period, so we were probably safe either way, but I didn't think it was right to take those chances with someone I couldn't commit to wholeheartedly.

His shoulders relaxed as he lowered me, then retrieved a condom from his wallet. He rolled it on and had me back in his arms in no time. "First like this, then I'll take you back to the bedroom. I need you too much to be gentle the first time." With those words, he plunged inside me, taking three long pumps to sheathe himself fully inside me.

I'd never felt so full and complete in my life—as if his cock belonged inside me. It wasn't just his cock. Having him there with me made my heart feel so much more capable of handling the other struggles in my life. Like a cracked glass that couldn't hold water, he sealed those cracks and made me a stronger person.

I clung to his shoulders as he pounded inside me, neither of us able to get enough of each other. After he brought us both to the blinding peak of the mountain and sent us careening down the other side, he carried me to the bedroom without missing a single beat. I, on the other hand, was a wobbly tangle of limbs.

I wasn't sure I could handle another round, but when his velvety tongue lapped at my slit, warm embers of lust began to ignite in my belly. He lavished attention over every inch of me—worshiped my body and lay siege to my heart. As if it wasn't his already.

Much later, when our bodies glistened with a sheen of sweat and the scent of sex saturated the bedroom, we lay entwined and talking softly to one another. I told him about my new job and the shelter. He gave me updates on his own life and what he'd heard from his friends.

"And what about your other job?" I asked the question hesitantly. "Have you been … working?" My meaning was clear. I wanted to know if he'd killed anyone since we'd come home.

His hand traced lazy circles on my back, only pausing

briefly at my question. "It's not like that. I don't take jobs all the time. Just one every couple of months."

I'd wondered about that. I'd wondered about all of it. I also wasn't sure I wanted to know, but at the same time, I didn't think I could make an informed decision about him if I didn't know the facts. I took a slow, steady breath and prepared myself for what I was about to say.

"Will you tell me about it? I want to know more."

THIRTY
Tamir

I wasn't sure where her line of questioning was leading, but she wasn't shutting me out, and that was all that mattered. There wasn't a day I hadn't laid eyes on her, but seeing her without being able to touch her was maddening. I wasn't sure how much longer I could take it.

If she wouldn't give in to being with me, I'd have to face the fact that I needed to leave. I couldn't be so close to her and not have her.

Telling her about my work could be exactly what we needed, or it could be the nail in the coffin that finally ended our chances. Either way, I agreed that she needed to know. I didn't want to finally let a woman into my heart just to keep secrets from her.

"I'm sent job offers by an entity who manages these things. I look through the file and determine whether the person they want dead has perpetrated acts heinous enough to justify their death, at least in my eyes. I've targeted political kingpins from other countries—like in the Congo, where the president was using children as soldiers, stealing them from their families, treating them horrifically to remove their humanity and training them to be ruthless machines. My last job, before I uncovered you, was a serial child rapist. He was a pharmaceutical executive, which is more likely the reason he was targeted, but his extracurricular activities were the important part to me."

"Do you trust the information this agency sends you? What if they make stuff up just to get you to do it?"

"I verify their assertions when needed. Often, like with the rapist, there was photographic evidence that made it perfectly clear just how guilty he was."

"What about sex trafficking? Have you ever killed anyone in that industry?"

I nodded. "I've snuffed out all types of evil. The government is limited in their reach, but I'm not. In my brand of justice, there is no judge or jury, but I accept that risk in the hope that I can help equal out the scales. It's too easy for evil to prevail and for the world, as a whole, to look the other way. Someone has to get dirty to truly make a difference."

She was quiet for a moment as she absorbed what I'd told her. "I suppose it makes sense, but that worries me, too. I spent a lot of years rationalizing my actions, telling myself I wasn't hurting anyone with my minor involvement in Los Zares. How am I supposed to know I'm not rationalizing myself into a bad decision now? When is it right to bend the rules, and when does it go too far?"

I traced my fingers in random patterns across her back,

loving the feel of her silky skin. "That's something we all have to figure out for ourselves."

"Lately, I've been wondering if it's enough to simply follow the rules and mind my own business. I can't help but feel like I'm perpetuating the problem by not doing something to stop it. My eyes have been opened to the horrible things that happen in our world, and I feel awful going about my day as if people aren't suffering. Am I accepting those crimes if I look the other way?"

"There's only so much one person can do—try not to be so hard on yourself."

"I know, but I also think maybe there's still more I could do."

I stilled, not sure I liked where her thoughts were taking her. "What exactly are you suggesting?"

"Nothing yet. Just trying to talk through my thought process." She paused, stumbling on her next words. "I found out earlier that a girl went missing from the shelter. The staff is certain she was taken by traffickers, and it breaks my heart. She was so young and sweet. Knowing those men I'd encountered are still out there, and so many others like them, has weighed on my mind. I just don't know how I can turn my back and not try to fight against people like that."

I felt the warm moisture of a tear hit my chest. My sweet Emily was too fucking compassionate for her own good. I hated to see her upset, but I was glad I could be there with her. I could tell she was more upset than she was letting on.

"There are organizations that work on taking down traffickers, but it's an ugly business and not often successful. The ruthlessness of criminals gives them an advantage over law enforcement. Keeps them one step ahead. You have to be willing to lose and keep fighting."

She lay still before lifting her head and meeting my eyes.

"But you don't. You walk straight up to them and do what needs to be done." There wasn't a hint of fear or judgment in her words, just cold certainty. It was sexy as hell.

"I do, but not everyone can sleep at night after participating in the type of violence I've known. I'm not like most people."

"The more I think about it, the more I realize I'm not either. Something about you speaks to me. There's no denying it or fighting it. I don't necessarily want a life of danger, wondering if you'll be hurt or killed, but I'm not sure I can live an ordinary life after the things I've seen. I haven't made my decision, but I'm getting closer. Knowing more about what you do gives me a lot to think about, but I swear, I won't make you wait much longer."

I turned our bodies so that I was on my side, looking down into her eyes. "My life isn't fairy tales and rainbows. I've lived in the shadows and seen my share of evil, but if it all had to happen for me to be right here at this moment with you, I wouldn't change a thing."

Pressing a kiss to her lips, I savored the heady taste of her and made sure she knew that I meant every damn word.

THIRTY-ONE

Emily

"YOU HAVE MY NUMBER NOW. I EXPECT TO HEAR FROM YOU."
Tamir leaned down and placed one last kiss on my lips, his
hand firm around the back of my neck.

I couldn't help but smirk as he pulled away. He wasn't
exactly the bossy type, but it was sexy as hell when he was.

He simply shook his head and walked down the hall
toward the elevator. My smirk blossomed into a full-blown
grin as I watched his breathtaking form from behind until he
disappeared into the stairwell. He truly was blessed
aesthetically.

"I see Mr. Handsome is back."

I had thought I was alone in the hall, so when Grace interjected her comment, my heart performed a trick Cirque du Soleil would have been proud of.

I slapped my hand over on my chest and laughed. "Grace, you scared me to death. Are you sure you aren't part ninja?"

The older woman stood in her doorway across from mine, grinning ear to ear. "Don't I wish. I think you being surprised had a lot more to do with his good looks than my stealthy abilities."

My eyes drifted back to where I'd last seen Tamir. "You might be right."

We both broke into a fit of giggles.

"Honey, I'm so glad you were able to come back. I know I told you already, but I sure did miss you."

I swept across the hall and wrapped my arms around the spindly older woman. "I missed you, too." In my heart, I could feel my tita smiling down on me, and it filled me with joy.

I returned to my apartment with a renewed sense of optimism, but my smile faltered when the implication of Grace's original comment hit me. *I see Mr. Handsome is back.* I didn't recall Tamir coming to my apartment before. Then it hit me. The attractive man she saw at my place the afternoon I was attacked. I had assumed it was my attacker looking for me, but of course, it hadn't been. Asaf had never truly been after me, so he would have had no reason to be at my apartment. It had been Tamir all along.

I shook my head and got out my phone.

Me: Exactly how many times did you break into my apartment before last night?

Tamir: Just once.

Me: My elderly neighbor caught you. You're not as stealthy as you think. I bit my lip to keep a stupid grin from spreading across my face.

Tamir: Maybe next time I'll come by in the middle of the night, and you won't know I'm there until I'm inside you. Then we'll see how stealthy I can be.

Sweet baby Jesus. My head spun as hormones overloaded my system.

Me: ~~Promise?~~

No, I was supposed to be taking a break from him and making a decision. But man, was it tempting.

Me: Touché.

It wasn't nearly as fun, but it was the responsible way to respond. Acting like an adult sure did suck sometimes.

My post-Tamir high quickly evaporated when I went back to daily life without the prospect of seeing him again anytime soon. I checked in with him via text each evening, and it was, by far, the highlight of my days.

The young girl never showed up at the shelter, and the police were unable to trace her whereabouts. It felt like a grave injustice to go on with my life as if she'd never existed. I felt helpless, and I hated that feeling.

I wrestled with my emotions each day, especially under the cover of darkness when I lay in bed alone at night. My tita would have wanted me to be happy, but she also would have wanted me to lead a life free of crime. Would she have seen Tamir's brand of justice as a good thing or a part of the problem?

There was no way to know. Plus, I had to accept that it didn't matter what Tita would think. This was my life, and I had to do what was best for me. My life had never been ordinary, and I was starting to believe ordinary was never in my stars.

The straw that finally tipped the scales was a simple encounter at an average coffee shop. I was pouring cream in my cup next to a man who spilled a portion of his coffee onto the table, burning the back of his hand. I quickly handed him napkins and helped clean up the spill.

"Thanks, I'm going to have to be more careful."

"Not a problem. How's your hand?"

"I don't think they'll have to amputate," he teased. "My name is Kyle." He held out his uninjured hand for me to shake.

"It's nice to meet you. I'm Emily."

"You have a minute to sit?" he asked, with a hint of awkwardness that often comes with putting yourself on the line.

I wasn't in a rush, and I told myself this was exactly the type of guy I needed to give a chance. "Sure." I nodded and followed him to a table.

We sat and talked for thirty minutes. I learned about his dentistry practice and told him about the restaurant I managed. He was undeniably attractive, with an easy grin and dimples that would have melted the iciest heart. He was stable and friendly and everything I should have wanted. Still, there was absolutely zero spark—that intangible chemistry between two people that made your heart race and your thoughts get sucked into that person's orbit until you could think of nothing but them.

Instead, all I could think about was how this ordinary man could never measure up to Tamir.

Tam was bolder than life itself. No dentist or salesperson or architect could ever compare to a man who tested the limits of life. No man could compare, and I was an idiot for even entertaining an alternative.

I didn't just love Tamir in spite of his job; I loved him

because of it. I loved him because he ravaged an army to bring justice to his sister's death. I loved him because he was the type of man who had lifelong friendships and the kind of heart that would go cross-country to help a woman in trouble. He would argue his actions were much more selfishly motivated, but I didn't believe it. He was genuinely a good person, looking to make the world a better place, and I wanted to be a part of that. I wanted to be a part of him.

The certainty of my revelation hit me with the force of a semi-truck, right there in front of Keith, or Kenny, or Kyle—whatever his name was. Once I gave in to my feelings and admitted there was only one man for me, I felt like everything else clicked into place, like a Rubik's Cube that couldn't be mastered until I'd completed the precise number of rotations.

I put a quick end to the coffee date, wishing I could go straight to Tamir and give him my answer, but I was due at work in a half hour. I walked with renewed vigor to the restaurant and worked my shift with so much enthusiasm that even Gordon Ramsay would have approved.

I'd only been working there for just over a week, so one of the owners was still present at closing to make sure the place was locked up and ready for the next day. The second I was given the okay to leave, I hurried straight to Tamir's apartment.

His building didn't have a code to get in, so I was able to go straight to his door. It was late, but I didn't care. I had to put an end to the floundering uncertainty. It would have been prudent to text him that I was coming, but I'd been too preoccupied in my haste to think of it until I was staring at the peephole of his dark green door.

Wisps of my hair flew in all directions, and my skin was dewy with sweat from my jog over, but none of that mattered.

The only thing I cared about was my resounding certainty that Tamir was the only man for me.

I lifted my fist and knocked on the door, butterflies wreaking havoc on my insides. I only had to wait a single, breathless minute before the door swung wide, and Tamir's guarded expression greeted me on the other side.

"Emily, is everything okay?" His eyes darted down the hallway behind me as he pulled me inside his apartment.

"Everything's fine—more than fine. It hit me today that I need to listen to my heart. Even though what you do scares me, I can't imagine ever being with someone else. You're it for me, Tamir. I love you, and every day without you was more painful than the day before. I'm sorry it took me so long to figure it out, and I hope that doesn't make you question the depth of my feelings, because I love you so much it hurts."

Tamir put an end to my rambling when he pulled me into his chest in a crushing hug, one of his hands cradling my head over his heart. "Shhhh, you have no reason to worry about me. I've understood from the beginning that you were in a traumatic situation. I would never have pressured you to make life decisions while you were still processing everything that had happened. I felt bad for pushing you when I came to your apartment, but I'd been weak. Desperate to see you. To touch you."

I pulled back and peered up at him through watery eyes. "I'm glad you did. I think our paths were meant to cross. Denying that felt painful and unnatural, which was all too obvious after being with you again. You're it for me, Tamir—" I stopped suddenly, and my eyes widened. "I don't know your last name," I breathed. "How the hell did I lived with you for almost three weeks, fall in love with you, and allow you to kill me without ever knowing your last name?"

251

He just grinned. "Because Emily Ramirez Rodgers Reyes, names mean nothing. But since one of these days, I'd like for you to carry my last name, I suppose you should know, it's Hofi. Tamir Hofi." Then he kissed me, and I'd never felt so happy in my entire life.

THIRTY-TWO
Tamir

3 Months Later

"I'm not going to be in town next week to train with you," I informed Maria as she practiced a series of punches into the pads on my hands.

"It's not like I can do much with this watermelon in my gut. It's made me slow, and my balance is shit."

"Only one more month." I smirked, knowing my sentiment wouldn't help.

"Don't remind me. I want my body back, but I'm terrified of having to care for a baby. We've hired someone to help out, and that's the only reason I'm not a total basket case right now." She stopped her strikes and went for her water bottle, squeezing a long stream into her mouth. Her hair was soaked, sweaty strands clinging to her face from all directions.

"You have nothing to worry about. You're going to be a wonderful mother." I held her eyes, appreciating the strong young woman she'd become. "It hasn't escaped my attention you've changed enormously over the past six months, and I don't just mean your belly. I'm proud of you, Maria. I know your life hasn't been easy, but you've persevered and become better for it."

Her eyes became glassy before sweeping the room for anyone who might be watching. "Fucking hormones," she muttered, wiping at tears before they could fall. "You can't go saying shit like that, not to a pregnant lady. And what about you? You don't think I haven't noticed how much you've changed in the past few months?"

I chuckled, placing my hand on her back. "Come on upstairs. I think it's time you and I had another chat."

I walked my protégé up to my apartment—the apartment I now shared with Emily. After spending two weeks together in the tiny cabin, living together felt more natural than being apart. We wanted to be together; there was no reason to keep separate apartments for some arbitrary courtship period.

The moment Maria entered, her eyes narrowed. "Are you living with a woman?"

I smirked. "Have a seat. There's a good deal I'd like to share with you."

A half hour later, I'd told Maria facts about me that, up until recently, I'd never considered trusting her with. Maria and I had reached a point in our relationship where I felt it was important for her to know the truth, and I knew I could trust her with the sensitive information. I wanted her to know. Wanted her to feel as though she was equally welcome to talk to me if she ever needed to.

"You sly bastard. All this time, you've been working as an assassin, and I never had a clue." Her eyes narrowed into slits. "Is that how you and my father came to know each other?"

"Your father is well connected in many ways. Perhaps he'd enjoy enlightening you about how our paths crossed, but that's not a story for me to tell." I smirked.

As expected, Maria huffed with agitation. She never liked being refused. "So this trip you're taking next week, will it be for pleasure or … work?"

"A little of both. Of course, I'm fortunate enough to enjoy my work most days, but this excursion will be particularly enjoyable."

Maria grinned, her eyes glinting with perfect understanding. "Well then, I look forward to hearing all about it when you get back."

Three days later, I was back in San Antonio. This time, I'd come alone. What I needed to do was a one-man job, and I certainly wasn't going to risk bringing Emily with me. In fact, I'd told her I was meeting up with Uri to help him on a project in Denver. I didn't want her to worry, but more than that, I wanted to surprise her when I got back, and that wouldn't have been possible if she'd known where I was.

I spent several days on reconnaissance, tracking Emily's uncle and learning his habits. Killing him would be simple, but only after I'd spent the proper time researching my target. It was crucial his death was unquestionably an accident. We didn't need anyone looking into why he might be killed if there was any chance it might point back to Emily.

Adrián drove his Harley almost exclusively, and like most bikers, he was highly territorial about the bike. No one else went near it, which made it a perfect means of execution.

He also never wore a helmet, making my job that much easier. I'd have to pass along my appreciation after his rotting heart beat for the last time.

Most modern bikes were almost entirely electronic and contained anti-tamper software that alerted the owner when the bike was moved. However, that didn't prevent someone from plugging into a terminal and entering a new code into the bike's primary computer system.

If someone, like myself, had the proper equipment to link a laptop to a motorcycle, they could tap into the acceleration and braking systems without the driver ever having a clue. It wasn't a simple task, so the risk to the everyday bike enthusiast was minimal, but I happened to have a friend who was exceptionally good with computers.

Before I'd even left New York, I'd had Uri get me everything I needed. I watched Adrián until I felt confident about the best opportunity for a motorcycle crash, then waited until three a.m. that night to set my plan into motion. Uri guided me through the process in my earpiece, instructing me on how to connect the electronics, then we worked on overriding the bike's programming.

Adrián Reyes had started each day with a drive to a mechanic's garage about ten miles from his home. The trip took him on a highway that curved through the hilly countryside.

The perfect setting for a fatal accident.

After I finished with the programming, I waited in my car, not allowing myself to sleep. Adrián rolled out of his house, as expected, just after ten in the morning. He hopped on his bike and pulled onto the road, completely unaware that this would be the last time he ever walked this earth.

I followed him at a safe distance. It was important that my timing was perfect so that I could pull over after the accident as a concerned citizen, ready to render aid.

I could tell the second our programming kicked in.

When Adrián's bike hit the seventy miles an hour mark, the computer initiated a dramatic acceleration. The motorcycle shot forward. Traffic at that time of day wasn't bad, so he didn't have to swerve to avoid other vehicles. He was going fast but maintaining control, that was, until he tapped the brakes. Following the commands of its new programming, the bike's braking system locked down the second the brakes were initiated. There was zero chance a driver could control the spinout of a bike locking up at almost ninety miles an hour.

The wheels wobbled, straightened, then caught a bump and sent the bike flying into the air in a twisting tornado of shiny chrome and black leather. Adrián was immediately thrown from his seat, launched forward like a child's toy, and sent careening onto the pavement before him. Even if he'd had a helmet on, the outcome would have been dire. As it was, there wasn't the slightest chance of survival.

I pulled my car onto the grassy median when I neared the wreck and ran toward the prone driver. His head was a mangled mess of grated flesh and oozing blood. I noted he wore a silver skull pendant on a black corded necklace, the same as he'd worn the day of Emily's staged death. Before other motorists approached, I yanked the necklace from his lifeless body and wadded it in my palm.

"Oh, Jesus. There's no way he's alive. Did you check for a pulse?" A young man in khakis and a polo walked up behind me with a fist pressed to his lips.

"Yeah. He's gone, but I hadn't had a chance to call the police—can you do that?"

"Sure, man. Fuck. I'm never gonna get that image out of my head." The kid pulled out his phone and began to talk to the operator while I slowly stepped back from the body.

More and more people gathered around, and before long, sirens wailed in the distance. Before the authorities had a chance to arrive, I slipped away, keeping my smile hidden, until I was safely back on the road.

"I never told you, but I knew something was up with you when we came back to your apartment, and I found the gun you keep strapped under the sink. I mean, I could tell you were different anyway, but that was the clincher. Who does that but psychos and assassins?" Emily stood at the stove, stirring a white sauce in a pan. She had on leggings with an off-the-shoulder baggy sweatshirt and stood with one foot propped against the opposite knee like a flamingo. She was talking absently, but I was steadfastly fixed on her as if she possessed the very meaning of life.

Fuck, I loved this woman.

"What that tells me is you went snooping in my cabinets," I teased her.

"I was looking for ointment for that cut on my cheek," she shot back in defense.

"Attached to the underside of my sink?"

"Well, that was kind of an accident. It just happened to catch my eye. I'm observant like that. It's a burden I bear."

As always, she brought a smile to my face. I crossed the room and wrapped my arms around her from behind. "And now, this apartment is yours, just as much as it is mine, so you can snoop any place you like." I grazed my teeth over her earlobe, eliciting a sultry moan.

"I'm cooking, Tam. If I don't keep stirring, this sauce will burn." Her words said one thing, but her arching backside said another.

I lifted one hand out in front of her and allowed her uncle's necklace to dangle from my fist. "Take the pan off the heat. There's something I need to do."

She held unnaturally still; the only sound in the room was the gentle hiss of the gas burner. Without taking her eyes from the silver skull pendant, she turned off the stove.

"You went back for him," she whispered, taking the necklace into her hands and turning to face me.

"I did, and I'll take care of anyone else who is ever a threat to you." I wove my fingers through her hair, drawing her gaze away from the pendant. "Instead of a ring, I'm coming to you with the ultimate statement of my love for you. When it comes to you, there are no boundaries. There is no measure for my love and no limit to what I would do for you. I want to be with you for the rest of my life. Marry me, Emily."

Two crocodile tears dropped from her lashes. "Yes." She nodded, then threw her arms around my shoulders. "Yes, I'll marry you. I love you so much, Tam."

We held each other for long seconds, simply enjoying the feeling of having everything we could ever want there in each other's arms.

"Just so you know, I have no intention of denying you a ring," I added. "I thought we could go shop for that together."

She chuckled before pulling back to meet my eyes. "I think that sounds perfect. You know I'm not all about material things, but I think I'd love to wear your ring."

The blood in my veins ignited with a ravenous hunger for the amazing woman before me. My woman. To love, cherish, and protect with my life. I'd professed my love and protected her; it was time to cherish … by worshiping every square inch of her body.

Diving in for a kiss so ardent it melded our souls together. We were both so frenzied in the minutes that followed that we didn't make it farther than the kitchen table. By the time we were done, the sauce she'd been cooking was a total loss.

I didn't regret it one bit.

EPILOGUE
Emily

THEY SAY YOU CAN'T MISS WHAT YOU'VE NEVER HAD, BUT I begged to differ. The second we landed in Little Cayman, I was acutely aware that I'd been missing out after twenty-seven years of life without stepping foot on a real beach. Sure, I'd been to Galveston, but the brown-water beaches of the Texas coastline didn't count. They didn't even remotely compare to this postcard-perfect Caribbean paradise.

We spent a full week relaxing on the beach, biking across the island and exploring the spectacular reef life. Our villa came with a stretch of private beach and a plethora of blue-tinged iguanas, the island mascot. The tiny resort provided breakfast, lunch, and dinner, each brought to our villa, so there was no need to see other people. We worked on puzzles at our glass dining table and lounged in hammocks beneath picturesque palm trees.

It had been the perfect honeymoon.

On July first, six months after I told Tamir that I loved him, I took his last name at a small ceremony at the courthouse. Neither of us had any family, so we had no interest in a formal affair. Grace joined us along with Uri, but Asaf and Alon were out of the country. Maria also joined us. I'd had the pleasure of meeting her when I started back at the gym. She struck me as an odd character but sweet in her own way.

Our ceremony was short, primarily composed of the vows we'd written for one another. Tamir wore a suit. It was the first time I'd seen him so formally dressed, and I nearly forgot my vows at the sight. He was the most handsome man I'd ever seen, but even more mesmerizing was the way his eyes lit every time he looked at me. I wore a knee-length ivory lace dress that Tamir took great pleasure in stripping off me later that evening.

It was the perfect start to our new life together, and it only got better when we got up the next morning for our honeymoon. It was my first trip to the Caribbean, and I could definitively say that it would not be my last.

I had adored every minute of our time together, but I had started to get antsy to get back home. The beach was beautiful, but the city had also grown on me.

"Put that thing away. I thought we were on vacation." For a stoic, assassin type, Tamir sure did enjoy teasing me. Fortunately, I had no problem returning the favor.

"I was just checking email, and I'm glad I did. I got a message from my bank asking to verify my login credentials so that my account wasn't frozen."

Tamir stiffened on the lounge chair next to me. "Em, tell me you didn't give them your login."

I slid my eyes to the side. "Gotcha." I grinned impishly.

He chuckled and shook his head. "Oh, you're going to pay for that."

"Before you dole out your punishment, we did get a job offer."

I'd taken on an active role on the administrative side of Tamir's contract jobs. As it turned out, Tamir had plenty of money for both of us. Apparently, contract killing was a rather lucrative business. I quit working at the restaurant and spent my free time volunteering at the shelter and serving on the board of a human trafficking task force. My part in Tamir's work didn't require all that much time, but I loved being a part of what he did. We discussed each job together, deciding as a team whether he would take the contract.

Every penny of my uncle's money was given to the shelter as an anonymous donation. The director and her staff were ecstatic. After spending plenty of time with them and the women they helped, I was confident the money was going to a truly worthy institution.

"Oh, yeah? Who's the mark?"

"A judge—a very, very dirty judge."

"Sounds promising."

"The only thing is, it's time sensitive. We'd have to leave first thing in the morning." Technically, we had one more day scheduled before our flight home.

Tamir swiped the laptop off my lap and snapped the lid shut. "Fine, but that still gives us one more night, and I have plans for you." He swept me into his arms, bridal style, and started jogging toward the placid water. "But first, I believe I owe you one."

I squirmed and giggled, no match for his strong arms. The moment he was waist-deep, he tossed me into the crystal clear water, then took my hand as I resurfaced and pulled me back toward him. He lowered himself to join me neck-deep in the water, allowing me to slip my legs around his middle.

"Such a bully," I teased with a smile.

He nipped at my bottom lip. "And you're the most beautiful woman I've ever seen."

My heart skipped a beat. "You're forgiven," I whispered.

"I was thinking, after this job, maybe we discuss having a family."

Between a full day of sun and the shock of his words, my head dipped and spun. "What?" The single breathy word was all I could muster.

"Family means a lot to both of us, and I know you miss Isaac and Averi. I thought maybe it was time we consider starting our own family."

"What about you and your job?"

"What about it?"

"I guess I assumed since you had gotten this far in life without children, that it wasn't something you wanted."

He pressed his forehead to mine. "It had nothing to do with want and everything to do with the right person coming along. I can't think of anything more fulfilling than raising a child with you."

I couldn't believe I could end up so lucky. I had wanted children, but Tamir was older, and I had accepted that being with him might mean not having children of my own. To have him and a child—I couldn't imagine a more perfect life.

"I'm ready whenever you are." I grinned.

Tamir's eyes lit with mischief. "We'd better get practicing, then." He scooped me from the water, plundering my mouth in a heated kiss. "They say it can take months, and I never was a quitter."

I threw back my head and laughed as he carried me to the outdoor shower. He made good on his promise three times that night. Two months later, we got confirmation that our rigorous efforts had paid off.

Tamir had given me my life back and then filled that life with immeasurable joy. I wasn't just lucky; I was the luckiest woman in the world.

Thank you so much for reading WHERE LOYALTIES LIE! *The Five Families* is a series of interconnected standalones— there are two directions you can go from here:
1. *Impossible Odds* (Giada & Primo)
2. *Forever Lies* (Luca & Alessia)
Read more about each option below.

Impossible Odds (The Five Families #4)
Giada learns what happens when you steal from the wrong man. He's got retribution in his sights, but a mafia princess doesn't scare easily.

Forever Lies (The Five Families #1)
Didn't catch the beginning of the series? When Alessia gets stuck in an elevator at work, she's trapped with Luca, the hottest man she's ever seen. But she can tell something dark

hides beneath his charming facade—especially once he decides he's not letting her go…

Stay in touch!!!
Make sure to join my newsletter and be the first to hear about new releases, sales, and other exciting book news!
Head to www.jillramsower.com or scan the code below.

ACKNOWLEDGMENTS

This book requires an extra special thank you to a number of people. As I wrapped up my first draft of this book, the world seemed to fall into yet more chaos than we'd already experienced during our two months in quarantine. Riots and outrage launched a surge of much-needed social reform, adding to the air of uncertainty we were already experiencing. Emotions were high. Patience was low. Many of us were simply doing what we could to process our current realities.

What do I do at that point? Start hitting up people to help edit my book. Talk about low on the list of priorities. I felt horrible asking favors when life had been tough enough on its own and totally understood that not everyone could give their time and energy.

To my alphas, Jason and Sarah. I am truly humbled by how readily you step up to bat for me. Without your frank, in-depth critical input, this book would never have evolved into what it was meant to be. Thank you, from the bottom of my heart.

To Leah and Kristi. How did I get so lucky?! I suppose I did have to weather an Austin flash flood to find you, but it was worth every harrowing minute! Thank you for everything you do for me. I am forever grateful.

Last but not least, I want to give a special thanks to three ladies who helped make sure my cultural references were on point. To Veronica, Erica, and Pnina, your guidance about

Mexican American and Israeli cultures was invaluable. Thank you for helping me represent Tamir and Emily as accurately as possible!

This was the most challenging book I've written to date, both because of the content and the times in which it was written. I'm thrilled with how it's turned out, but it never would have made it to this point without so much amazing help. Thank you all!

ABOUT THE AUTHOR

Jill Ramsower is a life-long Texan—born in Houston, raised in Austin, and currently residing in West Texas. She attended Baylor University and subsequently Baylor Law School to obtain her BA and JD degrees. She spent the next fourteen years practicing law and raising her three children until one fateful day, she strayed from the well-trod path she had been walking and sat down to write a book. An addict with a pen, she set to writing like a woman possessed and discovered that telling stories is her passion in life.

SOCIAL MEDIA & WEBSITE

Release Day Alerts, Sneak Peak, and Newsletter
To be the first to know about upcoming releases, please join
Jill's Newsletter. (No spam or frequent pointless emails.)
Jill's Newsletter

Official Website: www.jillramsower.com
Jill's Facebook Page: www.facebook.com/jillramsowerauthor
Reader Group: Jill's Ravenous Readers
Follow Jill on Instagram: @jillramsowerauthor
Follow Jill on TikTok: @JillRamsowerauthor